# THE ENDLESS SEASON

Freelance graphic artist Caitlin McGraw is living the hipster life in San Francisco when a jury summons brings her home to North Carolina. But doing her civic duty wasn't supposed to include a reunion with Seth Street, the celebrity Olympic medalist—and Caitlin's teenage love. She fell hard for Seth at thirteen, only to lose him when he left in the middle of that third summer…when everything changed between them.

You never forget your first love, and a decade of fame and fortune as the face of professional snowboarding hasn't dimmed Seth's memory of seemingly endless, perfect summers. Now, sequestered with Caitlin on a high-profile case, Seth could have a chance to rekindle those feelings and discover if what they once shared was meant to last. Amid family conflicts and hard-hitting revelations in and out of the courtroom, Seth and Caitlin face some tough hurdles. With so much at stake, can they trust in what they've reawakened in each other and turn this season of change into a lifetime of love?

# The Fourth Summer

## Kathleen Gilles Seidel

**LYRICAL PRESS**
Kensington Publishing Corp.
www.kensingtonbooks.com

LYRICAL PRESS BOOKS are published by

Kensington Publishing Corp.
119 West 40th Street
New York, NY 10018

First Electronic Edition: July 2018
eISBN-13: 978-1-5161-0733-9
eISBN-10: 1-5161-0733-0

First Print Edition: July 2018
ISBN-13: 978-15161-0736-0
ISBN-10: 1-5161-0736-5

Printed in the United States of America

*For Cynthia Matlack because when you need her,*
*she is always, always there*

# CHAPTER ONE

"I'm so screwed." Seth stared at his phone.

Nate grabbed the device and looked at the screen. "Oh, yeah, you are. Didn't your mom warn you about this?"

Ben was on the sofa, his feet on the coffee table, his hands linked behind his head. "I don't know how you clowns ever get women when you still count on your moms so much."

"I don't know either," Nate replied cheerfully. "But we do."

The three guys were hanging out in the chalet they shared on the grounds of the Endless Snow Resort on Oregon's Mt. Hood. They were wearing long-sleeved tees and hoodies, low-slung pants, and knit caps pulled over their shaggy hair. A snowboarding video was playing on the newest-model, wall-mounted TV. The front hall was carpeted with boots and wet coats. Medals of every color were draped over the necks of empty beer bottles.

They were professional snowboarders, three friends in their midtwenties who had trained together since they were kids. On the mountain they were disciplined, dedicated, and determined. They had to be. Snowboarding is dangerous. The rest of the time they felt contractually obligated to have fun. Fans expected snowboarders to be the pirates of winter sports: brash, reckless, and a little weird. This came quite naturally to these three.

"This isn't a joke." Seth shoved his phone back in his pocket. "Have some sympathy. You don't have to go home and report for jury duty."

"Because we already are home," Ben pointed out. "We changed our addresses. We are officially Oregonians. Have been for a couple of years."

"My mom did it for me," Nate admitted. "But relax. Why would anyone ever want you on a jury?"

Despite living in Oregon, Seth was still registered to vote in North Carolina where his parents lived, he carried a North Carolina driver's license, and he paid his income tax to the Tar Heel State. He had already burned through two postponements during the winter competition season. Now he was stuck. He either faced a contempt of court citation, or he went home, spent the night on the Luke Skywalker sheets in his old bedroom, and reported for jury duty. Luke Skywalker it was.

So on the last Sunday in June the male twig on the Street family tree flew home and spent the evening with his parents and his sisters' families. Monday morning he drove to the courthouse, found the jury assembly room, and got in line to check in like an actual adult. As he waited, he scanned the room, looking at—let's be honest here—the young women.

One blonde, pretty in a popped-collar-and-pearls way, nudged her companion, also a blonde, also with the popped collar and pearls. They recognized him. Seth tried to make eye contact; they looked away nervously.

He took another step forward in line. A dark-haired girl, wearing headphones, was working on her computer, using a wireless mouse. Her elbow was propped up on the table; that hand blocked a view of her face. The rest of her looked petite and hipster cute. She was wearing a short black skirt, retro sneakers, and a big man's watch on her narrow wrist. There were empty chairs at her table. He would go sit there.

Then she straightened, dropped both hands to the keyboard, and started to type...well, hello, was this possible? Yes, she was Caitlin, Caitlin McGraw, from the summers.

Suddenly he was a kid again, in his mother's kitchen, staring at the clock, desperate to have the minute hand move faster. *The bus from Charlotte gets in at...then her grandmother will pick her up...and it takes twelve minutes for me...* But he would still get there too early and have to sit on her grandmother's front steps, waiting.

An instant later he was at her table. "Caitlin?" He touched her shoulder in case she couldn't hear him over her music.

She looked up, pulling out her earbuds as she did. One of the cords got tangled in her hair.

Those eyes, those beautiful brown eyes...how could he have forgotten them?

"Seth." She stood up. "I heard that you were in town."

She had? Why hadn't she gotten in touch with him?

He wanted to sweep her up, spin her around, tell her great it was to see her, but they were in public, and for all he knew, she might not be so happy about seeing him. He shifted his backpack and pulled her into a quick one-armed hug, the kind you'd give anyone. "Why are you here? You don't live here, do you?"

"Only technically. I'm a twenty-four-year-old adult still using Mommy and Daddy's address."

He could hardly criticize her for that. "But your folks don't live here, do they? You were visiting your grandmother those summers."

"My dad retired, and they bought a house in that new golf-course community outside town."

He nodded. "My folks said that lots of retired military are out there. The golf course is supposed to be really good." Why were they talking about golf courses? He didn't give a crap about golf courses. "What about you? Where are you living?"

"Hadn't you better go check in?"

"I suppose." He dropped his backpack on the chair next to her. "Hold this place for me."

He returned to the line, and as he checked in, it occurred to him that if she knew that he had left the line without checking in, then she had seen him, been watching him.

*When we were kids you said that you wouldn't play games. Let's not start now.*

It took him a while to get back to the table. Too many people knew who he was. He sat down just as the jury coordinator called for their attention, welcomed them, then dimmed the lights in order to show a video. The screen was behind Seth so he had to turn his chair away from Caitlin. The video explained the court procedures and talked about how important it was for them to serve, how a trial by jury was a right first guaranteed by the Magna Carta, and—

Caitlin touched his arm and whispered. "You aren't supposed to say *the* Magna Carta. It's Latin so no article. Just Magna Carta."

He looked over his shoulder. "How do you know that?"

"I'm kind of nerdy."

One of their other tablemates gave them a stern look so they shut up and learned that if they were admitted to a jury, they would be issued red tags that they needed to wear whenever they were in the courthouse.

At the end of the video, the jury coordinator flicked the lights back on, and a different person, the Clerk of the Court, told them that there were two trials scheduled for that day, one civil, one criminal. He explained the difference between civil and criminal trials, repeating pretty much the same words that the video had just used. Then he told them about the little red tags, again using the same words as the video.

Within a few minutes fifteen people were called for the civil trial. Neither he nor Caitlin was called.

During the presentations he had been wondering if he should say something about what had happened. No, it hadn't "happened." He had done it. But, come on, it had been years ago, high school shit. There was no reason to mention it. Pretend that everything was fine. That worked for him. Ignore the sticky stuff, and it usually went away. Avoid the edges of the map; just have a good time with other people who wanted to have a good time. He was a snowboarder, after all. Having fun was part of the job description.

But when she started to lift the screen on her computer, he spoke quickly. "I kind of disappeared on you, didn't I?"

"You didn't disappear at all," she said evenly. "I knew exactly where you were. Your face was on the front of the Wheaties box, and you did start sending me form replies to emails."

"Oh, man, those autoreplies." He didn't like being reminded of them. *Hi, the Olympics were a great time for all the US teams, weren't they? Thanks so much for...* "I wish I hadn't done that. But it was a pretty bad time for me, and I did a lot of things wrong. "

"Bad time? You had just won an Olympic medal."

"Yeah. It was complicated. But tell me about yourself. What are you doing? Where do you live?"

She was a freelance graphic artist living in San Francisco. Yes, she liked it out there. And her parents and her grandmother, they were all fine. Her sister? "And her baby...who's probably not a baby anymore."

She smiled. "No, he's not. He'll be in fifth grade next year. My sister and Trevor, Dylan's father, actually got married a few years ago."

"They got married? After all the crap you went through, they're married now?"

"Yes, but if they had gotten married back then, they would be divorced by now."

Good point.

Seth noticed someone hovering by the table. He looked up. The man said that he worked for Seth's dad. Seth stood up and made nice. Caitlin put her earbuds in and went back to work. She didn't look up when he sat down.

He watched her work. Her fingers tattooed across the keyboard. Sometimes she would stop, hunching forward, staring at the screen, one hand over her mouth, obviously thinking. Then most of the time she sat back quickly as if she had had an "aha" moment and started the rapid-fire typing again. Other times she'd type slowly as if she wasn't sure of her solution.

The morning was starting to drag. He had stuff he could do, but he couldn't get started. This sucked. Such a waste of time. Since the assembly room had Wi-Fi, most people were on their phones or computers. A few older people had newspapers or actual books, the kind with paper and all.

Caitlin eventually took out her earbuds and stood up to go to the ladies' room. When she got back, he asked her what she was working on. She said that a lot of her clients designed video games, and she helped with the art and some of the coding.

"I had a game out there for a while." Kids were supposed to be able to get the experience of being Seth Street snowboarding.

"I know."

She did? "It wasn't very good."

"I know that too."

"We weren't on the same page as the developer." His family didn't make many mistakes, but that had been one.

The jurors were given an hour for lunch. He walked down to the basement cafeteria with Caitlin, but the other people eating there recognized him, and he had to go back to being the Olympic medalist, the face of Street Boards. Seth Sweep, the media had dubbed him after he had won Olympic bronze in a shocking upset. His bronze meant that the United States had swept the event, taking all three medals.

"You're certainly sounding grown up," Caitlin said when they were gathering up their trash.

"It's an act. If I were really grown up, I wouldn't be here. I'd have changed my address."

"They don't have jurors in Oregon?"

She knew where he lived. "Undoubtedly. And actually scruffy riders are a lot more mainstream out there. Someone might actually want one of us on a jury. So maybe procrastinating was a good choice."

"You don't want to serve?"

"God, no. Deciding if someone is innocent or guilty? If they deserve to be in jail? Talk about grown up, that's above and beyond."

He had to go out and feed his parking meter. He offered to take care of hers. No, she hadn't driven. Her mother had brought her; her grandmother would pick her up. "It's like being fifteen again," she said, "and having to call for a ride."

Oh, good, she didn't want a car. He had been looking for an opening. "Remember if you're fifteen," he said lightly, "then I'm sixteen and have a license. I can run you home."

*Sixteen...* Memories suddenly started swirling in his brain, shapes in a snowstorm. *Look up at me. Look at me with those dark eyes of yours and admit that you're remembering too, remembering how great that third summer was because I could drive and we could go anywhere.*

What was going on in his brain? All this past stuff...he was a here-and-now kind of guy.

But it was good stuff, wasn't it?

"It's completely out of your way."

What? Oh, she was still talking about him driving her home. "All of ten minutes. And then maybe you will let me take you out to dinner."

He hadn't been able to get a read on her. Was she going to agree to have dinner with him? He wouldn't be surprised either way.

"They are paying us a whole twelve dollars for our service today," she answered. "I can buy my own food."

So it was a yes to spending the evening with him, but no to something that would make it seem like a date. He could live with that.

The afternoon dragged on. People were talking to each other more, complaining. Seth looked at his email, then his social media accounts, watched a few videos that the up-and-coming kids had made and were always trying to get him to watch, checked on a couple of games he had going with friends, and then went back to his email.

He could handle stress. Pressure, fear...bring 'em on. But boredom? He wasn't so good at that. He wanted out of here. He'd take Caitlin with him if he could, but most of all, he wanted—he needed—to leave. Snowboarders weren't supposed to be model citizens. They were rebels, outsiders, countercultural iconoclasts, not jurors.

But Seth was the public face of his family's company, Street Boards. It manufactured snowboards and skateboards. His parents, his sisters, and his brothers-in-law worked there; it supported all of them. So there was no way that Seth could be a jerk here in the jury assembly room. If the moms and dads of America thought Seth Street was an asshole, they wouldn't let their kids put his poster up on their bedroom walls, and they certainly wouldn't buy a Street Board to put under the Christmas tree. Seth had to act like a good citizen even if it was driving him nuts.

There was a beverage station at the back of the room, just coffee and water. Seth didn't drink much coffee, but he kept getting water just to have something to do. Caitlin was still working.

By two thirty people were saying that if you didn't get called for a trial on the first day, you weren't likely to have to come back.

At three o'clock there was activity in the front of the room. The Clerk came back in and started talking softly to the jury coordinator. Surely they were going to be dismissed. A trial wouldn't start at three, would it? People at the tables started to put away their stuff, clear up their trash.

But when the jury coordinator stood up, she asked them to line up by the door as she called their names. She kept calling name after name until everyone in the room was standing in a line that snaked toward the back of the room. Caitlin's name had been called before his. She was too far ahead in line for them to talk.

And then they waited. And waited some more. Someone stepped out of line to get chairs for the older ladies. Seth winced. He should have thought to do that.

At three thirty, the jurors were all told to sit back down. At four o'clock, they were excused for the day. They could go home as soon as they signed for the little brown envelopes with their twelve-dollar payment. But the coordinator emphasized that they had to call the hotline or check the website later in the evening to see if they had to come tomorrow.

"But we won't have to come back, will we?" someone asked. "If you don't get a trial the first day, you're done, right?"

The coordinator said that that was not necessarily so and that they needed to check with the hotline or the website. Seth didn't like the sound of that.

"I came thinking that this might be kind of interesting," Caitlin said as they walked to the parking lot. She was carrying her computer in a messenger bag crafted out of an old Cub Scout backpack and a worn leather bomber jacket. "It wasn't."

"You got a lot of work done."

"It probably looked like it, but what do you know about the trajectory of bullets on a gravity-heavy planet?"

"Me? Nothing."

"The guy who designed the game apparently didn't either. Now it's too early for dinner. Do you just want to get a cup of coffee or something?"

No, he didn't want to get a cup of coffee. He wanted to spend the evening with her. He had already made a plan. That was one thing about three guys hanging out together. Someone needed to have a plan, or you never got out the door. "You remember the lake?"

"No. Why would I?"

She was being ironic. Of course she remembered the lake. "Let's pick up some barbecue and go out there. My parents have a lake house now."

"Their own place? So we don't have to trespass and eat on someone else's dock?"

"No." *Or have sex on a blanket back among the trees.*

Except they hadn't "had sex." They had made love. They had been in love.

That last summer he and Caitlin had been together, he had feelings for her that he had never felt again. Of course it was probably that your first love always did feel the most intense, the most consuming, but still...

\* \* \* \*

They had had three summers together from the time he had been fourteen and she thirteen, until he was sixteen and she fifteen.

He had grown up in the High Country of North Carolina and had started snowboarding when his uncles still had to lift him over the drifts at the edge of the parking lots. He had been a little meat torpedo in those days, fearless about height and speed, clueless about danger. At fourteen he had already been competing professionally for a few years. At the time he didn't—he couldn't—appreciate what sacrifices his family was making for his snowboarding. His dad worked in the furniture factory; it was a nonunion shop, and there wasn't ever any overtime. His mom had done alterations for the local bridal shop.

He had developed so quickly and so early that a lot of doors had opened for him. His mother had been great at negotiating tuition-free deals for him, but there was still travel and living expenses for both of them. In those days, few programs were set up for unescorted school-aged kids, so his dad had outfitted a pickup with a camper, and she made endless long drives, preparing meals in the little camper while he worked his way through the homeschooling curriculum. Pretty soon she had started escorting Ben and Nate too. Nate's mother was a schoolteacher; she couldn't take off during the school year. Ben's mother had five other children; she couldn't leave either. So the arrangement helped a lot with the expenses and certainly made everything more fun.

Although there was snow on Oregon's Mt. Hood year-round, his parents drew the line at the summer programs. Seth's two older sisters needed their mother too. So starting in April, Seth was back in North Carolina, attending regular school, trying to keep up his skills by skateboarding, while his mother turned her attention to the girls.

Each year it was harder to connect with other guys at school. Seth wasn't interested in ball sports, and this was a ball-sports kind of town. Of course he was better than the chumples, the slow, fat kids in glasses, but Seth wasn't used to being in the middle of the pack. He liked being the best, and although his mom kept preaching about this to him, he just didn't have as much fun when he was ordinary. What was so wrong with that?

The county had built a little skateboarding park back when skateboarding was a hotter fad. In the summer Seth was there all day every day, riding his bike over, often providing free unplanned entertainment for the little-kid birthday parties that were the main source of the park's revenue.

One day he noticed a kid, maybe eleven or twelve, on the other side of the fence. The kid was perched on his bike, with one foot on the ground and his helmet still on. Seth showed off for a bit—so what if this was an eleven-year-old kid, it was still an audience—then glanced over his shoulder to be sure that the kid was watching. The kid still was there, but he had taken his helmet off.

And he wasn't a he. He was a girl, slight in build but much closer to Seth's age than Seth had first thought. Okay. That was a better audience. Seth showed off even more, finishing a trick close to the edge of the skate park.

"Hi, I'm Seth," he said through the fence.

"Caitlin."

She was pretty with these really dark eyes. Seth wasn't sure what to say next. It was kind of awkward for a moment, but she spoke. "That's pretty amazing what you do. I suppose you've been doing it for a long time."

"Yeah, but some things aren't that hard to pick up. Do you want to try? I am happy to show you how."

"I don't have any of the stuff."

"That helmet will work. I'll bring a board and pads for you if you want to come tomorrow. And you need to grab a waiver from the front desk. Your folks will have to sign it."

"I'm spending the summer with my grandmother, but I don't suppose they'll care if she signs it."

"They won't notice."

They agreed to meet the next day. That night Seth started to have second thoughts. What if she were a major biff, a total Betty who couldn't learn anything? And what if she kept coming back to the park day after day anyway? What then?

He hoped it would rain, and the whole thing would fall apart. But it didn't. She showed up right on time wearing the same sort of cutoffs and T-shirt that she had had on the day before. Then she took off her helmet.

Oh. He had forgotten how pretty she was. Maybe this would be okay.

She handed the waiver to the kid at the counter and then took some dollar bills out of her pocket. Behind her head Seth waved a hand, and the attendant told her to go on in.

"How come I didn't have to pay?"

"Because you're with me. I don't pay."

"You don't? Why not?"

"They know me. I started here when I was four."

"Okay." She clearly didn't see how that added up. So she reached for the pads. "How do I put these on?"

She was a quick learner. She had strong legs and a good sense of balance, and since his mom was also nagging him to praise other people more, he told her.

She shrugged. "I've taken a lot of ballet."

"Really? Ballet?" She didn't seem like the type.

"My mom thought it would turn me into a lady."

"So how's that working?"

"Incredibly well. Can't you tell?"

He laughed and then showed her how to make a turn sharper. An hour later the park manager—an older man, a regular city employee—arrived, and he called them over to ask why "Mrs. Thurmont" had signed Caitlin's waiver. He seemed to know who Mrs. Thurmont was.

"She's my grandmother, but my parents signed a bunch of forms so that she can take me to the hospital or whatever."

The man smiled. "Let's not have any hospital trips from here, okay?"

A while later he came out again. "Seth, she's getting tired."

"No, I'm not," Caitlin protested.

Seth hadn't noticed, but now that Mr. Kendrick mentioned it, yes, he could see that her ankles were wobbling and they hadn't before. "Then we need to stop. Doing stuff when you are tired is the way to get injured."

How many times had he heard people say that to him? His coaches, his mom, they were constantly on him to stop practicing.

"I'm fine," she said. "Really I am."

"No you aren't." How wack for him to be acting like the grown-up. "We're stopping."

They met up every day for the rest of the week. He learned that her last name was McGraw and that her family lived in Norfolk, Virginia, but they had moved all the time because her dad was in the navy. He was a lawyer, a judge. Seth hadn't known that the navy had judges. Caitlin had an older sister who also took ballet. She was a million times better than Caitlin, but no—and suddenly Caitlin had gotten a little awkward, sending out all kinds of "I don't want to talk about this" signals—she didn't think her sister would try skateboarding.

She continued to improve, but it clearly bugged her that Seth was so much better than she was. She was pushing herself, and Seth didn't need Mr. Kendrick to tell him that she was trying too much too fast. She was going to hurt herself. "You're not ready for this kind of thing, not without a foam pit."

"Are you saying that because I'm a girl?" She looked pissed off.

"No," he lied. "I'm saying that I first got on a skateboard when I was four. And now snowboarding is, like, what I do. I am *sponsored*. That's why I don't go to school and shit." *So how can you think you could be as good as me?* He didn't say that last part.

She glared at him for a moment. Then she stepped up on her board and started again.

A second later he shouted at her. She was going too slow.

But she wasn't. She was so light that she didn't need tons of speed, and when she took off in the air, she didn't get much height, less than she had been getting, but she did something with her arm, letting it trail around her body, her eyes following her hand. Her fingers were gently curved, and halfway through she flipped her palm over. Her landing was soft, only the lightest sound.

When you analyzed it, it was nothing of a move, but he hadn't thought about it. He hadn't thought about anything. He hadn't been able to take his eyes off her. That's what it was like with the really epic guys, the top boarders. Whatever they were doing, even just their warm-ups, you had to watch them. You just did.

He wanted to be like that.

Long bike rides were a part of his summer training routine, and pretty soon she started to come. As long as she didn't do the sprints—he would do one sprint forward and then another back to her—she could keep up even through this hilly country.

The hills' winding roads would be dark with the shade from the birch and ash trees until around a bend everything would suddenly be open and light, and they could see, below them, town and the two ribbony rivers that met there. Further on was a Christmas tree farm with its regular lines of carefully trimmed Fraser firs marching up the lower slope of a mountain where Seth had first snowboarded. They would ride until they reached the lake. They would bring towels and wear their swimsuits under their clothes. In shadows of trees he tried to kiss her once, and she shoved him away.

Her grandmother, whom she called MeeMaw, lived in a big modern house on Pill Hill, which was where all the doctors lived. Caitlin's grandfather had been a doctor before he died. On wet days Seth would ride his bike through the rain, and they would sit at her grandmother's dining table, Seth supposedly catching up with schoolwork and Caitlin addressing envelopes for a benefit that her grandmother was running. She used special pens and had this major sick handwriting. Calligraphy, it was called. No one had taught her. She had learned it from a book.

He hated learning things from books.

One evening when he was at home, he heard his mother and one of his sisters in the kitchen talking.

"Mom, Seth is spending a lot of time with Mrs. Thurmont's granddaughter."

"I know," his mother answered. "It's usually the pregnant one who has to leave home, not the sister."

*Pregnant?* Was Caitlin *pregnant?* That couldn't be right. Of course, she was a girl. She used the girls' bathroom, and she wore a girl's swim suit, but still...pregnant? A baby? That would have meant that she had—

He couldn't think about it.

"Apparently"—his mother was still speaking—"her parents felt like Caitlin wasn't being supportive enough of her sister."

Oh, of course. Caitlin wasn't pregnant. Her sister was.

His aunt had been pregnant last summer. She already had three kids, and she was enormous. Her feet spilled over her shoes. She struggled to get in and out of a chair. Seth tried to imagine that happening to one of his sisters. He couldn't.

As soon as he saw Caitlin next, he asked her. It didn't occur to him not to. "So your sister is going to have a baby?"

"How did you know that?"

"My mom and sister were talking about it."

"How did they hear?"

Seth shrugged. "My mom seems to know everything. It's a pain." He started to put on his knee pads. They didn't have to talk about it.

"That's why I'm here, because of Trina being pregnant. My parents are all about how we have to show the world that we love her and we stand behind her. And they say that I am 'insufficiently supportive,' that I'm being a spoiled brat."

Seth wasn't sure what to say. "How old is she?"

"Fifteen, two years older than me, and I get that it totally sucks for her. I get that. But I didn't do anything wrong and yet everybody at school talks about me like I'm some kind of slut. I got invited to a rainbow party, and I don't even wear lipstick, much less do *that*."

Seth was not about to admit that he didn't know what a rainbow party was. That was the one bad thing about not going to school with the other kids. Sometimes you felt like a major stupid-ass dork. "Your folks...weren't they mad at your sister?"

"Who knows? My mom would go into their bedroom, she'd close the door and all, but I could hear her crying. And she kept asking my dad what they had done wrong. But they say that family problems stop at the front door. To the rest of the world we have to pretend that everything is okay, which is crazy because it's not."

"Is she going to keep the baby?"

"Yeah. My dad really thought that she ought to give it up, and this social worker came and talked to all of us. But Trina and my mom...so it's going to live with us. They're trying to figure out stuff like health insurance because the military will go on covering Trina, but not the baby. That's all anyone talks about, Trina and the baby. So that's why," she finished, "I'm not going to let a guy do stuff to me."

"It's okay. I get it."

"Good. Then we don't have to talk about it again."

Seth went home and looked up rainbow parties...and then since the whole family used the same computer and his sisters knew how to check browser histories even if his parents didn't, he instantly did some searches on rainbow photos and rainbow physics as if he were suddenly interested in meteorological phenomena, which actually were pretty cool when you learned about them.

But the rainbow parties thing...why would a girl be willing to do that at all, much less on a bunch of guys and in public?

One afternoon at the skate park he looked up and saw that his dad was watching him work with Caitlin. Usually in this part of town you could hear the factory whistle signaling the shift change; Seth must have missed it.

For someone who couldn't afford to come to any competitions, his dad was stoked about Seth's career. Early on he had taken Seth's cheapie boards and tinkered with them in his garage workshop, putting better edges on them and the like. Now he was making them from scratch, layering and laminating the wood.

He also made the skateboards Seth used in the summer, and a week after coming to the park his dad gave him a skateboard he had made for Caitlin. "She's small for her age. This is a better board for her."

And it was.

She had to leave in the middle of August. She was taking the bus to Charlotte, and her parents were driving to meet her there. He rode his bike to the bus station to say goodbye. She was going to keep her skateboard on the bus with her, and her grandmother suggested that Seth carry it out of the terminal for her. Mrs. Thurmont turned away as if there were something on the station's bulletin board that she just had to read. She was chill for an old lady—although it wasn't like he was going to kiss Caitlin goodbye or something. He walked out to the bus anyway, handed her the board, and punched her lightly on her arm.

"Next summer?" he said. Her eyes really were something. He had gotten used to them so he didn't notice them all the time, but now, standing here...

"You'd better believe it," she said.

# CHAPTER TWO

And now eleven years later, Caitlin still had those eyes.

His family's house at the lake was timber and stone with lots of windows and a big screen porch. Seth retrieved the key from the hiding place. He gave Caitlin a quick tour of the house, but she said that after a day of sitting around the courtroom, she wanted to be outside. Seth picked up a blanket in case they wanted to sit down by the shore.

"I'm a city girl," she said. "I'm going to need bug juice."

"Oh, of course." There were at least seven cans of insect repellent by the door. His sisters used all-natural products on their kids; his mom liked the scented products; his dad didn't. Seth let Caitlin pick one, and he grabbed another for himself.

Then a memory hit him again. *That night in the park we only had one can for the two of us.*

What kind of romance had bug repellent as one of its highlights?

His and hers.

The property was bordered by birches, maples, and white pine. A few scraggly rhododendrons blossomed where the shade was the lightest, and one big oak tree sat off by itself. Seth's brothers-in-law took turns mowing so there was an open, sunlit stretch of grass leading down to the dock and the big rocks by the shoreline.

"So where on the lake are we?" Caitlin asked when they got outside. "I'm a little turned around."

"The public beach is that way." He pointed.

"Okay." She was looking around, getting oriented. "So the place that you and I used to sneak into is over there...and is this the tree we could see from that dock?" She gestured over her shoulder toward the oak. "The one that we thought must be so great for climbing?"

"It is that tree, and it is great for climbing, although it's gotten harder since Dad had to take off the bottom branch last year. How much of a city girl are you?"

"If you are asking if I can still climb a tree, I assume so, but you'll need to give me a stirrup." She cupped her hands, showing what she meant.

He did so. She put one foot in his hands and then sprang up, catching a limb with her hands.

How light she was, like a plastic beer mug, the kind that you're expecting to be glass so when you first pick it up, you almost throw it over your shoulder.

He looked up. Her calf muscles were strong and defined, curving down to her ankles. She was testing a big knot in the tree to see if she could use it as a step. He caught a glimpse of red panties.

"Did you pick your underwear to match the juror tag?"

She looked down at him, blank for a second. "Oh, right, yes. I called ahead."

In a moment she was standing on one of the limbs, holding on to a branch overhead, inching her way out to make room for him. He took another good look up her skirt, then jumped, grasped the lower limb, and hoisted himself up.

"This is really stupid," she said.

"Why?"

"We could fall."

"But we won't," he said confidently. And if they did...well, he had face-planted from a lot higher up than this.

He gave her a hand so that she could sit down. It could have been a tricky maneuver, but she did it gracefully. *You can take the girl out of the ballet studio, but you can't...* Then he reached through the leaves, grabbed another limb, and swung across so that he could sit facing her.

She was trying to wriggle her skirt down over her thighs. The big watch on her wrist made her hand look small. "I'm not wearing the right clothes for this."

"I think you are."

She stuck out her tongue at him.

It was nice, sitting here in the tree, watching the water. Bulldozers had been brought in to carve out the little public beach across the lake; everywhere else trees, grasses, and wildflowers sloped down to the rocky shoreline, the gray and brown rocks etching an undulated border between the patches of sun and shadows on the green slopes and the flat blue water. In the distance above the tree line were the Blue Ridge Mountains, their slopes covered with fine North Carolina hardwoods.

Snowboards were made of layers of resin, fiberglass, carbon, and glue, but at their core was wood. Some pros liked wood from obeche trees, but that wood had to be imported from Africa. That seemed wrong to Seth, snowboarding on something from a continent so dry and hot. The core of his boards was close-grained yellow birch from the High Country's cool mountain slopes. His dad always had a couple of trees in the commercial forests flagged, and he and Seth would watch their growth. For Seth that was part of the magic, knowing the tree, feeling like it was your partner.

He heard the faint chug of a trolling motor, and in a few minutes a fishing boat eased around the point of an inlet, its little motor making a ruffled wake on the surface of the water.

"You must have visited your grandmother after you all moved to San Diego," he said. "Why didn't you ever stop by and see my parents? They liked you."

"Seth, you dumped me. I wasn't going to go sit in your mother's kitchen and have your sisters feel sorry for me."

He winced. "I didn't really mean to dump you. I was a mess."

"There's no need to rehash this. We were kids. It was a teen romance. Teen romances end. That's what they do."

"Apparently your sister's didn't."

She shook her head. "The teen-romance part blew up the minute she found out that she was pregnant, but they had to stay in touch because of the baby. Years later they came together as actual adults."

Seth was twenty-five. In plenty of places that qualified for being an actual adult. He changed the subject. "On this gravity-heavy planet of yours, why are people using something as low tech as bullets?"

"It's not my planet. I'm just paid to make it gorgeous, and who says that they are people?"

"Good point. How did you get into this?"

"I started in college, doing it for other students. After I graduated, I got what should have been a dream job in Silicon Valley. The work was good, but even though people wore flip-flops and board shorts to the office, it was still totally corporate with insane office politics and people stealing credit for your work. So I decided to go out on my own."

"Is it going okay?"

"It's a bitch and a half, especially in San Francisco, which is beyond expensive, but I'm doing okay. Now I'm ready to get down." She was clearly done talking about her life in San Francisco. "How do we do that?"

"You can climb down by the same route, but I'm going to jump. It's faster." He switched his hand position and then lowered himself, extending his body so that he could drop and land lightly. "Now scoot down your branch and I will catch you."

"Are you going to look up my skirt?"

"You bet."

She eased herself down to the branch. He got hold of her legs as she dropped and eased her down, sliding his hands up her body.

"You don't have a car in San Francisco, do you?"

She looked surprised and started to step back, but a light pressure on her waist kept her in place. "I'm a freelancer. Even if I could afford a beat-up junker, a parking space is way out of reach. Why are you asking?"

"I keep noticing how strong your legs are. Isn't San Francisco pretty hilly?"

"For sure. We all have gorgeous butts out there because we walk up and down hills all day."

How normal this felt, standing close to her, his hands on her waist. "You don't really care that I saw your underwear, do you?"

"Of course not."

He kept his hands at her waist. "It's really good to see you again."

"Same here."

Were they going to play games? When they had been kids, she had promised that she wouldn't do that. She had said she would be straight with him when she was ready. And she had been.

She put her hands on his shoulders. He could feel the weight of her big watch. "I'd like us to be friends," he said.

She knew what he was asking. "With benefits?"

"If that works for you."

"It works for me," she said. Her hands started to move, caressing his shoulders.

He bent his head and kissed her.

And suddenly it was like being a boy again, that fierce magic, that ache, that overwhelming sense of desire, to smell the magic of her hair, feel the firmness of her arms, the trim curve of her waist and back, his fingers seeking the softness of her breast.

He felt her hand on the hand of his neck, her fingers separated and moving slowly. Her other arm was curved around him, and it was as if no woman had ever touched him before, as if it was all as new as it had been back when they had been in the woods together before.

"Do you want to go inside?" he whispered.

She shook her head. "We have the blanket."

He took her hand and led her back among the trees. These trees were all younger than the oak, and their roots had dug deep into the light, sandy soil, leaving the earth smooth. He kicked aside a few pinecones, unfurled the blanket, and let it float to the ground. Then he unzipped her skirt and pushed it down over her hips. Her red bikini underpants weren't designed to be sexy. They didn't have lace or skimpy strings at the sides, but they curved under her crotch with a snug, neat fit. As soon as they were lying down, he put his hand over the curve, and he could feel the warmth there and then all through her.

He knew that it would be all right to slip the panties off, open his khakis, and enter her now. She was ready. But then it would be over. And he didn't want it to be over.

Or so matter-of-fact. *You wanna have sex?* This ought to mean something. Things didn't mean enough anymore.

She was reaching for his zipper. He batted her hand away and sat up, pulling her with him so that she was straddling him, facing him. "Do you remember the first time you came?" This was how they had been that night, when they were sixteen and fifteen, her facing him, her knees on either side of him.

"I guess...yes, yes, of course, I do."

They had already had intercourse, but they had never had enough privacy to be fully undressed together, and he still hadn't been comfortable with her body. He hadn't known any specific ways to stimulate her, and so when it did happen for her, it was almost by accident.

He had been kissing the upper curve of her breast that night, and then she had shifted a bit—maybe by accident, maybe on purpose—and suddenly he was feeling the little firm tip of her nipple against his tongue, and her hands dug into his hair, supporting herself, and she moved against him.

She had probably been wearing a T-shirt that night; she would have pulled it off over her head by herself. Tonight he unbuttoned her blouse. Her bra was flesh colored, lacier than her panties had been, but not matching them. When she had dressed this morning, this was not what she had expected.

He unhooked the bra...and then was suddenly confused. How had this worked back then? Her pressing her crotch against him, and him being able to—

Oh, right, of course. Even though he had started his growth spurt then, he hadn't been finished. He had kept growing; he was taller now than he had been on that summer night so long ago. But he could make this work. His back was flexible and strong, and he was comfortable grasping her hips, bringing her closer to him, positioning her in a way that he wouldn't have had the nerve back then.

An instant later he was both a boy again, arousing a girl for the first time, and a man, sure and confident, cupping the breast he was kissing while teasing the other with his free hand.

Was all this happening then or now? Both. The blanket was green wool; it was blue fleece. The afternoon sun was on his face; it was at his back. Her hair was pulled back; it was tumbling over her shoulders. She smelled like Dove soap; she smelled like grapefruit and lime. Both moments, then and now, happening as one.

Just as before, her fingers nestled into his hair, gripping his head, relying on him for support and balance. But she was experienced too, and in a moment she let go of his head, pulled back, and started to search for his zipper again. She wouldn't have done that back then.

"No, no," he said. "Let's do it like before."

So she relaxed into the glories of being pleased. Last time she had been able to move against his body. Now because of his height she had to kneel, but only the lightest flick of his fingers against her still scarlet-covered crotch left her gasping and her muscles convulsing.

Afterward she leaned against him, settling back on his thighs.

"What was that all about?" she asked.

"I don't know for sure." It had been almost eerie, the feeling of two things happening at once, but she couldn't have been talking about that. "It just suddenly seemed like a good idea to do what we had done before."

"It's hard to believe that it was exactly like that." There was a smile in her voice. "Surely you weren't that good as a kid."

"No, but I was shorter and that made it easier."

"Okay." She didn't get it. Obviously she hadn't been thinking about the logistical difficulties. "But I've learned some things too," she said.

And she had; of course she had. He had a fleeting thought about other men, other penises, but it was pretty easy to let that go because what she was doing to him was...well, it was pretty hard to think anything.

They lay quietly for a bit. Then she rolled to her side, facing him. "You know, I don't think I have had sex outdoors with anyone but you."

He thought for a moment. "I haven't either...but I spend a lot of time in the snow, so outdoor sex might not be a great choice."

"Are you in a relationship?"

"No." What did she think of him, that he would have done this, if he were seeing someone? "What about you?"

"I live in San Francisco. All the men I meet are not only married, but they are married to each other. I'm usually the one straight chick in a room full of gay guys."

She admitted that she was getting cold. They organized their clothes and went inside, eating on the screen porch, talking some, not about much or anything in particular. Afterward she carried the trash bag out to the car while he circled around the house to hide the key. When he came back, she was looking at her phone, leaning back against the car, one foot cocked behind her. Her leather purse was on the ground. Her retro sneakers were black canvas with white laces.

Seth thought of himself as a here-and-now kind of guy, live in the moment and all that. He was practical, down to earth. He gave little enough thought to basic Christian theology, much less anything woo-woo about a spirit world. But out there on the blanket it had truly seemed as if two moments were happening at the same time. It must be that the memories were so strong; that could be the only explanation.

Caitlin picked up her purse to put her phone away. She made a face. "I have to go back to court tomorrow."

Seth cursed and pulled out his phone. He had the hotline number and his ID code on an old email, and yes, he had to report back tomorrow. "This is so wack. They're not going to pick us."

# CHAPTER THREE

Caitlin did not have sex with men she had only known for an evening. It wasn't any big moral issue. When you had sex with strangers, you didn't know what you were getting into. The guy might turn out to be a Silicon Valley asshole or a clingy type who wasn't going to let you catch your breath, wanting to see you on Tuesday...oh, you are busy on Tuesday, what about Wednesday? Thursday?

It had been great to be young and living in San Francisco. The city was beautiful, and there were always people on the streets, other young people ready for adventure. Caitlin liked prowling through the thrift shops, not caring about fashions or trends, but then having other girls stop her on the street asking her where she had gotten something. She could step into a crowded restaurant at brunch, and people she didn't remember meeting would remember her and call her over, making room for her at their table.

Of course, you could go out for a long, boozy brunch every Sunday when you had a Silicon Valley paycheck. Not when you were freelancing. San Francisco was a lot better when you had money. Her apartment was tiny, tiny, tiny, but for the rent she was paying, you would think that it came with a herd of dairy cattle. She was able to get her health insurance under her father's Navy's Young Adult program, but that would end in another eighteen months. She had no idea what she would do then.

She stayed out of credit card debt. Too many women her age seemed to think of the money they spent on their clothes, their hair, and their bar bills as an investment, what you had to do to make sure that someday your prince would come. Caitlin viewed that as an extremely poor investment. Most princes these days had student loans to pay off.

If she had ever thought about having a prince for herself, it would have been when she was fifteen and in love with Seth. So technically this evening didn't count as having sex with a stranger. But did she know what she was getting into? Absolutely not. Not a clue.

She had acted all cool and hip as if seeing him hadn't mattered. But this was Seth. *Seth.* How could he not matter? She just didn't know if it was going to matter good or matter bad. Really, really bad.

Her parents asked about him, but they were only mildly interested. During those years when all she wanted was to spend the summer in North Carolina, she had always tried to conceal the fact that she wanted to come because of him. Then when her dad was transferred to San Diego and she was so devastated about Seth not calling, they didn't really know how desperate she felt because Trina was still home, sucking all the oxygen out of the room.

Her parents were more interested in her day in court. When she said that the next case was a criminal trial that seemed to be having trouble getting off the ground, her mom said, "That must be—"

Her father interrupted. "That Caitlin doesn't follow Carolina politics is in her favor. Let's keep it that way."

"I don't like the sound of this." She looked at him. Unfortunately he had his judge face on. He wasn't going to tell her anything. "Is this going to be some big murder case where I am going to be sequestered for a year?"

"No. Not at all. And North Carolina doesn't sequester juries. Of course judges could, but they don't. It's expensive, and the current thinking is that sequestered juries render bad verdicts."

\* \* \* \*

Her grandmother had more of a clue of how intensely Caitlin had cared about Seth back when they had been kids. So when she was driving Caitlin to the courthouse the next morning, she had questions.

"Did you have a nice evening with him?"

"Yes, I did."

"He has turned into a very good-looking young man, hasn't he?"

"Yes, he has."

"I like a tall man."

"Actually his height has been a problem for snowboarding. He is taller than most."

"And he must be very fit."

This conversation was getting weird. "Of course. It's his job."

"Your grandfather was athletic, very fit. I enjoyed that."

Dear Lord in heaven. Was MeeMaw saying what Caitlin thought MeeMaw was saying? It didn't matter how progressive a thinker you were, how strong your claim to being a hipster was, you didn't want to hear your grandmother talking about your grandfather in bed. That took a bit of doing to get out of her head.

The jury coordinator was surprised to see her. "But you didn't need to come for the informational session. You've already heard it. You could have waited until eight thirty. We must have told you that yesterday."

Caitlin glanced around the room. There were a lot of familiar faces, people from the Monday group. The coordinator's "must have" obviously meant "we were supposed to." That was no way to run a zoo.

Seth wasn't there. She put her laptop bag on the chair next to her, saving it for him. But when the lights dimmed for the video, he hadn't shown up.

This was what happened after one-night stands, wasn't it? The guy made all kind of promises and then didn't show up the next day. Of course she had leverage that most women didn't. If Seth didn't appear, the court could issue a summons and throw him in jail. Too bad women everywhere didn't have that option.

The video was exactly the same as it had been on Monday. There was still a "the" in front of "Magna Carta," and the Clerk of the Court repeated the same parts of it that he had repeated on Monday.

At 8:26 Seth strolled in. "Hey," he said.

MeeMaw was correct, at least about Seth. Caitlin supposed she was also correct about PopPop, but Caitlin did not want to think about that.

Seth was indeed a very good-looking young man. He still had the puckish air he had had as a kid. He was clean shaven today, but in most of his pictures his chin and jaw were slightly scruffy, giving him the air of an engaging rascal. Despite his WASPy name, he had a lot of Scandinavian blood. His hair bleached quickly in the sun. His eyes were light, green with a touch of blue. His cheekbones were open, and his skull long. She had used the shape of his head in a lot of the games she animated, varying his features so that it never looked like him.

But it was a little hard to get overly giddy about seeing him when she had just wasted half an hour, and he hadn't. "How did you know to come in late?" she whispered.

"My mom told me."

He could have shared that information, couldn't he? She watched as he plugged his extension cord into the wall socket.

In terms of technical activity, last night had pretty much been parking-lot sex, not that Caitlin had much experience with that given the hourly rates at garages in San Francisco. But there had been something so—could she use the word "sweet" to describe a professional snowboarder?—about him remembering their past.

He sat down and then leaned close to her, his forearm brushing hers. "I hope you need a ride when we're done here. I threw some skateboards in the car. We could go to the park like we used to."

"That sounds like fun." It really did. "I'll have to go home and change." It was one thing to climb a tree in skirt, but skateboard in a park where the thirteen-year-old boys hung out? Ah, no. "But only if this doesn't last all day. We're going to have dinner at my grandmother's."

"It better not last all day. I will hang myself. I Googled you last night. There's nothing about your work."

"No."

"Why not? You do work, don't you?"

Did she work? She did nothing but work. "Of course I do."

She must have snapped because he immediately apologized. "I'm sorry. Was I wrong to look you up?"

"No, it was fine. Really." Didn't she do online searches on people she met? She hadn't searched on him last night because she did it a couple of times a year. "I have two sets of clients, and they don't need to know about each other. So I use pseudonyms for both."

"That sounds interesting."

"It's not." But she explained. There was enough resentment and distrust of women in the video-game community that she identified herself to clients as "Tlin" and never spoke to them on the phone or met them in person.

The games she worked on were violent and aggressive. It was draining. So she went to the other extreme and designed covers for romance novels. It required less sophisticated computer skills and didn't pay as well, but the covers were luxuriantly rich. Lovers embraced on green paths in front of covered footbridges. Silken dresses slid off ivory shoulders; cravats were unloosened; kilts were unbuckled. To those clients she was "Aurora."

"Aurora?" Seth asked. "That's so...so—"

"So lovely? Yes, it's supposed to be. I can be lovely when I try."

"I'm eager to see that...but aren't you concerned that by using a male pseudonym for the video games, you aren't doing anything to help other women get into the field?"

Was she having her feminist creds questioned by a snowboarder? Seriously? "I wanted a way out of a corporate job." She forced herself to speak mildly. "This didn't seem like a huge compromise."

The Clerk of the Court was speaking again. Today there was only one criminal trial, and he said that it could be lengthy. People could be excused, the Clerk continued, if they had long-scheduled vacations or medical procedures.

"What do you think 'lengthy' means?" someone else at the table whispered.

Caitlin shook her head, and Seth shrugged. They didn't know. But it didn't sound good.

The Court would need documentation for excuses, the Clerk said. And being busy at work was not an excuse. And no, a letter from one's boss would make no difference.

"I'm supposed to go to New Zealand on Monday." Seth leaned toward her. "It's work, but shall I lie and say I am going on vacation?"

"That's on your conscience."

"I don't have one of those. My moral code is based on what is good for Street Boards. If it won't hurt the company, I do it."

Within minutes people were at front table showing the jury coordinator images from their phone and tablet screens. They were pleading, trying to be excused. About a third were allowed to pack up and leave. The rest had to sit back down.

Forty-five minutes later all the remaining people who were holdovers from Monday were called to line up. They followed a deputy to the courtroom, stopping to hand over their phones and computers.

Caitlin only knew about courtrooms from TV, but the layout was what she expected. The judge's bench and the witness stand faced the lawyers' tables, behind which, separated by a railing, were the benches for the observers. The jury box was perpendicular to everything else. It had two rows of chairs, and the second row was elevated. Caitlin noticed that there were eight chairs in each row, sixteen in all. They must be planning on picking four alternates.

The potential jurors filed in to sit on the observers' bench. The judge repeated some of what had been in the video, making it now the fifth time Caitlin had heard it, although he solved the whole Magna Carta issue by not mentioning it. He then explained the procedure for the day. Sixteen people would be selected at random and questioned. Some would be accepted, some excused. This would continue until twelve jurors and four alternates had been selected.

Names were being called. "Darrell Truckee, Nancy Kingsley, Susanne Nugent, Cameron Edwards, Caitlin McGraw, Richard..."

Oh, that was her. Caitlin stood up. Apparently she had been the tenth juror called. Her seat was in the back row second closest to the front wall. From his place on the observers' bench, Seth gave her a fake Cheshire-cat grin.

*That keeps you in the parking lot, boy-o. Bedroom sex requires more.*

One of the lawyers stood up and introduced himself as the prosecutor and explained what a prosecutor and a defense lawyer did. None of it was new information to anyone who had ever watched one minute of television.

They were first asked if they knew personally the defendants or the lawyers. Could they disregard any media accounts that they had read? That was easy for Caitlin. She had no idea what the case was about. Did they know anyone in law enforcement? Caitlin raised her hand and said that her father was a retired navy judge. Would that influence her decision? No, she answered honestly.

The lawyers gathered to talk among themselves. A man and a woman remained seated at the defendants' table. They must be the defendants. They were both middle aged, well preserved, and well groomed. The man had thick silver hair and looked like a successful executive. The woman looked equally successful in a nicely cut black suit with a feminine white blouse. Her necklace was a twisted rope of silver and pearls.

Caitlin didn't want to have to judge these people. Or anyone. She didn't belong on a jury. Why hadn't she lied and said that her father had always said that all defendants were always guilty? Why hadn't one of the lawyers asked her something that would reveal that she really had no right to claim North Carolina residency, that she was defrauding the state of California, and that she should be the one to need a jury of her peers?

Eventually the lawyers were finished, and the judge began calling names, "Darrell Truckee, Susanne Nugent...." Was it good or bad to have your name called? None of them knew. He droned on and then finally said, "If I have called your name, you have been excused. Thank you for your service."

Her name hadn't been called. She and the man in the first seat in the front row were the only ones left. Did this mean she was on the jury? Yes, it must. She had been selected, empaneled. Sixteen down to two, and she had been one of the two. How had this happened? Last night she and Seth were so sure that they wouldn't be chosen.

Why had they thought that? Because they were too young? They weren't. She had started voting at eighteen and legally drinking at twenty-one. Wait, what about renting a car? If she was too young to rent a car without a premium, surely she shouldn't be on a jury.

She looked at Seth. He grimaced in sympathy.

*He's twenty-five. He can rent a car. Pick him.*

Except there was no way they would ever select him. Forget the age thing. Who would want a snowboarder deciding their innocence or guilt? And even more important he was part-owner of the town's biggest employer. Street Boards had taken over the furniture factory when it closed. Wouldn't having a Street on the jury throw off the negotiations?

Fourteen more names were called. They were questioned, and then twelve of them dismissed.

The woman to Caitlin's right was still seated at the end of that round. "They didn't call my name," she whispered to Caitlin. "What does that mean?"

Caitlin turned to look at her. She was younger than Caitlin, and the slant of her thin chin gave her face a weak backwoods quality. "It means you have been selected."

"But that can't be." The girl was shaking her head. "I have a terrible time making up my mind about anything...why would they take me?"

Caitlin couldn't answer that.

Seth was going to be able to go home pretty soon, and she would be stuck here. No skateboarding today. And what about the rest of the week? Was he going to stick around and fly to New Zealand from here, or go back to Oregon?

It didn't really matter, did it? Not really. She would miss out on some fun, but "friends with benefits"—when did that ever work? She'd seen people try it. Sometimes your "friend" was suddenly picking out china patterns with someone, leaving you feeling like a loser. Or neither one of you tried very hard to find someone else, and then whenever you were together, you both felt like failures.

Why would she want to put herself through that? A one-night stand might be a better choice.

\* \* \* \*

They only had two weeks together during their second summer.

By the time Caitlin got home from the first summer, her family knew that Trina was going to have a boy. Caitlin expected that Trina and Mom would have gone crazy decorating the fourth bedroom with rocket ships or little blue ducks. The two of them had always done all those things together, choosing paint color, sewing new throw pillows. The family's furniture was very neutral, and each time they moved, her mom would pick out a bold color for the walls so each place felt exciting and not at all like a place you were only going to be in for three years. Caitlin was always dragooned into helping with the actual painting, but she never went to the paint store or the fabric store. Trina and Mom took forever to make up their minds, and they clearly had a good time taking forever, whereas Caitlin spoiled all the fun because she knew immediately that that white had too much yellow in it and that that wallpaper would make everyone dizzy if the ceilings and walls weren't perfectly plumb.

But when she got back from MeeMaw's at the end of the summer, instead of the back bedroom being an explosion of baby froufrou, it still had her father's desk and the pullout sleep sofa. The baby—his name was going to be Dylan—would sleep in Trina's room.

Except he didn't sleep. He had to be jiggled. He needed motion to calm him down. One time, out of frustration, their dad had put him in his car seat and went on a drive, but Trina didn't have her driver's license. At night she had to jiggle him. Sometimes she would come into Caitlin's room and wake her up. "Please, I can't do this anymore, but don't tell Mom and Dad." Caitlin was stronger and so jiggling a baby didn't tire her out, and honestly—although it made her feel pretty heartless—she could block out Dylan's crying even when it was right in her ear.

Trina was being homeschooled. The county sent a tutor a couple of days a week, but mostly it was on Mom, and so she had to nag Trina both to do her schoolwork and to get Dylan on a firmer schedule. Trevor, Dylan's father, came over twice a week even though he clearly didn't want to. His mother had to drive him, and she always came in. Before her visits there was a frantic forty-five minutes of tidying up, the sort of thing that they had never had to do in the past because before Dylan had been born, Caitlin's mom had never been one to leave dishes in the sink or the newspaper on the kitchen table.

Caitlin felt ignored by everyone in the family. If she hadn't had the skateboard Seth's father had made, she wouldn't have been able to do anything or go anywhere. She started wearing black to school, hanging out in the art room, eating lunch alone. Finally one day about a month into school, her mother was handing her a load of laundry to put away when suddenly Mom stopped. "Caitlin, how are things with you?"

"Fine," Caitlin snapped and reached for the laundry basket.

Mom wouldn't let her have it. She put it back on top of the washer. "But this is your first year of high school, and we haven't signed you up for any activities. Do you want to take ballet again? I could call the studio."

"No, I do not want to take ballet."

"What about that skateboarding that you're doing? Would you like to see if I can find lessons?"

"I already looked into it. The closest decent place is sixty miles away. Everything around here is all little kid shit."

"Caitlin!" Mom's voice was stern. "I know that this is hard on everyone, but there's no call for that kind of language."

Oh, for God's sake. Her sister had gotten pregnant, and Caitlin was being scolded for saying "shit"?

"Oh, I am sorry," Mom apologized instantly. "I shouldn't have said that."

"But you did." Caitlin grabbed the laundry basket and stormed out of the room.

She and Seth usually just kept in touch by trying to be on computers at the same time, but that night she took the family's phone into the front hall closet and called him on the cell phone he and his mother shared.

"I'm not having kids, not ever." Dylan had a cold, and his nose was almost as disgusting as his butt.

"Okay," he said. "But you should get something out of this. Your mom feels guilty. If you want something, ask. She's going to be a soft touch."

"I want everything to go back to normal, to how it was. That's what I want."

"Well, good luck with that one. You want your own phone, don't you?"

"I don't want anything from them," she grumbled.

"What about some other kind of dancing? Did you want to do that?"

She did. She wasn't trying to get herself to a competitive level at skateboarding. Even if her parents would have been willing to drive sixty miles—and there was no way they felt *that* guilty—she was starting too late and, in truth, she didn't have the competitive fire, the drive to win that Seth did. What she wanted from skateboarding was to practice and get better and to be awesome, scarily awesome. She remembered how Seth had looked at her the first time she stopped trying to skateboard like him. She wanted people to watch her and be blown away, even if it were only the moms at the birthday parties.

Ballet had made her graceful, but she wanted to develop style, something like those sexy Latin dancers she'd seen on TV. She knew that Jazzercise was aerobics for people her mother's age, but it seemed like her best option to learn something different. The classes weren't as expensive as ballet, but they were in the evening and on the other side of town. Her parents would never let her cruise over on her skateboard.

She waited until Trina was putting Dylan to bed. Her parents had already gone into their room, but the door was open. Her mother had her back to the full-length mirror, twisting her head over her shoulder to look at what she called her fanny.

Her pants were too tight. Even Caitlin could see that. It was strange. Mom was gaining weight. Here she was, this superdisciplined navy wife, and she couldn't fit into her pants.

She must hate that. She must really, really hate that.

Caitlin was the weird art student who wore black. She was the one who was supposed to be depressed, except she was—she knew perfectly well—playing at being depressed in order to punish her parents. But her parents didn't seem to be noticing...probably because her mother actually was depressed.

Her father spotted Caitlin first, and when he said her name, her mother instantly did the mom thing, trying to look like she didn't mind having pants she couldn't sit down in.

Mom knew about Jazzercise. Some women she knew took one of the morning classes.

"So I thought," Caitlin said, even though she had never planned this, it hadn't occurred to her until this second, "since you would have to drive me there, that maybe we could take the class together."

"What a great idea." Dad was instantly enthusiastic. "You were just saying that you needed to exercise more, Sharon, and to do it with Caitlin..."

"I don't know." Mom was shaking her head. "I feel like I have way too much to do."

"But if you have to drive her anyway," Dad said, "why not work out too?"

Mom was still shaking her head.

By now Caitlin was convinced that this was a good plan, a very good plan. Mom being bummed all the time was as big a problem as Dylan screaming all night. "Then will you come with me the first couple times? There won't be any other kids in the class, and I will feel weird with all those grown-ups. Would you come just until I don't feel so out of place?"

"Oh." Mom knew that she was boxed in. How could she say no to that? "Well, sure, sweetie. If you need me, of course."

The teacher was from Latin America, and she was using her hips and shoulders in the way that Caitlin wanted to. So Caitlin liked the most dance-type moves, but her mother was—amazingly enough—totally into the kickboxing, kicking her leg off to one side with her fists clenched up in front of her. Mom the warrior...Caitlin couldn't have predicted that.

Within a week her mother was going to a morning class as well and within a month was wearing her pretty clothes again. Trina started to say that she needed exercise more than anyone, but Dylan was too young for the child-care program offered at the studio. Caitlin could tell that Trina wanted Mom to drive her to the classes and then—what?—sit in the car with Dylan while Trina exercised? Even Trina wasn't going to ask that.

Caitlin stopped the depressed art student act. It wasn't necessary. The high school was more than twice the size of her middle school, and being close to a military base, there was a big turnover in the student body every year. No one was very interested in what her sister had done last year. So instead she was known as the cool girl who came to school on a skateboard.

In January Trina got her driver's license, and their parents bought her a used car, emphasizing that she would have to share it with Caitlin when Caitlin was old enough to drive.

*Yeah, right,* Caitlin thought.

Suddenly Trina was going to the morning exercise classes while Mom was staying home with Dylan. It made Caitlin furious. What about Trevor's family? Why weren't they doing anything? Trevor himself was worthless. He hardly even touched Dylan, but what about his mom? She was a nurses' aide at the hospital, but why wasn't someone expecting her to rearrange her schedule and take care of Dylan sometimes?

Now that she had the car, Trina was trying to connect with her old friends after school. So more and more she was asking Caitlin if she could come straight home to sit with Dylan, or, as long as she didn't have plans on Friday or Saturday night, why couldn't she...

Mom and Dad stepped in. Just because Caitlin was home didn't mean that she was available to take care of Dylan. Caitlin was to be home alone with Dylan no more than one evening and three afternoons a month.

So instead it was Mom and Dad who took care of Dylan while Trina went to the mall. Caitlin asked why they kept giving in to Trina all the time. They didn't have a good answer.

One day in April her parents sat down with her. "I know you're looking forward to go back to North Carolina, but we think it is Trina's turn."

She stared at them. "You're kidding, right? She's going to MeeMaw's and we're going to be stuck here with Dylan?"

"No, Dylan will go with her, of course. You deserve a summer at home, a summer of just being a teen."

"But that's not what I want." Caitlin felt desperate. She and Seth...they had such plans. His older sister had already agreed to drive them to the Highland Games at Grandfather Mountain. They also thought that if they took the whole day, they should be able to bike to Boone and back. Boone was a college town; Seth had already gotten a schedule of their summer concerts. And there was skateboarding and the lake, and being together... she had to go. She had to.

"Why don't I go and help Trina? MeeMaw shouldn't have to do that. Let me go with them. I will help. I really, really will. I don't mind. You can't dump all this on MeeMaw."

"Trina will have her car. She can be self-reliant." Dad was speaking in his judge's voice. "We've made up our minds."

The poor schmucks in his courtroom at least had had some rights of appeal. Caitlin didn't.

She went straight into Trina's room. "Do you want to go to MeeMaw's?"

"No. I'm totally pissed about it."

"Then why—"

"Because they think I need to accept more responsibility for Dylan. And this was MeeMaw's idea. She thinks that Mom is having 'boundary issues.' Apparently she doesn't plan on helping me at all. They want me to manage on my own."

Caitlin's strategy of offering to help had been completely wrong. She had said the worst possible thing.

Once again she took the phone in the closet and called Seth. A lot had been happening in Seth's family. His dad, who had always made Seth's boards, was opening a small factory to produce both snowboards and skateboards. A snowboarding family who had a kid Seth's age had been super encouraging, helping with the business plan, the paperwork, and the financing. Seth had said that he would need to work in the factory some.

"I will too," Caitlin had promised. "I don't know what needs doing, but I am an awesome housepainter."

But it was Trina who was going to North Carolina. Caitlin called Seth to tell him.

"Shit," he said. "Shit. Shit."

"And she doesn't even want to go. That's the bitch."

"Can't you talk to your folks? Explain how important it is. You could stay with us. I'll ask my mom. I'm sure it will be okay."

"Oh, right. Your mom is going to be totally on board with helping me to disobey my mom."

"Oh..."

They were powerless. There was nothing they could do. They were kids.

Her parents had her ask her art teacher about summer programs. The teacher was not very enthusiastic about her abilities. She could draw meticulously, but apparently she didn't have "original vision" or "her own voice." Caitlin wondered if he would have thought that if she had continued to wear black and eat lunch alone.

She should, he suggested, aim for a career as a commercial graphic artist. She knew that he intended it as a putdown, but after she had read about that kind of work, she decided that it sounded pretty awesome.

The photography course the teacher recommended was full, so she signed up for a class about computer programming because the description had the word "graphic" in it. She couldn't imagine herself being interested in computer programming, but at least she got a cell phone out of her parents feeling bad.

The class was clearly a summer camp for nerds. There were no other girls. Not one. Caitlin did not understand a single word of what the teacher said in the first hour. After he assigned them to individual computer stations, he came over to Caitlin. He squatted down next to her, his hand on the edge of her desk. "Your paperwork says that your art teacher recommended you?"

Caitlin glanced down at his hand. She wished that he would move it. "Yes, sir."

"Well, if you find this is not the right class, you have a week to withdraw and get your fee back."

"Yes, sir."

*Withdraw? Give up?*

*I'm not my sister.* And she wasn't thinking about the pregnant Trina, the depressed teen mom, but Trina as she had been before, the pretty one, the happy one, the B student who expected, who needed, everything to come easily.

Caitlin was not a quitter. She was *so* not a quitter. The first few days were unbelievably hard. Her dad thought he might be able to help her, but he was even more lost than she was. So she focused on the vocabulary, trying to understand the words that everyone was slinging around. Then there was some grunt memory work. She could do that, but there was so much that she simply didn't understand.

She wasn't about to ask the teacher for help. He would just suggest that she withdraw. There were two guys in the course who were better than the rest of them. One was an arrogant preppy type. Caitlin hated him. He was a Seth-gone-wrong, too big, too bold, too bright, a Seth who didn't give a shit about anyone else as long as they were watching him. The other guy was East Asian Indian, slender and quiet, nothing like Seth except that he was willing to explain the stuff he was good at. She chose him.

They did their final project together at the end of the session, and it was the best in the class. Of course, the teacher assumed that Dev had done it all, and while he had done the trickiest programming parts, the design had all been Caitlin's. Commercial graphic art might be the thing for her.

There would still be three weeks left to the summer after nerd camp was over. Her parents asked her if she would like to spend two of them in North Carolina.

"Yes, yes, of course. That would be great."

"We haven't forgotten how generous you were to offer to help with Dylan. We think Trina needs it."

So the big experiment had failed, and now Caitlin the babysitter was going to the rescue. Oh well, if it got her down there to see Seth...

She flew to Charlotte and then took a bus the rest of the way across the state. MeeMaw had some kind of committee meeting, so Trina and Dylan came to the bus station to pick her up.

"You know why you're here, don't you?" Trina asked as soon as Dylan was back in his car seat.

Caitlin fastened her seat belt. "To help with Dylan."

Trina nodded. "MeeMaw wanted to send me home. I'm just no good with him. Now that he's crawling, you have to watch him all the time. He doesn't want to be in the stroller so I can't even take him for a walk. I'm sixteen and I feel like my life is over."

Trina had been saying that ever since she found out that she was pregnant. "What did you do all summer?" Caitlin asked. "Did you make friends?"

"Who is going to be interested in me?"

Caitlin might be really sick of hearing Trina whine about how her life was over, but sometimes she would remember what her sister had been like before, glowing, gorgeous, and graceful. Caitlin might have resented all that glowing gorgeousness, but she didn't want to see her like this. Then they turned the corner, and on MeeMaw's front walk she could see Seth's bike, a skateboard tied to the little rack, and sitting on the front steps, a backpack at his feet, was Seth himself.

She was out of the car before Trina had turned off the engine, dashing up the sidewalk. Seth was coming toward her, and she threw herself at him, hugging him just as she had hugged Dev a few days before.

But he wasn't Dev. He was nothing like Dev. She pulled back. "You've gotten so tall."

"I grew five inches. It was a bitch. My center of gravity changed every week."

It was so strange standing next to him having to look up. She almost felt a little awkward.

"Come get your suitcase," her sister called out. "I want to lock up the car."

"Oh, right." She started back to the car.

"I'll get it," Seth said.

And that was weird too. She could carry her own suitcase. She had gotten herself from the airport to the bus station. But he was already at the car, lifting it out of the trunk with one hand, slamming the lid with the other.

Trina and Dylan were in the room she had had last summer, so she was in a smaller room at the other end of hall. That was fine with her.

"Do you want to unpack or something?" Seth asked after he put her suitcase on the bed.

"No. Let me just get out my skateboard. I took the wheels off, so we will have to put them back on, and then let's go."

She handed Seth the sweatshirt-swaddled board while she fished around the suitcase for the wheels.

"You've used this a lot," he said once he had unwrapped the board.

"I love it. I would have been lost this year without it. It's how I got every place on our side of town."

"Are you going to the skate park?" Trina was at the door, Dylan on her hip. "I would like to come."

"Ah..." Caitlin did not want Trina to come. "We were going to bike over."

"I can drive us. I just have to change Dylan and fix a bottle."

Caitlin knew that that could take forever. "How about if we meet you there?"

Out in the garage Seth pumped up the tires of the bike while she put the wheels back on her board and blew the dust off the bike helmet. "I'm sorry about my sister," she said. "I guess she's had a pretty crappy summer. I may be babysitting a fair amount."

"That's okay. I'll babysit with you. "

There was a new sign hung along the skateboard park's fence, advertising Seth's family's business. The logo had "STREET BOARDS" in clean black type—Helvetica, Caitlin now knew that it was—but then inserted in red between the two words was a caret and "& Snow." The red letters looked like graffiti, as if someone had whipped it onto the logo with a can of spray paint.

Caitlin stopped in front of it. "Oh my God, that is so awesome. I love it."

"So do I. It was my mom's idea, but it took her forever to get the graphic artist to understand what she wanted."

"They probably had to design the font, but it was only four letters, and there are no ascenders and all the letters have a similar mass." She was holding her hands up as if she were curving her fingers around the letters, getting a feel for them.

Seth was staring at her.

She dropped her hands. "Some of us do go to school, you know."

She had told him that she wouldn't have room in her suitcase for pads. One of his sisters had dropped off a set the day before. He went behind the counter and got them, coming out with a new skateboard as well.

"I told my dad that you were focusing on footwork. He said that you should try this board. You can keep it if you like it."

Caitlin hadn't realized how scuffed, even nicked, her old board was until she looked at this sleek one with the wonderful Street & Snow Boards logo.

She couldn't wait to try it. She pulled the pads on and tightened the strap on her helmet. "Now you have to tell me everything I am doing wrong. I want to get better."

It had never occurred to her that he wouldn't be a great teacher. He would tell her to change something, and of course she would mess up at first because she would be concentrating so hard on the new thing that she would do everything else wrong, but then suddenly everything would feel right and he would be clapping and laughing. It was wonderful, and it seemed impossible to imagine that they hadn't seen each other in a year.

Then Trina showed up.

She took Caitlin's pads and helmet, and Seth had to show her the basics while Caitlin sat with Dylan. It was no fun.

Trina didn't want Caitlin to babysit. She didn't have any place to go. She wanted to tag along with Caitlin and Seth. It was almost as if she were the bratty little sister. Caitlin did put her foot down about one thing. Trina could come to the skate park with them—it was a public place—but she could not ask Seth to teach her. It wasn't fair to him. If Trina wanted to learn, she should go to the park on her own, rent equipment, and pay for lessons. Caitlin would stay home with Dylan.

So Trina stopped trying to learn, but she still came to the park. She didn't have anything else to do. If Caitlin and Seth were biking out to the lake, she would drive and meet them there. In the evenings she would try to get them to stay home and watch a movie with her.

The only time she couldn't try to join them was when Seth's mother invited Caitlin to supper. But then, of course, they were with his family. They were almost never alone. And there didn't seem to be much they could do about it. They were kids.

One night toward the end of her stay she had stayed at the Streets' until after dark, and she didn't have lights on her bike. Seth loaded the bike into his mother's station wagon, and the two of them sat on the old swing set, waiting for his sister to drive Caitlin home. The lights from the kitchen windows etched white bars on the dark grass, but if Caitlin turned her head, she could see the fireflies flitting near the bushes.

"What's the strangest thing that happened to you this year?" Seth asked.

She had been turning around in her swing, letting the chains twist overhead. She dug a heel into the ground to hold still. "I suppose deciding to be the tragic art student." But he knew all about that. "What about you?" He would have asked the question for a reason.

"I had sex."

"*What?*" She must have lifted her foot because suddenly the swing was whipping her around, house, bushes, garage, house, bushes, garage. Even when the chains had untwisted, the swing kept going, the chains wrapping around each other in the other direction. She had to put both feet on the ground. "With who? Why?"

"Why did I have sex? Why do you think? Because I could."

"You have a girlfriend? Why haven't you said anything about her?"

Seth with a girlfriend? She didn't like that. And him having sex, him taking his pants...she didn't want to think about it. Not at all. No.

"She wasn't really my girlfriend."

In fact, she wasn't even a girl; she was in her early twenties, one of the established pros. Apparently she and one of her girlfriends had been joking about his friend Nate and him, and it wasn't quite a bet, maybe more like they dared each other. "It wasn't romantic or anything. Some people were hanging out in one of the condos, and she grabbed my hand and took me into one of the bedrooms."

Caitlin didn't want to hear about this. "At least I hope you were smart about things."

"I wasn't."

"You didn't use a condom?" Caitlin stood up from the swing. "Seth, are you kidding? Don't—"

"Don't I know about your sister? Yes, I do. I didn't think about it. But apparently she told some other people about it afterward, and one of older guys came and talked to me, saying that she knew that she was okay, on the pill, and tested for stuff, but that I shouldn't assume that that was always true."

"You were really stupid."

"I know that, and it wasn't much fun having everyone know about it either. "

He clearly wanted to—well, confess or something like that. It had been a crappy experience for him, but she couldn't listen. It was all too... What had actually happened? Had they undressed all the way? No, why was she thinking that way? She didn't want to know.

Her phone buzzed. She pulled it out of her pocket. It was Trina. She didn't always answer her sister's calls, but anything was better than sitting here trying not to look at Seth's crotch.

Dylan was asleep, and MeeMaw was home. Trina could come over and pick Caitlin up. Then they could go to the Dairy Queen or something.

"I've got my bike," Caitlin told her, something that Trina knew perfectly well. "It's too hard to fit it into your car. And Becca's got to take a friend of hers home anyway."

"She doesn't give up, does she?" Seth asked when Caitlin had hung up.

Caitlin shoved her phone back in her pocket. She might have been bitching about Trina the whole time she had been here, but for someone else to be criticizing her... "You can't blame her. She's lonely."

"But it's not fair to you, that everything is about her all the time."

"Well, what about you and your sisters? Isn't everything about you and snowboarding?"

"They don't mind."

"How do you know that? How did they feel about your mom being gone so much? I treat my mom like she is the enemy, but I would have *died* if I'd had to go to my dad when I started my period, and I bet that your sisters had to."

He muttered something. She wasn't fighting fair. What could he possibly say about his sisters' periods?

Well, he had had sex, hadn't he? "And what about the money?" she demanded. "Aren't your sisters in the same boat as me? Only a lot more so. All your skateboarding has to have cost tons more than Dylan does."

He glared at her. "You're wrong. I got all my expenses paid this year, and on top of that—"

"But you've been doing this for years, and your family never said that you had to quit, and they could have. We can't quit. We can't tell Trina to stop being a mom and turn Dylan over to Social Services. We can't do that."

Just then the kitchen door opened. More light flooded the grass. His sister and her friend were ready to leave. Becca asked Seth if he wanted to ride with them, but he said that he needed to help their dad with something.

Trina was waiting on the front porch. She still wanted to go to the Dairy Queen.

"Won't it be closed?" Caitlin did not want to go.

"No, I called. They're open until ten."

Caitlin was suddenly weary. *I can't fix this. I can't make you like you used to be. I can't.*

But she could go to the Dairy Queen, couldn't she?

Trina just ordered a Diet Coke, so it wasn't as if she wanted ice cream. Caitlin went full out with a banana split, three scoops of ice cream with three different toppings and whipped cream. Caitlin didn't know what thrilling things Trina thought would happen—the kids hanging out in the DQ parking lot were the sort that Trina wouldn't have said two words to back home—but they sat at one of the picnic tables, and Caitlin ate slowly so they could stay until the place closed.

Her phone buzzed. It was Seth. He must be calling to apologize. Caitlin longed to talk to him, but no, this was her sister's time. She couldn't see that sitting here was doing Trina any good, but Caitlin taking a call from Seth would make it worse.

She called him the instant she got back to her room.

"I don't like fighting with you," he said.

"No. Me neither."

"You've got to try to come back for longer next summer."

"It's not up to me. You know that."

"This really sucks. It seems like we never get to see each other. Why can't we decide things for ourselves?"

"Because we can't. Because we're kids." Caitlin was feeling sick. She hadn't finished the banana split, but she had eaten too much of it. "But you go to more places and do more things than most kids."

"But they don't involve seeing you."

# CHAPTER FOUR

Seth was called to the jury box immediately after lunch on Tuesday. He was seated in the back row with one person between him and her.

He was asked if he had ever been victim of financial fraud. "If I have been, I don't know about it yet."

Caitlin could see people start to smile.

Then he was asked if he knew anyone who had been the victim of financial fraud. He thought for a moment. He knew some people who had lost a lot of money, he said, but he had no idea if they had been defrauded or had made bad decisions. "Knowing the people involved," he added, "I'd bet it was bad decisions. Really bad ones."

People in the room started to laugh a bit, but the judge frowned and cut it off.

The lawyers had their usual little meeting to discuss the jurors. Then, as before, they approached the judge to share their conclusions. Every other time this conversation only lasted long enough for the judge to glance at the list of names before reading them aloud. But now the judge was frowning, gesturing for the lawyers to step closer, wanting to talk to them.

It was pretty clear to Caitlin that they were talking about Seth; two of the lawyers kept glancing at him. Did the lawyers want Seth on the jury, and the judge didn't? It couldn't be the other way around. Finally the judge waved the lawyers back to their seats and began to read names. Everyone now knew that it was good to hear your name. The person to Caitlin's left gasped with happy surprise when her name was called. Then the clerk started reaching into the box to call up more people.

Seth's name had not been called. He was on the jury too. She looked over at him. He was sitting upright, his head pulled back; he was not expecting this. The woman who had been sitting between them had to ask him to pull his feet back so she could get out.

Maybe this served him right for assuming that he wouldn't be seated. Would it have made a difference if he had explained about New Zealand? He wasn't just "busy at work." He was going to make a video of himself snowboarding in the backcountry as a promotion for Street Boards. The company had gotten permits, arranged transport and lodging for a crew, and hired guys who were willing to hang out the open door of a helicopter with a seventy-thousand-dollar camera in one hand.

But she was glad. Of course she was. They could have fun in the evenings. Why had she been so worried? A week, maybe a bit more, however long the trial was going to last, wasn't too big a challenge for a "friends with benefits" relationship, was it? That wasn't long enough for things to get messy, for people to have their hearts broken because someone else was deciding between Lenox and Kate Spade china.

The chair between them was now vacant. More names were called. After the empty seats in the first row were filled, a heavyset red-faced man approached the second row. He had to hitch his way up the little step. He rested his hand on the back of a chair in the first row, which caused that occupant to turn her head sharply. He was having trouble moving past the other jurors, so Seth stood up and started to move to the seat next to Caitlin.

That would be nice, to be sitting next to him.

"No, Mr. Street," the judge suddenly barked. "You must stay in your assigned seat. You can't move to sit next to a pretty girl. This is a court of law, not a dating service."

*Pretty girl...dating service...* Caitlin couldn't imagine her father ever talking like that in his courtroom.

"Yes, Your Honor," Seth said and stood in front of his own chair to let the man pass.

The heavyset man collapsed onto his chair. A musty, acrid scent came down with him. He was a smoker.

*Please dismiss him. Please. Please. Don't make me sit next to this.*

He was seated. Apparently smoking and being overweight were not disqualifying conditions.

A whole new set of people had to be called into the juror room, and they went through the judge's welcome and the prosecutor's explanation of the court system yet again. As the next round of jurors was being questioned, Caitlin noticed that the heavyset man had inched his chair close to hers. He must be trying to give himself more room for his bulk. A few minutes later he put his forearm on the right arm of his chair, jutting his elbow out until it hit Caitlin.

*No. You do not touch me.*

This morning Seth had let his arm rest against hers. That was different, so different. She shifted in her chair and sat up very straight so that the man wasn't touching her.

In another twenty minutes the man forgot about his turf war. He started to fidget, then grew agitated, clearing this throat, pressing his fingers to his temples as if he had a headache. He needed a cigarette.

When only two seats remained to be filled, one of the candidates interrupted the lawyer, "No, I can't give a fair verdict." He was a young man. "I couldn't sit still. I won't be able to listen."

The judge reminded him that it was his civic duty. "You are an American citizen, aren't you?"

"I don't care about that." The man was not shamed. "I've been going nuts today. This has been the worst day of my life. I can't do it again. Put me in jail if you want. That has to be better than this."

The heavy man was slumped forward, his hands gripped behind his fleshy neck, desperate for a cigarette. Over his back Caitlin could see Seth.

"*He* can't sit still?" Seth said softly. "What about me?"

The judge motioned the lawyers forward, and after a brief conference, he dismissed the juror. He was harsh, criticizing the man's citizenship, but it didn't matter what he said. That young man was free. He had gotten out of serving. This was not sitting well with the other jurors. *Why didn't we think of something like that?* Caitlin glanced at Yvette, the juror sitting next to her. She was sitting like an obedient first grader, her hands neatly folded on her lap. At lunch she had said that she worked on the line in a poultry processing plant. It was a horrible job. She didn't care how long the trial lasted, anything to keep her from having to go to work.

At four o'clock they finally had all sixteen jurors. They were sworn in again and given the red badges that they were to wear on lanyards around their neck whenever they were in the courthouse. The judge admonished them not to talk about the case among themselves, which wasn't a big challenge for Caitlin because she still hadn't a clue what the case was about. He then told them about the procedures for the next day, where they could park for free, how they were to report not to the assembly room, but to their own jury room off the courtroom, et cetera, et cetera. They could use their phones or the internet as long as they signed affidavits, pledging not to research the case. He said that the testimony would probably last until the middle of the following week.

When he finally excused the jury, the smoker next to Caitlin was on his feet, shoving his way past Seth and the other jurors, all of whom drew back to let him pass except for a tiny middle-aged Asian woman at the end of the row. She thrust out her arm, making it clear that he was to wait his turn.

It was late enough that she called her parents to pick her up on their way to MeeMaw's. When she told her parents that Seth was also on the jury, her father cautioned her. "You know you can't see him. No judge is going to like jurors socializing with each other during the trial."

Wait, no? Not see him? "We wouldn't talk about the case." *I just want us to have bedroom sex.*

"I know that. But it wouldn't look right. You can't do it."

* * * *

"Are you kidding me?" Seth said when she told him the next morning. "We can't see each other?"

"That's right."

"What is this? Some kind of flashback? Are we kids again?"

"No, we aren't kids. We are a jury of someone's peers."

He ran a hand through his hair. "I really wanted to spend more time with you."

"It's not going to happen."

Of the sixteen people on the jury there were ten women, six men; ten whites, five African Americans, and one Asian; four seemingly retired people, two women and two men. The rest of the women were of various ages while among the men, besides the two retired ones, were Fred the Smoker who was probably in his forties, and three young men, Seth, an African American man dressed with quiet elegance, and a sandy-haired, rabbity-looking fellow.

Except for the nicely dressed black guy, none of them were the sort that Caitlin had ever had any dealings with back in San Francisco. They were so...she didn't want to finish the thought because it made her sound like the artisanal/organic/vinyl-records San Francisco snob that she had probably been back when she'd collected a Silicon Valley paycheck.

But good military kid that she had once been, she did make an effort to learn names, starting with the older people. The men whom she assumed were retired weren't. Keith, the white one, was still farming his lands, and Dave, the black one, was driving an interstate truck. Apparently farming and trucking didn't have the pension plans that the navy did.

As to be expected in a room with at least one Southern woman, there was food. One of the two older women had made brownies, and the other one had made banana bread. A young woman who worked in a bakery had gotten her boss to contribute a platter of little Danish pastries.

"We need to set up a snack schedule," Kim, the Asian American woman, announced. She already had a piece of paper and was drawing lines and writing dates. She passed the paper to the young well-dressed man on her left.

"What should I do?" Yvette whispered to Caitlin frantically. It seemed that Yvette was going to cling to her throughout the trial. "I live with my sister. She doesn't like me to use the kitchen."

"Sign up for the last date," Caitlin suggested. "Maybe the trial will be over by then."

The paper had now reached Keith, the farmer. He was shaking his head. "There's no way I am going to ask my wife to do this. She's going to have to kill herself to keep up with the chores, what with me not being around during the day."

"Then you shouldn't have been taking any of what was here today," Kim snapped. "Not if you aren't going to take a turn."

The women who had brought the food were all insistent that they had brought for everyone, that they didn't expect, et cetera, et cetera.

"Then from now on we will do it this way," Kim announced. She clearly did not tolerate being disagreed with.

So exactly how did that make her a good candidate for a jury? Caitlin couldn't imagine entering in deliberations with her. Or with Fred. How could they ever reach a unanimous verdict?

Unless that was what someone was hoping for. Was a hung jury part of a strategy? Were they being set up to fail?

A middle-aged woman in a deputy's uniform asked for their attention. Her uniform was exceptionally unflattering. The khaki color washed her out, and the tucked-in shirt emphasized her low bust and barrel waist. She identified herself as the lead deputy, but said that it was fine if they called her Sally.

She collected their affidavits about the internet and said that court might be starting a little late.

"What time will you usually start?" someone asked.

"The official start time is nine."

"But then why do we have to come in at eight?" The man speaking was the sandy-haired, rabbity one. Caitlin thought his name was Teddy.

"Because they can't get started without you."

"But then it is okay if we come later, just so long as we are here by nine?" His voice had a thin, whiny sound. "My wife really hates getting up this early. She can't do it."

"No," Sally said patiently. "You need to be here by eight."

She then told them that during testimony they would be allowed to take notes; notebooks and pens would be on their seats in the courtroom. Caitlin was glad of that. She could listen better if she had something to do with her hands.

Then she tried to settle down to work. It was a little hard to concentrate. A lot of the other jurors, especially the women, were chatty, and one of them, a redhead, had an annoying laugh, like a hyena having an asthma attack. Fred was already asking for a smoking break.

The morning dragged on. Finally at eleven Sally came back and told them that the trial was about to start.

The jurors put their belongings in the bins assigned to them and got in line in the order in which they were seated. It took them a minute to get this straight. Caitlin supposed that they would soon get pretty good at it.

She was surprised to see how full the courtroom was; the observers were crowded close to one another on their benches, and there were more lawyers at the tables. So this trial must be some big deal.

Everyone was looking at the jurors as they filed in. Caitlin took her seat between Fred and Yvette. She felt a sudden thrill. *This is it. We are the jury of your peers. We represent the community; we enforce the laws and the standards. We matter. This is a service.*

Was this how her father felt when he arrived at the Naval Academy, very young, but determined to serve his country? Or her something-great-grandmother who had nursed with Clara Barton during the Civil War? Okay, this wasn't much compared to those, but Caitlin never did anything out of patriotism. She only bothered to file an absentee ballot for the national elections and any time her parents told her that a race was contested. This was something she was finally doing because she was an American.

This was justice, not the violent revenge that counted as justice in a computer game, but real justice, grand and solemn. She looked around the courtroom, at the observers, at the lawyers. She wanted to believe that everyone felt this way, felt that they were all a part of something important.

If this trial were such a big deal, the lawyers should be charged up, full of adrenaline. But they weren't. One man's tie was crumpled; he must have loosened and retightened it several times. One of the women's hair was mussed in back; she had been rubbing the back of her neck. The defendant had on fresh lipstick, but none of the other women did.

Although the lawyers had all been sitting up straight when the jury had entered, they were, only a minute or so later, resting their chins on their hands, looking down blankly at their papers. Because of her work with games, Caitlin observed people carefully, wanting to be able to convey emotions through expressions, gestures, and postures. These people were frustrated and exhausted.

And the judge—he was sitting forward in an aggressive stance, his jaw out, as if he were in midcombat.

This was not starting out well.

Fred's elbow was a good five inches into her space.

The judge welcomed them, talking about how he ran an orderly trial. Then he told them that this was a joint trial with two different defendants, and that they need to consider each defendant separately, that the verdict for or against one should have no bearing on the verdict for or against the other. Both defendants had their own team of lawyers, and each would be allowed to have one of their representatives question each prosecution witness and to mount their own defense. It would make this one trial longer, but certainly not as long as having two separate trials. So the trials had been joined in the interest of the taxpayers of North Carolina.

But not apparently in the interest of the jurors.

He went on for thirty-five minutes. Then he called on the prosecutor to give his opening statement. That lawyer asked to approach the bench. The judge gestured, and in a moment a gaggle of lawyers clustered around the judge's bench. Then they returned to their places, and the judge announced the first big decision of the trial.

They would break for lunch so that the prosecutor's opening statement would not be interrupted. The judge told them to leave their notebooks on their seats and then cautioned them not to discuss the case among themselves or with anyone, which would yet again be easy advice for Caitlin to follow as the only thing she would have to say was that the female defendant's shoes looked very expensive.

They were given ninety minutes for lunch so Caitlin ate quickly, wanting to get some more work done. Seth scooped up the rest of his lunch and rode up the elevator with her.

"What are you doing about New Zealand?" she asked him softly.

"Not go."

Seth no longer competed in many events. Instead he focused on "parts," videos of himself snowboarding. It was a big part of the snowboarding world now. The newcomers made them, wanting to get noticed by sponsors, while established people like Seth made them to promote their current sponsors. As the videos were posted on the internet, she had seen most of Seth's, and they were really beautiful. They were shot in the backcountry, Seth gliding through pristine snow, then taking off, soaring against a blue sky. The Street Boards logo was on his helmet, jacket, and board. There was never any red in any of the shots except the graffiti-like "& Snow" of the logo.

He used his height, a problem in competition, to make his moves big and graceful, and sometimes he turned his left hand in a way that she knew, she absolutely knew, he had learned from her so many years ago.

"But what about all the helicopters and cameramen, all that? Are you canceling them?"

"That's what my dad and I were going to do because nobody's ever done a Street Boards part except me. But my mom thought that canceling was too expensive so she told me to get someone else. My friend Nate is going to do it."

"Your mother makes these decisions?" Caitlin remembered Mrs. Street as an ordinary Southern fry-chicken-and-bake-cookies kind of mom.

"When she's right. Dad still doesn't like it, but I can see her point. Maybe our marketing plans don't have to be about me all the time."

"That's starting to sound pretty adult, Seth."

He grinned. "I'm hoping that it's a temporary thing."

One woman had apparently never left the jury room. She had brought lunch with her.

"You were smart to bring your own food," Caitlin said to her, remembering that her name was Elizabeth. "The soup downstairs was liquid salt."

"Salt I can handle," Elizabeth answered. "I have celiac disease, which I know is supposed to be a white people's thing"—she was African American—"but if I have any gluten, I will be in the bathroom the rest of the day."

The afternoon court session actually started on time. The lead prosecutor, the oldest man at that table, rose to give his opening statement. He confirmed that the defendants were indeed the people Caitlin thought they were. The woman was the wife—or ex-wife, she wasn't sure—of a former congressman, and the man was the congressman's former law partner, and they were being accused of—

Caitlin had absolutely no idea what they were being accused of. It was something financial, falsifying depreciation schedules, capitalizing rather than expensing, bid rigging. All those words were coming out of the lawyer's mouth. Was it an accounting issue, a stock purchase issue, or something else altogether? She had no idea.

What on earth was she doing here? She didn't understand a word of this.

The only thing that emerged with any clarity was a picture of the defendants as people you could love to hate. They were greedy and materialistic, arrogant and selfish.

None of these struck Caitlin as indictable offenses. If they were, Silicon Valley was going to need to build a lot more prisons.

She glanced at her fellow jurors. Yvette had hands folded neatly in her lap. Her eyes were open, and she was sitting up straight, but Caitlin couldn't see anything in her body language that indicated she was paying attention. She was probably just happy not to be surrounded by dead chickens. Other people had their heads forward, their eyebrows lowered, trying to follow the argument.

After two hours the judge interrupted the lawyer, reminding him that a time limit had been agreed on. The lawyer said that he was nearly finished. Ten minutes later the judge prompted him again, and again the lawyer said that he was nearly finished. Seven minutes after that the judge told him that he was finished and excused the jurors for the afternoon break.

As they stood up, Yvette whispered to her. "I'm so con—"

Caitlin interrupted her. "We can't talk about the case."

"Oh."

Back in the jury room everyone was looking a little shell-shocked. Caitlin glanced at Seth; he shrugged. He hadn't understood anything either.

After the break they were told that only one of the defense attorneys was going to give his opening statement now; the other would speak after the prosecution rested. This lawyer began by saying that the prosecutor had deliberately been trying to confuse them when in fact the case was fairly simple.

But instead of explaining capitalization and expensing, he argued that this was a case of overzealous prosecution, that there had been a vendetta against the defendants because of their powerful friends. The irregularities that the prosecution would cite as evidence were minor, probably typos made by a data entry clerk. He was angry, and Caitlin never liked being around anger.

She left court that afternoon, as confused as ever, but also feeling as outraged as she had when a coworker in Silicon Valley had taken credit for her work and as unclean as she had when her pediatrician had tried to hand her a prescription for birth control pills.

Her sophomore year, the year between her second and third summers with Seth, went well. The art teacher who had sneered at commercial graphic art had left, and the new teacher was impressed with the things Caitlin was doing on the computer.

Her birthday was in February, and her mother made an appointment for her annual checkup. She still saw a pediatrician; she and Dylan had the same doctor. After examining her, he said that she needed to be more regular about taking a multivitamin and that she should either start eating more red meat or take a small iron supplement a few times a week. Then he asked if she was sexually active.

"No, never."

"I still recommend that you start taking birth control pills." He started writing on his prescription pad.

"No, really," she said. Of course lots of girls had sex at fifteen—notably her sister—but no. No. "I don't have a boyfriend."

"At least consider it." He tried to hand her the prescription. She wouldn't take it. He kept his hand out. He wasn't giving her a choice. So she took it and crammed it into her pocket.

Her mother was in the waiting room. She paid the bill, and out in the car she asked Caitlin what the doctor had said. Caitlin told her about the multivitamin and the twenty-eight milligrams of iron. "But I don't need to take the iron every day."

"Was there anything else?"

"Not really."

"Caitlin."

So Mom already knew. It must have been on the bill or something.

"He gave me a prescription for birth control pills."

"I know. I talked to him about it."

"You did? Mom! You think I should be on birth control? I'm not having sex. You know that."

"Yes, yes, I do. But, honey, we can't go through this again, and so many girls after their sisters—"

"But not me, Mom. Not me." Caitlin was really offended.

"I know you say that, but it only takes one time. It will give your dad and me such peace of mind."

"Dad! He doesn't know, does he?"

She nodded. "He says we need to protect the family. Give me the prescription. I'll fill it, and then you can decide."

On the phone that night Seth asked her a couple of times if she was okay. She said she was fine, but of course she wasn't. She had always told him almost everything; it was odd not to tell him about this. But she couldn't.

What if it made him wonder? She couldn't stand the idea of him thinking about her that way.

The next day her mother handed her a narrow white bag with the vitamins, the iron pill, and the circular packet of birth control pills. "It's your decision, Caitlin, and I honestly don't know if we're doing the right thing, if we are just making it too easy for you to start having sex, but you're already older than Trina was."

"I'm not Trina."

"I know. I know, but..." Her mother looked very uncertain.

"I wish you trusted me," Caitlin said, mostly because she knew that that would really hurt her mother.

She started taking the supplements right away, leaving them in the bathroom she shared with Trina and Dylan's diapers. She shoved the birth control pills in the back of her underwear drawer.

The following week her father got his orders. The family would be moving to San Diego after school was out. That's what happened in military families. It had been unusual for them to have been in Virginia for six years.

Like everything else in this family, the only thing that seemed to matter was Dylan.

His other grandparents were stunned at the thought that he would be moving all the way across the country. They consulted a lawyer. As long as the McGraws were open to them visiting—which, of course, the McGraws were; they just weren't buying the plane tickets—there wasn't much Trevor's family could do. Trevor could sue for joint custody if Trevor wanted joint custody—which he didn't—but he probably wouldn't get it. The courts did not look kindly on fathers who didn't pay any child support.

So there were tears and pleas, which grieved Caitlin's mother and enraged her father. Did these people seriously expect him to refuse a lawful, in fact, a desirable reassignment? Trevor's parents bought Dylan cute clothes and enormous toys, but what paid for his health insurance, his diapers, his baby food? That navy paycheck.

Caitlin liked seeing her dad so angry. It was about time that somebody got mad at that other family.

Not that anyone cared, this move would be okay for her. The skate parks in San Diego were amazing, and the school she would be going to had very sophisticated technology. She'd be fine...as long as she could spend the summer in North Carolina.

Seth's parents had decided that he was old enough that his mother didn't have to travel with him, and so he had been in Oregon from April until June when they insisted that he come home for two months, believing that taking a break from intensive training was important for his long-term health. That drove him nuts. Everyone else was training year-round. But it meant that he would be there. She had to be there too.

When things calmed down with Trevor's parents, Caitlin raised the issue with her parents. "I will be able to spend the summer with MeeMaw, won't I?"

"Ah..." Her parents looked at each other, and Caitlin felt sick. Were they going to say no? How could they?

"For a week or so," her mother said, "of course."

No. That was not what Caitlin had in mind, not at all.

"We were thinking," her father said, "that you ought to get a job this summer. If you start saving now, you will have a little bit of extra spending money in college."

"You won't mind working," her mother said. "You'll probably like having a job."

"I could get a job in North Carolina. MeeMaw would help me find one." Or she could work at Street Boards. Seth's parents would give her a job.

"But don't you want to meet other kids?" her mother asked. "Working at a mall...that will be a great way to meet other teens."

The kind of teens who worked at a mall. Those were Trina's friends, not hers.

"We're a family, Caitlin," her father said. "We have to do what's right for the family as a whole."

"No," she snapped, "we do what's right for Dylan and Trina."

She stormed upstairs and slammed the door of her room. A half an hour later she heard her mother coming upstairs. She went out to the hall to meet her.

"Caitlin, I—"

"Listen," Caitlin interrupted. "Those pills. If you let me go, I'll start taking them."

The next afternoon her mother came into her room. "Your dad and I talked about it. You can go, but you don't have to make a bargain with us over the birth control pills. You don't have to take them if you don't want to. It's totally your decision."

It didn't feel like it. "I took the first one this morning."

MeeMaw said that she could easily get Caitlin a job in one of the doctors' offices, but she would look around to see if she could find a place that employed more teens. A day or so later she called back to say that the Dairy Queen manager used to be a patient in Caitlin's grandfather's practice, and he would take her on without her having to fill out an application in person as was the usual requirement. She could start as soon as she arrived, but she would have a weeknight schedule at first.

So in early June Trina and Dylan went to the mall with her to buy the black jeans and midthigh black shorts that she would need to work at the Dairy Queen. And new bras. Thanks to the birth control pills, her old ones were too small.

The bus ride from Charlotte seemed to take forever. MeeMaw picked her up at the station. Caitlin could barely answer MeeMaw's questions about her school year and the move to San Diego. All she could think about was seeing Seth.

Once again he was waiting on her grandmother's front steps.

"Go on. Go on." MeeMaw stopped the car in front of the garage to let Caitlin out.

She seized the handle of the car door. It was stuck. How could it be stuck? Of all times, not to be able to get out of the car. Oh, right. Out and then down. She went running up the sidewalk.

Then stopped. Seth...he wasn't Seth.

Of course he was taller. She had expected that. That had happened last year. But this year he was so...so grown, so manly. His jaw was squarer, his face fuller, his shoulders broader. She felt awkward.

He didn't. He threw his arms around her, squeezed her, and—not even intending to, he just straightened his knees—lifted her off her feet.

"Whoops, I didn't mean to do that," he said, putting her on her feet, steadying her for a moment. "You're so light."

"I weigh more than I did last summer."

"Really?" He stepped back and looked at her. "You look the same."

*Because I have a sweatshirt on.*

MeeMaw left the garage door open and asked Seth to carry Caitlin's bags upstairs. He swung them out of the trunk easily and answered MeeMaw's questions about his family.

"Your mother did call me," MeeMaw said.

"She did?" Suddenly Seth looked a whole lot less adult and a lot more like an annoyed teen.

Mrs. Street had called to alert MeeMaw that Seth had a driver's license now, but that they would understand if Caitlin's family wouldn't let her ride with him.

Before Caitlin could protest, MeeMaw said that she had told Mrs. Street that it would be fine.

"I'll bet anything that MeeMaw didn't ask my parents," Caitlin whispered as they headed to Seth's car. "They probably would have said no."

"Your grandmother knows me. Your parents don't."

"And that's all it takes to assess your driving skills?" Caitlin felt that being his friend entitled, even required, her to call him on his cockiness. "Being introduced to you?"

He grinned at her, knowing exactly what she was up to. "Absolutely."

They stopped by the Dairy Queen so Caitlin could get her training schedule. They bought their supper there, and they drove out to the lake just because they could.

A gang of high school kids was at the public beach. Seth said that he sort of knew them and that it would be weird, so he drove farther around the lake, looking for a weedy, unused-looking driveway. When they found one, he parked on the side of the road. They slipped under the chain that stretched across the drive and skirted around the padlocked cabin to sit on the dock, hoping that the owners wouldn't appear.

It was still early enough that the sun was shining on the dock, but it was gritty, not exactly what a proud Dairy Queen employee would put food on. Caitlin unthinkingly pulled off her sweatshirt and started to spread it out.

"Cait—"

She looked over at him. His eyes instantly shifted away, and he seemed to flush.

Oh, her sweatshirt. She had taken off her sweatshirt.

Okay, she was going to be cool about this. She spread the shirt out, using it as a tablecloth, and started to unpack the food. "I told you that I'd gained weight. I wasn't kidding."

"Yes, but..." He didn't know what to say.

"My boobs? It's birth control pills. My parents made me start taking them."

"Hold up." Now he was looking at her again. "Birth control? You have a boyfriend? Why didn't you say something?"

"Because I don't." She explained what she hadn't been able to tell him on the phone.

"So they don't trust you?"

"I guess I get it." Caitlin suddenly wanted to defend her parents. "Dylan makes things hard. We have to plan everything around him, especially since he isn't a military dependent like the rest of us. So I understand that my folks feel that they couldn't face that again. I just wish that they believed I had enough sense not to let that happen."

"My folks told me not to do anything stupid with you."

"They did?" Caitlin really didn't like that. "Didn't you tell them that it's not like that between us, not at all?"

"I did, but they're super concerned because of who you are."

"Who *I* am? What did they mean by that?"

"We're a factory family, or we used to be, and you, you're a Thurmont. It's not just that the Thurmonts belong to the country club, but your grandfather, Doc Thurmont—well, people thought the world of him."

"My name is McGraw, and the McGraws are south Boston dockworkers." It was always a bit of a culture shock to visit her father's family, but they were Caitlin's only cousins and she liked them a lot. "Now can we talk about something else?"

There was lots to talk about. Street Boards was doing really well; Seth's dad was looking for more factory space. The Forrests, Seth's friend Nate's family, was negotiating to buy a bankrupt ski resort on Mt. Hood in Oregon, the one place in the United States where you could count on snow year-round. They wanted to turn it into a snowboard park. If it all worked out, Seth and his friends were going to live there someday.

Seth also asked her about the move to San Diego, and they talked about what computers they would buy if they had all the money in the world.

It had been light when they arrived, but the sun was sinking behind the tree line. The boats on the lake soon turned their lights on, and a campfire flickered to life at one of the cabins along the shore. The parking lot at the public beach was momentarily flooded with light as people turned on their cars and then pulled out of the lot. Caitlin could see their red taillights flickering through the trees. They would be going into town to catch the late movie, Seth said.

The campfire was shooting red-orange flames, and the people were dark outlines moving around it. Caitlin had been a Girl Scout, and she knew that the fire was bigger than it needed to be, but she liked watching it. Seth was watching it too, and she could feel him next to her, breathing the slow, deep breaths of an athlete.

*We're both growing up. Pretty soon we can stop being kids.*

# CHAPTER FIVE

Once all the jurors arrived Thursday morning, Kim, the tiny woman with a massive need to be in charge, started passing out copies of her completed snack schedule. She had written each person's name on top as a way of knowing who had gotten theirs. Caitlin supposed that saved them from having to sign a receipt for the document.

Then Kim reached into her tote for a second handout. "I got this off the internet. It is some definitions of—"

"Whoa," Seth said just as others were sitting up in alarm. One deputy was moving toward Kim, his hand out for the paper, while the other was lifting up the court phone on the wall by the door.

"I thought we weren't supposed to do our own research," said the woman Caitlin was thinking of as Chatty Heather. "Didn't the judge say—"

"This wasn't research," Kim protested. She turned her back toward the deputy. She didn't want to give up her handouts. "At least not into the case. It's just defining the terms that they are using. It will be so helpful because I know that Yvette here doesn't understand anything."

Yvette looked up, startled.

It wasn't fair to single out Yvette. None of them understood anything.

The second deputy hung up the phone and said that Kim needed to go speak to the judge.

"I don't see why," Kim protested. "I was trying to help. Some of them need help."

The deputy escorted her out, and twenty minutes later Sally, the lead deputy, came back. "Juror Fourteen has been excused. I need to pick up her things."

"You mean she's leaving?" one of the younger women gasped.

"The judge takes his cautions to you very seriously," Sally said.

"It's like on TV," April, the redhead, said and laughed nervously. April laughed at everything, and the sound was loud and grating. "On those reality shows where people get voted off, and then they just disappear."

"That's right," Chatty Heather agreed. "That must be so strange to have people be gone like that. I've never understood—"

"Well, at least," Fred the Smoker interrupted her, waving his copy of the snack schedule, "we will have this to remember the bitch by."

* * * *

The prosecution started calling witnesses, and Caitlin could tell that the first witness really wanted the jurors to understand the issue. She looked at them when she spoke; her shoulders were open, her gestures were generous. She talked slowly and tried to explain each piece of jargon that she used. But then the prosecutor would follow up with a jargon-filled question, and after a while the witness gave up and just answered the questions, her arms now close to her body.

How could anyone become a prosecutor and be this bad at things? If the courtroom worked as things did on TV, all the lawyers at that table were assistant district attorneys. The actual district attorney would have been elected. Caitlin had no idea if she had voted for the current incumbent or not.

What a godawful citizen she was, voting mindlessly, not being a resident of the state where she truly lived. She could not think of a single way to justify herself.

It was now the defense lawyers' turn with the first witness. Because there were two defendants, two lawyers questioned the witness separately, and as far as Caitlin could tell, they asked almost the same questions. If there were a difference that was going to let her conclude that one defendant was guilty and the other one not, she wasn't hearing it.

And Fred was desperate for a cigarette.

At least the snacks in the jury room were great. Marcus, the quiet young African American whom Caitlin assumed was gay, had bought delicate, little, obviously homemade quiches to start the day with, and at the midmorning break he brought out beautifully colored French macarons.

"Did your mother make these? Your wife?" one of the older women asked innocently.

Marcus shook his head. He was a chef and had come to town in September because he had gotten a job at the town's one very good restaurant.

He had only been in the state ten months, and he had already changed his driver's license and his voter registration. That's what grown-ups did.

After the break, having had his morning cigarette, Fred was back to thrusting himself into Caitlin's space. She knew it had to be deliberate. She wanted to shove him, pinch him, bite him, except that last one felt too unsanitary.

She was usually capable of standing up for herself. But confronting him would only make him worse.

She was now starting to hate the defense lawyers as much as the prosecutors. One of them was always trying to make the witness answer yes or no, when the witness wanted to say, "Yes, that is possible, but highly unlikely." Then when the witness finally gave up and answered yes, the lawyer would look triumphant as if he had scored some major point.

*Do you think that we are idiots?*

Apparently they did. Caitlin started to play games with the clock. She would not look, not look, not look, then try to guess how much time had passed. She was always wrong; she always overestimated.

The prosecution was introducing a great many documents as evidence, and Caitlin's extensive legal training, that is, watching *Law and Order* reruns, had taught her that the defense would have seen them all ahead of time. Nonetheless, someone from both defense teams felt it necessary to examine each page of the document as if wanting to signal to the jury that the prosecution was not be trusted. It just made Caitlin hate them even more. Of course she hated the prosecutors too, so this wasn't going to get in the way of her fair and impartial verdict. Fair, impartial, and totally ignorant.

What was an "impairment charge"? Was that something that a normal human being was supposed to know about? She wished she could ask someone.

After lunch, and an hour or so of more testimony, the bailiff handed the judge a note. The judge unfolded it, read it, folded it back up again, and told the jury that they would be taking their afternoon break a little early. As they were filing out, he hurriedly motioned to Sally, and while they were waiting in line to pick up their phones and computers, she asked them to put their internet-enabled devices on airplane mode. One of the older women had to be shown how.

Caitlin kept copies of her current projects not only in the cloud, but also on her hard drive and on a thumb drive. So she was able to work. Having figured out the trajectory of a bullet on a gravity-heavy planet, she could start coding all those changes.

Breaks were only supposed to last fifteen minutes, but the little timer she had on her computer for billing kept clicking, an hour, an hour and fifteen minutes. After two hours she stopped the clock and went with Sally and the other female jurors to the restroom. A male deputy was escorting the men. The hall was completely empty.

But Sally wouldn't tell them what was going on.

People were getting restless. One of the younger women had had a movie downloaded on her computer so several people were gathered around her small screen trying to watch it together. Fred said that he didn't care how long the trial lasted. As long as he was making twelve dollars a day, his bitch of an ex-wife couldn't expect him to pay her anything.

Caitlin went back to work. In another fifteen minutes, she finished with the not-so-speeding bullets. She filled out an invoice and updated her own records. Of course she couldn't send it to the client yet, but she could do it as soon as she got back to her parents' house.

She started chatting with some of the other jurors. One of the older women, Joan, a former third-grade teacher, was a knitter, while the other older woman, Delia, had a crocheting project with her. Norma, a nurse who looked to be in her late fifties, was working on professional course material.

Finally at five o'clock Sally came to get them. "Do we need to put our phones in the bins?" Seth asked. "Can we leave them on the table so we can grab them and go?" Surely the judge was simply going to call them back in, admonish them not to talk about the case, and then dismiss them for the day.

"No," Sally said. "Please use the bins."

The observers' benches were empty, which wasn't too surprising since there had been no testimony since the first hour after lunch. The lawyers were sitting behind empty tables; they had cleaned up all their papers.

The judge turned to them. "Ladies and gentlemen, I am sorry to tell you that a situation has arisen that will require that we sequester you. This means—"

Sequester? Caitlin sat up. Sequester? What? This wasn't possible. Hadn't her father said that North Carolina didn't sequester juries, that it was expensive, that sequestered juries came up with bad verdicts?

They would be moved to a motel, the judge was saying, where they would be housed and fed entirely at the state's expense.

Was he serious? This couldn't be happening.

"I know you are going to be asking why we are doing this," the judge continued, "but that is what we can't tell you, except to assure you that it had nothing to do with Juror Fourteen being dismissed."

Juror Fourteen? Oh, right, that had been Kim.

The judge was still talking. "Of course this will be frustrating, and some of you will have some financial hardship."

"*Some* hardship?" Dave interrupted. He was the older African American man who drove an interstate truck. "What about bankruptcy?"

The judge ignored that. He acknowledged that they would need their belongings, and deputies had been working all afternoon with their families or colleagues.

"And what about Monday?" one of the women asked. "It's the Fourth of July and my family always—"

The judge held up his hand, silencing her. "You may take up individual cases with Deputy Burke. Now, Juror Five"—that was Elizabeth—"I am told that you have a food allergy. You will be able to manage, won't you?"

"No, sir, I will not. I would have to bring all my own food, and that is too much to ask of my family."

"Can't we find a food service to accommodate you? Don't most restaurants have gluten-free dishes these days?"

"There is an issue of cross contamination, sir. And those traces would build up if it was three meals a day. My doctor will provide any documentation that you need."

The judge did not look happy. "Then I suppose I must excuse you."

"Thank you, sir." Elizabeth stood and moved along the railing of the jury box. At the door to the jury room she turned and lifted her hand in farewell to the others. Then she was gone.

Back in the jury room, the jurors pummeled Sally with questions. Shopping for a grandchild's birthday present...finding a new grain supplier... refilling prescriptions... Sally had no answers.

Caitlin asked about the internet. "If we sign those affidavits again, we can go online, can't we?"

Sally shook her head. "I'm afraid not."

"But—" Caitlin broke off. Sally would have no answer.

Caitlin's rent was due tomorrow, July 1, and her health insurance was due today. Both were on an autopay system. She had money in her account to cover this month's debits, but not next month's. The gravity-heavy planet designer might take two weeks to pay; then her bank might sit on the money for a few days. If she couldn't invoice the client immediately, next month's rent and insurance would roll over to her credit card, which had a Shakespearean interest rate. If she got behind on that credit card, what a nightmare that would be.

Was living in San Francisco worth this stress? Why hadn't she saved more when she worked in Silicon Valley?

Sally was answering a question from one of the other women. "I know, I know. My husband couldn't pack for me either, but we will let each of you have a fifteen-minute phone call tonight."

"What about dinner?" the young rabbity-looking man asked. "My wife and I, we always eat at the same time every night. That's what I am used to."

"Oh, grow a pair," Fred mumbled.

Sally ignored that. "We are having meals delivered to the motel."

"What motel are we staying at?" someone else asked.

She said that she was not authorized to release that information. "And I am afraid that you will have to leave all your internet-enabled devices with the court."

"Can't we just put them on airplane mode like we did this afternoon?" Seth asked.

"I'm sorry."

"Can our families come pick them up?" Caitlin asked. Her computer was the most valuable thing that she owned, and she was dependent on it for her income. She couldn't let anything happen to it.

Sally said that she believed that that would be possible, but it was the judge's decision.

So into plastic bags went phones, computers, MP3 players. Some of the older jurors had books and magazines that they could keep. Delia and Joan had their handicrafts, and Norma had her geriatric wound care text, but all the younger people were left with nothing, nothing to read, nothing to watch, nothing to listen to. At least Caitlin had never indulged in a watch with internet capability. Seth and Marcus had. They weren't even going to know what time it was.

They filed out of the courthouse through a small side door. A bus was waiting for them. Caitlin made sure that she got to sit next to Seth. It was good to feel his arm against her arm, his thigh against hers.

"This blows, doesn't it?" he said.

"I wish I had my computer and my phone."

"This will be a test. Is our generation as addicted to constant stimulation as people say we are?"

"I'm sure that I am," she answered.

Sally boarded the bus last. "Now I have your room assignments."

"What?" It was a voice from the back of the bus. "Are you serious? We don't even get our own rooms?"

"It's the Fourth of July weekend," Sally reminded them. "We were fortunate to get this many rooms." She started reading off the names. Caitlin knew that there was no chance that she would be with Seth—which might make all this not just worthwhile, but potentially rather glorious—and she was happy to be with Joan, although she was surprised that Joan and Delia, the two older women, had not been put together.

The bus headed east. People had questions for Sally. They were pretty much the same questions that they had had earlier. How was anyone supposed to pay their bills on $12 a day? How was Keith's wife going to manage the farm without him there at all? Sally had no answers.

The bus went through a seedier part of town and then pulled into the parking lot of an older Best Western. The driver parked by a side entrance and waited while Sally went in to get their keys. It was a while before she came back. People were starting to complain about being hungry.

Sally returned full of apologies. "We had wanted to organize a common space for you to relax and eat in, but unfortunately we could not make that happen on such short notice. I am afraid that you will have to stay in your rooms this evening. We don't have the manpower for anything else. Your dinners will be delivered to you. And we have to ask you not to leave your rooms except in the case of fire or some other emergency."

"Can you do this?" Teddy, the young rabbity-looking one, asked. "This is like being in jail. Don't we have rights?"

The judge, Sally said, was fully conversant with the extent of his legal authority.

Caitlin had traveled a few times on Silicon Valley business, and this room was nothing like the sleek hotels she had been booked into then. The two double beds had matching floral spreads, the kind where the quilting is done not by actual stitches, but by little broken lines that had been heat-stamped into the synthetic fabric. There was a desk and a desk chair that had arms so that it could serve as a reading chair as well. If Caitlin had been here of her own free will, she would have been annoyed by the lack of electric outlets, but of course she had nothing to plug in, and there were now plenty of outlets since the radio had been removed, the phone had been removed, and there was a big blank space on the wall where the television had been. Even the chain on the door had been removed. This really was like jail.

Caitlin supposed that they were lucky to be allowed to keep their belts and shoelaces. Apparently the judge was not worried about suicide attempts. Maybe he should be.

A few minutes later one of the deputies handed them a bag from Subway. "Sally says to tell you that we are really sorry. We've never done anything like this. We will do better tomorrow."

"What about our luggage?" Joan asked.

"And the phone calls?" Caitlin added. She realized that if she gave her parents access to her cloud storage accounts, they could deliver her latest project and invoice the client. At least she hoped that they could. They were both a good five years behind on the technology curve. And maybe more than five.

The deputy said that the luggage was being searched now and that the phone calls were already starting. Someone would come get them when it was their turn.

Joan had opened the bag of food, and Caitlin could see that she was hovering uncertainly. Oh, of course, there was only one chair.

"You take the chair," Caitlin said. "Really. I'm fine sitting on the floor or the bed."

The sandwiches came with potato chips and a cookie, but no beverages. Caitlin went into the bathroom to get water for both of them.

Joan thanked her. "But we're outside the city limits, and the rural water is pretty bad."

It was. It had a bitter bite followed by a metallic aftertaste. Caitlin had to force herself to drink it.

After they ate, Joan sat down with her knitting, and Caitlin took the little sketch pad she always carried in her purse and started making a list of everything she would need her parents to do in the next few days. Some clients required detailed messages while the rest could get something generic.

Of course Tlin wrote in a different style than did Aurora. Then it occurred to her that this was a lot to convey in a phone call, so she started to rewrite her messages to make them shorter...except now she was using up a lot of her sketch pad. Did she need to worry about that? Should she be writing on the Subway bag? No, surely, her mother would think to send some more drawing paper. And if the deputy had explained that the jurors would not be able to use their phones and computers, her mother would also know to send her some books. Her mother had always been great at things like packing for long car trips. She had been a navy wife, and navy wives could pack.

But when the deputies arrived, they only had the carry-on bag that Caitlin had brought from San Francisco, and in it were only the things that Caitlin had brought from San Francisco.

*Oh, Mom... You couldn't have at least sent me a book? Dylan's in elementary school, and he lives in Atlanta. You have time to think about me now. Isn't it my turn?*

So what was she going to do with herself? If there had been a Bible in the nightstand drawer, she would have read that, but either the Gideons had stopped putting Bibles in motel rooms, or the judge had declared that the Holy Book was potentially subversive reading material. Caitlin sighed, took her sketch pad, and wasted another sheet of paper drawing her suitcase in excruciating detail.

"It's nine thirty," Joan said at last. "I guess we didn't get to make our phone calls."

"Shall I go out and ask?" Caitlin was starting to stand up.

"They did tell us to stay in our rooms."

That was true. Caitlin sank back to the floor.

At ten they decided to go to bed. This was Joan's usual bedtime, and Caitlin didn't have anything else to do. They took turns in the bathroom, and Caitlin had to ask Joan for some toothpaste. Her mother had simply repacked the toiletries that Caitlin had brought, and Caitlin didn't bother to bring toothpaste and deodorant when she was visiting her parents.

The bed wasn't uncomfortable, but Caitlin wasn't sleepy. Not at all. She lay on her right side for a while, then turned over to her left. That was fun. Now what?

Apparently the critics of her generation were right. She was addicted to external stimulation. Didn't she have any inner resources? Why hadn't she learned to meditate?

*Pay attention to your breathing.* That's how meditation classes began. Caitlin inhaled, then listened to herself exhale. It was not interesting.

The air-conditioning unit switched on, fluttering a little burst of air. Then it stopped. No, it wasn't the air-conditioning. It was Joan, Joan breathing. The flutter became a sigh, and a moment or so later Joan was full-out snoring. There were rattles, snorts, grunts, a whole symphony.

Okay. So how were you supposed to pay attention to your breathing when someone else was going at it too?

*Grrru-th...hahhuh...* This was getting hard to listen to. Why did cartoonists represent snoring with a line of peaceful *z*'s?

If she turned on the light, she could use yet another page of her sketch pad. But she couldn't turn on the light. Although each bed had its own sconce, they were mounted together with one knob. One turn of the knob turned on Joan's light, the second turn added hers as well, then the third turn left her light burning and Joan's off, but by then Joan would be awake, and Caitlin would have to apologize when what she really wanted to do was shoot Joan.

What kind of person wants to shoot a retired third-grade teacher?

If Joan's snoring was regular, Caitlin thought that she might be able to block it out, but there were gasps and wheezes, followed by periods of stone silence that went on long enough that Caitlin would start to wonder if her roommate had died.

What was she going to do in court the next day? How was she ever supposed to listen to the testimony if she hadn't slept? And she wouldn't be wearing deodorant. Maybe she would stink enough that Fred would stay on his side of the armrest.

She tried putting the pillow over her head. It didn't help. She was going to sleep in the bathroom. That was the answer. She scooped up her bedding and tiptoed across the room. As she was spreading the quilt across the bathroom floor, she couldn't help noticing that the underside of the sink surround was unfinished particleboard. The floor was clean enough, but the underside of the countertop? Who cleans that? And who actually sticks gum there?

Sights you wish you hadn't seen.

The heat-stamped quilt didn't have enough loft to soften or warm the hard tile floor, and even as small as Caitlin was, she had to think about how to lie down. Should she put her head next to the toilet or underneath the old chewing gum? Her something-great-grandmother and Clara Barton would have been happy to do either.

Well, good for them. She was going to sleep in the hall. What could the court do to her? Throw her off the jury? Oh, darn.

She picked up the bedclothes again and opened the door as quietly as she could. The hall was carpeted, which was good. Cone-shaped sconces shone on the vinyl wallpaper, making it brighter than she would have liked, but she was not going to let herself mind.

Midway down the hall, a desk was set up perpendicular to the walls. A deputy was on duty, guarding access to the jurors' rooms...except that the deputy had crossed his arms on the desk and was resting his head on them. If he was snoring, Caitlin couldn't hear.

He had a bottle of water next to his clipboard. Would he wake up if she tried to steal it? Probably.

She spread the quilt on the carpeted floor and lay down, pulling the sheet and the blanket over her face to block out the light. The sheet had a slight metallic smell. It must have been washed in the local water.

At the least the sheets were clean. She should celebrate that.

She heard a sound, another door open. She peeked out from her blanket. It was Seth, also carrying a pillow and a blanket. She sat up and put a finger across her lips, nodding her head toward the sleeping deputy.

"Snoring?" she whispered.

He nodded. "Do you know what time it is?"

"It's only ten to eleven." She watched him as he laid out his quilt. "Your parents didn't send you anything to do?"

"It must not have occurred to them that we won't have our computers. Did you try the water?"

"Isn't this starting to feel a bit postapocalyptic?" Caitlin had worked on several postapocalyptic games. "We are stranded somewhere with crappy water, only fast food to eat, and nothing to do."

"So you are assuming that McDonald's will survive the apocalypse?"

"Seems like a good bet."

This was nice talking to him like this. If the deputy hadn't been there... motel-hallway sex? She didn't know what that involved, but it might be fun to find out.

"*Jurors!*"

The deputy had woken up. He was getting up from the desk and moving toward them. "You need to return to your rooms. Immediately."

Seth shook his head. "No. Our roommates snore. We can't sleep. But we are going to be right here in the hall. You will be able to see us every second."

"I know we aren't supposed to roam around," Caitlin added, "but we aren't going to do that. It's the last thing we want to do. We want to sleep."

The guard shook his head. "I don't have the authority to authorize this. You need to return to your rooms."

"Is there some way we can figure this out?" Seth was trying to negotiate. "We understand that you don't want to wake up your boss, but is there some middle ground? We'll stay on opposite sides of the hall, we won't speak to each other, we can even come closer to the desk. Would that work for you?"

"You need to go back to your rooms."

Caitlin looked at Seth. He was looking at her. *Which one of us is going to make a scene?*

He shrugged. *The face of Street Boards and all that. I have to behave.*

And she shrugged back. *I am turning over a new leaf in the citizenship department. I am going to be worthy of the gold eagle on the front of my passport. I don't really know what that involves, but assaulting a deputy in the hall of a Best Western probably isn't the place to start.*

She doubted that her telepathic connection to him was strong enough to send this entire message, but he understood the shrug.

At least he had thought to bring his room key out with him. Caitlin hadn't. Apparently part of her new leaf involved being an idiot tourist. The deputy had to call the night manager to let her back in her room.

Back in the room, she made a nest for herself between her bed and the wall...and tried to listen to her breathing and think of someplace beautiful.

San Francisco was beautiful. But San Francisco was far away. And too expensive. So the lake...the lake was beautiful, with the grass running down to the rocks at the water's edge, the birds, the wind in the trees, being in the tree with Seth, being on the grass with Seth. And the water, above all the water...they had never drunk the lake water, had they? No, agriculture runoff and all that.

Couldn't she find something else to think about besides crappy drinking water?

* * * *

"Honey lamb, what are you doing down there?" Joan looked upset to see Caitlin on the floor the next morning. "Is your bed too soft?"

Caitlin sat up. "I just couldn't get comfortable."

"Let's talk to someone about getting you a bed board."

A deputy, a tall, fit-looking woman whom Caitlin hadn't seen before, had woken them up. The jurors were to eat breakfast between six and six thirty, at which point the motel's breakfast room would be open to the public. The jurors were to return to their rooms and wait there until it was time to leave for court.

The breakfast was typical motel fare, cold pastries, oatmeal packets, yogurt so sweet it might as well have been ice cream. There was a toaster and a waffle maker, but Caitlin felt as if she were swimming through molasses. If making a piece of toast felt too hard, how was she ever going to stay awake during the testimony today?

Chatty Heather and red-haired April with the hideous laugh were all bright and perky on one side of the room.

*Shut up. Please. For fifteen minutes could you just shut up?*

*I am an awful human being.*

Caitlin opened the little refrigerator, hoping that there would be some bottled water, but there were only juices. She took her yogurt to sit next to Marcus, the slender, quiet chef, guessing that he would not want to talk.

Delia, the other older lady, came over and asked them if they had gotten their phone calls.

"No," Caitlin said. "Did you?"

"I did, but there were others who didn't."

"What happened? Do you know?"

"I certainly do. That young man, Teddy. The one that can't make a move without talking about his wife—"

Teddy walked into the room in time to hear his name. "Oh, are you talking about me?" he asked innocently.

"Yes, I am," Delia said firmly. She was a majestically built African American Southern grandmother radiating a "say grace before dinner" ethos. "You owe some people in this room an apology."

Teddy, slight and pink cheeked, looked startled. "Me? For what?"

"Because there were only two phones. Other people didn't get to speak to their families because you wouldn't get off."

"And the deputy kept telling you to get off," Chatty Heather said. "The rest of us got off after our fifteen minutes."

That certainly must have been a different deputy than the one who wouldn't let Caitlin and Seth sleep in the hall.

"Yes, but it was important"—Teddy was pleading his case—"and my wife said that they couldn't make me, that we still had rights. And Dave, he didn't get off. I heard the deputy tell him to, and he stayed on."

"For an extra five minutes." Delia defended the trucker before he could speak. "And he has to get his son-in-law to take over his business. That's not like you needing to tell your wife what you had for supper."

Caitlin looked at her watch. They had been at the motel for twelve hours, and people were already bickering.

Seth came into the room and sat down next to her. He hadn't shaved, and he must have taken his contacts out because he was wearing narrow, square-framed, silver-rimmed glasses. None of his pictures had ever shown him in glasses, but she liked the look.

She twisted her wrist so he could see her watch. "Did you get any sleep?"

"Who cares about a little thing like that?" he said, clenching his fist in some kind of power salute. He got up to get some coffee, and right away the new deputy joined him, the tall female one.

And in a moment she was touching her hair. Then her tongue flicked across her lips. Caitlin knew how to animate attraction. This was textbook.

*Leave him alone, will you? He's probably had five minutes of sleep.*

But the deputy was fascinated. Here he was, this good-looking celebrity. Seth had to eat standing up.

At six thirty, another deputy told the jurors to go back to their rooms and then be ready for court at seven thirty. Someone would knock on their doors when it was time. Caitlin used Joan's toothpaste again, but decided that she would fly solo on the deodorant issue. She and Fred could have a competition. Who smelled worse, him from smoking, her from a natural glow?

No one came to the door at seven thirty. Nor at seven forty-five. Her dad had run his courtroom on time.

At eight the tall deputy did knock on the door. She told them to come to the breakfast room.

Seth and Marcus were already at the table they had sat at for breakfast. Seth had shaved and put his contacts back in. Caitlin sat with them. The deputies on duty stood near the walls. The tall woman took a place near the table where Seth was seated.

Sally was waiting for everyone to arrive. Her uniform was neat, and the hair at the back of her neck was damp, but the skin under her eyes was gray, and she looked as if she needed to remind herself how to walk. She must not have slept either.

If North Carolina never sequestered juries, Sally would have had no training or preparation. She had probably spent the night on the internet, trying to find out how it worked in other states. Some of these crazy rules, like confining them to their rooms last night, were probably a result of no one knowing what the rules were.

Sally gestured for them all to sit down. That didn't seem like a good sign. Why weren't they lining up for the bus?

"The judge has informed me," she said, "that the court will not be in session today."

"What?" About six voices spoke at once. People wanted to know why and when was the case ever going to be done if they took the day off, and didn't anyone realize that this was like being in prison, and what were they supposed to do with themselves all day? Couldn't they go home just for the weekend?

Sally shrugged. There was nothing she could say.

"Farmers don't get to take the day off," Keith muttered.

But they would be allowed to use this room all day, she said, and they could move freely between it and their own rooms, but no juror should go into a room that was not his. A deputy would escort the smokers outside for smoking breaks, and they were trying to get a TV in here so that the jurors could watch a movie. She had heard about the issue with the phone calls and was looking into that.

"And you're going to have to be patient with us. We are trying our best to make this more comfortable for you, and it will get better."

"What about exercise?" Seth asked. "There are signs for an exercise room. Can we use that?"

She said that she would look into it.

"And could we get some bottled water?" Marcus asked.

Caitlin could have kissed him.

"I will see," Sally said, "but we are going to run into some price issues at some point."

"But the deputies are bringing their own water," he pointed out.

Sally shot a guilty glance over to her clipboard and stack of folders. She had indeed brought a water bottle. "We'll see," she repeated.

"One more thing, Deputy," Norma said. She was the nurse. "I would say from the look of things that some of us were unable to sleep."

People looked around, wondering who she was talking about.

"Oh, no," Joan gasped suddenly. "I snore, don't I? Oh, no. Caitlin, dear, is that why you were... My sister said—I'm a widow, I didn't know. I'm sorry, I'm so, so sorry."

Caitlin wasn't sure what to say. "I know that you can't help it."

"But no, no—" She looked at Sally. "Please, can you do something?"

"I'm sorry. We are trying to get more rooms, but so many people are in for the Fourth. You need to be patient."

Joan looked truly mortified.

"Excuse me. Excuse me." Yvette had her hand up as if she were in grade school. "I sleep like the dead. That's what everyone says. I could trade with Caitlin. I don't mind. Really."

Yvette was rooming with Norma. Norma didn't mind the switch.

"So that takes care of it, does it?" Sally asked.

"I think there is also a problem with the men," Norma said, pointedly looking at Seth.

"I'm fine," Seth said. "I'll be fine."

"Are you sure?" Sally asked him.

"Absolutely."

What a jackass. That was one reason Caitlin liked gay men. They didn't need to be so Clint Eastwoody about everything. Well, Seth was doing this to himself. He was the one who would suffer.

Caitlin packed her clothes back up and traded places with Yvette. Norma told her to try to get a few more hours of sleep. "But if you sleep all day, you will be miserable tonight. Do you want me to ask one of the deputies to come wake you up at ten or so?"

"If they will."

* * * *

She fell asleep immediately and had to struggle to wake up when the deputy knocked on the door. She wasn't wildly eager to go back to the breakfast room. She knew that if she started to sketch—and what else did she have to do?—she would be surrounded by people who wanted to watch and ask questions. She wouldn't live alone and work as a freelancer if she wanted to be surrounded by people asking questions.

But she should at least let Norma know that the room was available if Norma wanted to study.

"Oh, you're awake," Chatty Heather exclaimed as soon as she saw Caitlin coming down the hall. "Caitlin's up," she called out to the others. "I was wondering how long you would sleep. I know people who can sleep forever. I don't understand that. I can't. Your boxes are here. We can't wait for you to open them. So, come, come." She started tugging Caitlin over to the corner of the room.

Caitlin pulled herself free and glanced around the room, looking for the tall deputy. She must be off duty. "What are you talking about?"

"Those. Those. Your boxes."

Next to the little refrigerator were two big cardboard boxes with Caitlin's name on them. One was in her mother's handwriting, the other in her grandmother's.

Apparently not only had Caitlin's mom not let her down, she had issued an "all hands on deck" call. If Caitlin had both her mother and her grandmother packing for her, she might be able to colonize Mars with what they had sent.

Apparently the boxes had come with her luggage, but deputies hadn't had time to search them last night. "I'm sorry," Sally apologized. "Someone was supposed to tell you about them."

"That's okay," Caitlin said. Sally must be getting sick of apologizing.

"We did have to take out a few of the movies, the ones with courtroom drama. We will return them to your family."

"Fine."

April was getting the boxes out of the corner, putting them on the table. "Caitlin might want to open them in private," Norma said.

"Oh...but we have been looking forward to it all morning."

"And it's fine," Caitlin said. Even if her mother and grandmother had thought that they were equipping a years-long Mars expedition, they would not have sent any sex toys.

The first thing was a soft mohair throw blanket and a small pillow. That was nice. Sequestered-jury sex was looking about as likely as Mars-expedition sex, but at least she now had something more cuddly than the heat-stamped polyester bedspreads. Then came her favorite shampoo and conditioner, toothpaste, deodorant, dental floss, and a box of tampons. Navy wives thought of everything, didn't they? There was the portable CD player that she had last used in fifth grade along with a zippered case of CDs. The case was bright purple with Trina's name spelled out in crystals. That had to be full of boy-band music. There were a book light, plenty of batteries, and a collection of books and movies from home along with a very old portable DVD player. She had read a lot of the books and seen all the movies, but who cared? Her mother had also gathered up whatever art supplies Caitlin had had in North Carolina; there were half-used pads of good paper along with Faber-Castell colored pencils, M. Graham watercolors, and brushes. The pencils had been sharpened to different lengths, and some of the tubes of watercolor had been squeezed down to half capacity, but it didn't matter. Caitlin did most of her work on the computer these days; it would be nice to play around with the old-fashioned way of doing things. In San Francisco she felt that she couldn't do anything creative unless she was billing someone for it.

*Thank you, Mom. Thank you, thank you, thank you.*

People were passing around the books and the movies, asking Caitlin if they could borrow this one or watch that one. "Let me catch my breath," she said.

Everything in the second box was new. Apparently as soon as they had gotten the call, her mother and grandmother had started packing, and her father had gone to Target. He must have spent several hundred dollars. Or more. All the movies were new releases, chosen at random as her father knew nothing about new movies. When he had come to the book section, he had probably just scooped up everything off the top-sellers rack and then a few nonfiction titles with interesting covers. There was a book about rules for card games and four new decks of cards. At the bottom of the box were board games, Scrabble, Monopoly, a fifteen-hundred-piece jigsaw puzzle, which someone grabbed from Caitlin, and then a boxed game with a note from her mother taped to the shrink-wrap.

"Oh my God." Teddy knocked over the stack of books to get to the game. "That's Revelation."

He jerked it out of her hand. "I *love* this game." He started to claw the shrink-wrap off.

"Could I have the note on top, please?" Caitlin asked.

"Oh, sure." He handed her the wad of shrink-wrap in which her mother's note was crumpled.

Caitlin smoothed it out. *The clerk at Target told Dad that this was hottest new game. But it looks pretty hard. We can return it if you don't open it.*

Too late for that. Teddy was already tugging the box lid off.

Marcus and Seth were with him. Seth picked up the lid. "This is a new version. Good for your parents, Caitlin."

"So you two play?" Teddy was excited. "We need a fourth. Does anyone already know it?"

"Oh, I'd love to learn," Heather gushed. "I adore games."

"And I would too," April joined in, laughing her horrible laugh.

"We need someone who already knows," Teddy said. "It takes a long time to learn."

"Actually," Keith said, "believe it or not, I've played with my grandsons. I'm pretty cool for an old farmer."

"This is awesome." Teddy was already opening the board. "I've never had a chance to play this version. Mandy"—that was his wife—"says we shouldn't spend the money on it."

The four men cleared the coffee cups off one table and started to set up the board. Everyone else was looking expectantly at Caitlin. Which one of her toys could each of them play with?

"I really love jigsaw puzzles," Stephanie said.

Caitlin did too. She handed Stephanie the puzzle. Stephanie worked at the bakery, and with her soft cheeks and curvy mouth, she always looked pleasant and patient, as if she didn't mind if you took forever to choose between a maple sour-cream cake doughnut and a raised one glazed with rainbow sprinkles. She would have never jumped on a patron's first choice as Caitlin had always done at the Dairy Queen.

"And this Maria Murphy book," Delia said, picking up a hardback book, "this is the new one, and I never get to read them until the paperbacks show up in the used-book store."

Caitlin nodded. What else could she do?

*But my Mommy and Daddy brought these for me. Me. It's my turn now, and you all are taking my turn from me. Just like Trina and Dylan did.*

How mature was that?

Fred told—as opposed to asking—Caitlin that he was going to watch one of the movies even though the little DVD player looked "like a piece of shit."

April and Heather pulled up chairs to watch the Revelation game. Heather kept asking questions, wanting to learn the game, and when Teddy was rude, April laughed. Caitlin asked Norma and Joan what they would like to do. Norma said that she was willing to take a study break to play a game, and Joan admitted that she did enjoy a good game of Scrabble.

Caitlin didn't particularly like Scrabble—she was a visual person, not a verbal one—but somehow she found herself picking out seven Scrabble tiles.

How had this happened? Why was she playing Scrabble when she would much rather be working on the jigsaw puzzle?

Were her mother's boxes turning her into a good navy wife? Or was it because she had been a Girl Scout and still remembered some of the laws? "Help other people at all times, especially those at home."

Delia, the other older woman, joined the game, but she and Joan were a little more interested in whispered gossip.

At first they only talked about the deputies, how much they liked Sally, the head deputy, how they wished that Ryan, who was in the room now, weren't so nervous, and how tall Andrea was.

"I hope Seth Street already has a girlfriend," Delia said.

Caitlin almost knocked over her letters. "Why do you say that?"

"Didn't you see that deputy Andrea with him this morning? She looks like a pretty determined gal."

"I imagine that he can take care of himself," Caitlin said. *And I'm here.*

"I'm surprised that he is on the jury at all," Joan said. "I didn't think he lived here anymore."

"He doesn't. He lives in Oregon. He's like me. He's still using his parents' address."

"So you know him?"

Caitlin shook her head. "Just summers when we were kids. I hadn't seen him in years."

"Well, if he wants to go back to Oregon," Delia said, putting down a word that used the only free vowel on the board, "he needs to tell that deputy that he already has a girlfriend."

Caitlin stared at her tray. There was no way she could make a word now...especially when all she could think about was the time when she was the one needing to pretend to have a boyfriend.

\* \* \* \*

On the first full day of their third summer, Caitlin got her Diary Queen uniform, a black knit shirt with the DQ logo and a black ball cap. She and two other kids were being trained for three days, and Caitlin, being Caitlin, wanted to be the Best Trainee Ever. By the end of the first day she mastered getting a perfect curl on top of a soft-serve ice-cream cone, something that took some people weeks to learn. That night she took home the price chart and memorized it. The second night she studied the manual on making Blizzards.

Seth laughed at her. "You're taking this pretty seriously. It's just a Dairy Queen."

"It's my first job, and I assume it won't be my last. Why shouldn't I take it seriously?"

The manager had initially said that the new employees would be cleaning, hauling trash, and unpacking supplies. He put Caitlin on one of the registers as soon as training was over.

Clearly a problem at the Dairy Queen was getting the little kids to make up their minds. Gone were the days when there was chocolate, vanilla, or a swirl of both. There were about fifty million flavors of Blizzards, most of them well-known candies. Caitlin learned to praise the kids' first choice to the ends of the earth to keep them from changing their minds. She rang up more sales on her register because she could keep her line moving.

The other problem was Gabe, the assistant manager who worked the evening shift. He was a college student and the franchise owner's nephew, so no one was going to complain about him. Two of the other girls told Caitlin to tell him that she had a boyfriend. Otherwise he would pester her endlessly to go out with him, and then he would be determined to score. Caitlin, grateful for the warning, told him right away that she had a boyfriend.

She usually went to work on her skateboard—Seth's father had made two more new ones for her, one for the park and one for cruising—and then either her grandmother or Seth would pick her up.

Of course she liked it when Seth did. He usually went to the gym after dinner, and he would shower there. So the ends of his hair would be damp, and he would be feeling loose and easy as he did after a vigorous workout. He would wait for her, sitting on top of the picnic table. The lights inside the store would be off, but the big security lamps in the parking lot would be on, and she could see him swinging his feet or hooking one arm across his chest to stretch the back of his shoulder, chatting lightly with other boyfriends or girlfriends waiting there too.

The other couples would always greet each other with a kiss and then walk to the cars, their arms around each other. Seth would stand up when she came out and say, "Hey." She would say something, and they would walk to his car, not touching.

She wanted him to touch her. She wanted him to kiss her. She wanted him to put his arms around her, not like the first big bear hug he gave her in front of her grandmother, but to touch her like he meant it, his hands on her arms, her back, exploring. She wanted to touch him. She wanted to press her body against him.

She wanted them to kiss as one of the couples in the parking lot did, the girl sitting on the picnic table, her legs apart, the guy standing between her legs, his hands low on her back, so low that they were really on her butt, cupping her, pulling her close to him down there. She wanted to do that with Seth; she wanted him to touch her breasts. Her body was urging her to do this, to do more.

Yet how could he? After the conversations they had had? *We're friends... we aren't like that...it's different for us...* She had set those rules, but she had been thirteen, now she was fifteen. And she didn't want to lose his friendship, not ever, but she also wanted to sit on a picnic table with her legs apart and feel his hands cupping her.

For all that she dressed like a tomboy, she had never minded being a girl; she just had had enough of all the ruffled pink hand-me-downs that she had to wear when Trina had outgrown them. Couldn't Seth see that? He had seen her figure. Why couldn't he see that she was ready for the rules to change?

Most nights Gabe, as the shift manager, was the last to leave, but one evening Caitlin stayed an extra few minutes to figure out someone else's register. So Gabe left with her.

Seth hopped off the table when she came out and took a step toward her.

"So this must be the boyfriend," Gabe drawled, and as he spoke, Seth had come close enough for Gabe to recognize him. "Oh...you're—" Gabe's voice was less cocky. He turned to Caitlin. "You didn't tell me that *he* was your boyfriend."

Caitlin shrugged.

Seth stepped forward, his hand out. "Yes, I'm Seth Street. It's good to meet you." He was sounding very poised, very grown.

Gabe muttered something and shook Seth's hand without making eye contact.

"So you work here?" Seth said, trying to make conversation.

"Yeah"—Gabe still wasn't looking at Seth—"I run the place, and Caitlin, tomorrow you need to do what I said."

What he had said was that someone needed to retrain Cyanne on the register. Cyanne was the girl who had messed up her drawer. Retraining her was not Caitlin's job, and until this minute Gabe hadn't thought so either. He just wanted to boss her around in front of Seth.

"Are you ready to go?" she asked Seth.

"Sure." He took her skateboard from her as he often did, but when they reached the car, he came around to her side and opened the door for her, something he had never done before.

"Okay, let me explain," she said as soon as he was in the driver's seat. "The other girls told me to tell him that I had a boyfriend. So I did. That was all. I didn't mention any names or say anything else. But, of course, he would think it was you. I hope—"

"I don't mind," he interrupted. "Why would I? If I needed to tell someone that I had a girlfriend, I probably would tell them that it was you. It doesn't seem like any big deal." He started the car and pulled out of the parking lot.

It did seem like a big deal to Caitlin. She wouldn't want Seth telling people that she was his girlfriend. She wanted to be his girlfriend.

"You were awfully smooth back there," she said.

"I've been meeting with sales reps, and Nate's mom set up some media training for some of us. I told you that."

"Yes, but—"

"You thought it sounded arrogant and pretentious."

"Okay, I did."

"The guys on top, Caitlin, they are awesome riders. They're so much better than anyone else, they really are. But they do more than go out there and shred. They sit for interviews, they give speeches, they even model clothes from their sponsors. I want to be ready for that."

"And isn't it going to help that you've gotten so good looking?" They had talked about her boobs; they could talk about how he was turning out.

He shrugged. "People say Ben is the best looking of the three of us."

They usually had an hour before MeeMaw expected her home. The skate park was closed, and an hour wasn't enough time to go out to the lake. If the night was nice, they sprayed bug repellent on their ankles and went and futzed around on the children's playground equipment in the park; in bad weather they would go to MeeMaw's and play cards or work on a jigsaw puzzle.

They only had forty minutes tonight, but the night was warm and dry. Seth parked along the curb near the playground. When they were out of the car, Caitlin reached out her hand for the bug juice, but instead of handing it to her, he knelt down and sprayed her ankles himself. First he sprayed above her sock. Then, lightly, without touching her, he hooked the cuff of the sock with his index finger, pulling the sock open so he could spray more deeply.

Then when he went to spray himself, Caitlin took the can from him. She knelt down.

How strong his calves were, almost out of proportion to his lean torso. He wasn't wearing socks, just the battered Sperrys he wore when he didn't feel like lacing up athletic shoes.

She was going to touch him. She put her hand on his ankle and started to ease his foot from the shoe. She heard him inhale sharply. She let his foot rest on her thigh while she sprayed it.

She was too close to the spray and its sharp metallic vapors, but she didn't care.

When she had finished, she put her hand out for him to help her up. Even when she fell at the skate park, she didn't do that. She always preferred to get up herself.

Not this time.

She felt his strength flash through her as she let him pull her up. They stood there for a moment, looking at each other.

"My folks," he said at last, "already think we are boyfriend and girlfriend."

Caitlin imagined that her grandmother did as well. "They're just words, Seth."

"No. It's a lot more than that." And he bent his head to kiss her.

How hungry they were for each other. Where to kiss, what to touch, hands, lips, everything was urgent, fevered. The slow, sweet kisses that they might have shared two years ago were swamped by the tidal wave, the whirlpool, of passion, longing, waiting. Everything was dark; nothing was enough.

Headlights from a car swept over them. A horn honked. A jeer splintered across the park.

Caitlin didn't care.

Seth did. "People can see us." He was breathing hard. "This isn't right. Not here. Not like this." He shook his head, trying to clear his mind. "Let's go sit for a minute."

They went over to the children's swings, sitting side by side, just as they had in his backyard at the end of last summer.

"How far do we—do you—want to take this?" he asked.

"I don't know," she sighed. "It's what I want, you know it is, but I don't want to be like my sister."

"But aren't you taking the pill?"

"It's more than that. Trina said that she couldn't help herself. I don't want to be like that. Ever. To feel like I have no choice."

He was shaking his head. "That's not us. We're strong, both of us."

"We are, aren't we?"

He nodded.

"Then let's not play games. I'll tell you when I'm ready."

"That sounds fair."

"I'm assuming that you're already ready."

"Yeah, pretty much."

* * * *

Revelation was clearly as complicated a game as Teddy had said. It had world-building characters set in what was indeed a postapocalyptic setting. It also featured all kinds of historical losses: the Alexandrian library, Sappho's manuscripts, and the paintings that Savonarola had had burned in the fifteen-century Bonfire of the Vanities. The unwritten *Canterbury Tales* and the seven deadly sins figured in the game in some bewildering way.

Thanks to a series of moves involving the paintings stolen from the Isabella Stewart Gardner Museum, Seth won the first game. Teddy wanted to play another round. Caitlin watched as the men reset the board. At noon, one of the deputies brought in several big bags from McDonald's. This was their third consecutive fast-food meal. Someone had purchased big two-liter plastic bottles of soda, but the water was in the motel's pitchers.

Seth, Marcus, and Keith all stood up from the game.

"But we will go on playing while we eat, won't we?" All morning Teddy had seemed more like a kid than ever, so happy to have his favorite toy that he hadn't cared about anything else.

"We don't want anything to get on Caitlin's game," Marcus said quietly.

"Oh, we will be careful."

"Not with french fries we can't," Seth said.

The deputy had menus from a Chinese restaurant and told them that they should order their dinner now.

"Let's each pick one," Joan suggested, "and then we can see if we have a decent mix."

"But if we each pick one, we will have way too much food," Delia said. "I don't need to pick."

And instantly all of the women said that they didn't need to pick either. How were they ever going to agree on a verdict if they couldn't order Chinese?

"I don't like having all that different food jumbled on my plate," Teddy said, "so I'm just going to order for myself."

"Me too," Fred said. "Because you know that whoever is first in line will pick all the good stuff out and just leave sauce for the rest of us."

Caitlin thought that the person most likely to do that was Fred.

After lunch she sat down at the jigsaw puzzle. But the people who had been working on it were being territorial and assigned her a part that was too easy. A deputy wheeled in a television with a DVD player. That began the discussion of what movie to watch, which took a while.

*This is Friday, Friday afternoon, and we still have to survive Saturday and Sunday before we get back in the courtroom and be bored out of our skulls.*

And Monday. Monday was the Fourth of July. Caitlin had forgotten. Court wouldn't meet then either.

The movie was mildly amusing, but April found it riotous. *Ah hee. Ah hee. Ah hee ha.* It was worse than Joan's snoring.

In the middle of the movie there was a shout from the Revelation table. Marcus had won. "Well done, man!" Seth congratulated him. "I never saw that coming."

Teddy was frowning at the board. "I don't see how you did that."

Marcus, Caitlin noticed, had a very pleasing smile, slight and sweet. His skin was much darker than many African Americans, and so when his lips parted, the whiteness of his teeth emphasized the gentle curve of his lips. Caitlin thought that he would be someone worth getting to know, but Teddy was clamoring to play the game for a third time.

Then the people who didn't get their phone calls were allowed to go out to the lobby to the two pay phones. A deputy monitored the call, but could only hear the juror's side. Caitlin supposed that it would be possible for a family member to just start talking about all the things that the jury wasn't supposed to know. If Caitlin's family did that, knowingly violating a court order, she would have hung up and dialed 911. Her parents' brains had been taken over by little green Martians.

But they weren't answering the home phone. They did have cell phones, and Caitlin had their cell phone numbers programmed into her own phone, but she didn't remember what they were.

That left her sister, whose cell phone number she did know.

"Oh my God," Trina gushed. "Mom said that you'd been sequ—"

"Trina, I'm sorry, but I need to you to listen. I've got some important professional stuff that has to be taken care of. Are you someplace that you can take notes?"

"No. I'm at the grocery store. But I have an app on my phone so I can record the call. Shall I do that?"

"Oh, yes, please. That would be perfect."

So Caitlin read through her lists and messages as quickly as she could, giving her passwords in code...*then the two-letter abbreviation for the state where Dad was born and the four-digit street address for the house we visited in the summers...* In the background she could hear Trina continue to shop for groceries.

But Trina had been listening. "It's a little late," she said when Caitlin was done, "but I'll make sure that someone gets to the courthouse before five to pick up your computer today. I think I can handle the rest of it."

"Thank you, Trina. Thank you. Thank you. I don't know what I would do if I couldn't get that invoice out. I hope it isn't too much trouble."

"No, no," Trina said. "I want to do it. You've never asked me to do anything before."

"That can't be true."

"No, it is. Even when I got my driver's license, you didn't even want to ask me for a ride."

*I had my skateboard,* Caitlin started to say. But no, not now. She wasn't up for reviewing family drama. "Well, thank you. I do need you now."

She walked back to the breakfast room, struggling between gratitude and guilt. She decided to focus on the gratitude. It was comforting that her sister would know where their father had been born and what their grandmother's street address was. For most people the longest relationship that they would ever have was with their siblings. Maybe Caitlin should try to make a little more of hers.

The Chinese food arrived before anyone was hungry. Once again the other three men made Teddy stop playing. Teddy took his container of General Tso chicken and ate that and only that. Fred kept his shrimp in lobster sauce by his side, but then took some of all the other things, too.

"We knew that would happen," Norma whispered to her. "Don't get upset by it."

She had a point. But it was hard not to feel bad for Yvette. The girl went through the line last. By then there was no more plum sauce for the moo shu pork even though that's what Yvette had wanted to order. Clearly she almost never went out to eat, and even crappy Chinese food was a treat.

"Is something wrong?" Seth asked her. "Are you getting dehydrated?"

She looked at his plate for signs of excessive plum sauce—had he been the selfish plum-sauce pig?—but he had loaded up his plate with vegetables... not that the vegetables, gleaming with sesame oil, were all that healthy. "Probably, and all this soy sauce isn't going to help."

"Marcus is filling his glass full of ice so the water is really cold and then adding a little bit of juice. It helps."

Caitlin tried that, and it did help except when it was that cold and sweet, it was hard to drink enough.

Why was she being such a princess about the water? How spoiled could a person be? Very spoiled, apparently. Her friends in San Francisco were all aficionados of bottled water, each person having a preferred brand.

After dinner the men went back to their game and Stephanie to the jigsaw puzzle. Caitlin felt as if everyone else was looking at her, waiting for her to tell them what would be fun to do.

*Why are you looking at me? I'm not the popular girl. That was my sister.* Trina had been the fun one, at least until she had gotten pregnant. *This isn't my job.*

She had been coxswain on her high school and college crew teams. The coxswain was the one person on the boat who didn't row. The coxswain's job was to motivate the rowers, keeping them functioning as a team. She had been good at it, and that skill had paid her way through Stanford. It didn't seem to be helping her now. The eight rowers in her boat had been driven athletes with bitingly competitive natures and the capacity to keep rowing with perfect technique when their muscles were shrieking. What could she do with this crowd?

"I'm not a teacher like Joan," she heard herself say, "but would anyone like to have a little drawing lesson?"

The drawing lesson was a great hit. Dave, the burly trucker who loved his outdoor grill and his smoker, proved to have a fair bit of natural talent.

At 8:00 p.m. Andrea, the tall deputy, came back on duty. She seemed disappointed that Seth was so involved in the game.

The motel staff had said that Caitlin could store the boxes in their supply closet and could even leave the jigsaw puzzle out, but if one of the other guests wanted to work on it during their breakfast hour, the staff wouldn't stop them.

"That's fine," she said. The puzzle had fifteen hundred pieces and would take hours and hours to finish.

At nine thirty, people helped her pack things up, although Stephanie, who seemed to be the helpful type, was clearly having trouble pulling herself away from the puzzle. Teddy picked up the Revelation game, said good night, and started to leave the breakfast room.

"That's Caitlin's game," Keith said. "She may want to keep it with her other things."

"Oh." Teddy looked disappointed. "Could I at least take the instruction book? I want to reread it."

Seth and Marcus had won the first two games. Then Keith had won the third; good farmer that he was, he had paid attention to the food supply. So everyone had won except Teddy. That clearly bothered him. But his taking only the instruction book seemed like a great way for the instruction book to get lost. "No, just take the whole thing."

Caitlin had kept out the book light and some books for herself. Then she handed Seth the CD player.

"What's this?" he asked, looking down at the sparkling "TRINA" on the front of the purple case.

"Music. In case you can't sleep."

"Don't you need it?"

"I have the book light, and Norma doesn't snore."

She slept surprisingly well, and in the shower the next morning she resolved to take better care of herself. She would force herself to drink the water; she would ask Seth to design a series of exercises she could do on the floor of her room without any equipment. She would play one game of Scrabble, but then work on the jigsaw puzzle. She would be a healthy, well-adjusted person who could help other people and still meet her own needs.

But Stephanie had finished the jigsaw puzzle. All fifteen hundred pieces. It lay on the table, a swirl of blues and lavenders, the overhead light reflecting off its glossy surface.

Caitlin wasn't the only person disappointed. "That really wasn't fair," someone grumbled. "It was here for all of us."

*Actually, no,* Caitlin thought, *it was here for me. And I worked on it for fifteen minutes.*

"She must have stayed up late," was all she said.

She went to sit by Marcus, and a few minutes later Seth joined them. He handed her the CD player and Trina's sparkling purple CD case. "I shouldn't be an ingrate, but that was some kind of heinous music."

"I'm sure it was, but my sister was a major teenybopper. What did you listen to when you were eleven?"

"Metal. It scared the shit out of me, but that's what the older guys were listening to, and I wanted to be cool. But seriously, thank you. It made a big difference."

"Then keep it. My folks sent plenty of batteries."

He took it and reached to put it on one of the empty tables. He had to stretch and tilt his chair back on two legs. The move was effortless, graceful. He seemed refreshed, energized, far beyond the healing capacity of Trina's boy-band music.

Caitlin waited until Marcus stood up. "You've been outside," she whispered. "You got some exercise."

"How did you know?" He looked puzzled.

"You're looser, lighter. I don't know how I know. I just do. I'm right, aren't I?"

He nodded.

"Are you out of your mind?" She was still trying to keep her voice down. "Are you trying to be thrown off the jury?"

"No, of course I'm not. It was legit. I was with Andrea. We went for a run. It was her idea. She suggested it last night. She's training for a marathon. She said that she wanted a training partner."

A training partner? If Joan and Delia were right, a training partner wasn't all Andrea wanted. "Why didn't you ask the rest of us?"

"She's the deputy. I don't know if she asked other people or not."

Oh, she didn't. Caitlin could pretty much guarantee that. "And I suppose she brought you water."

"Yes, as a matter of fact, she did."

Caitlin could not compete with this, someone who could get Seth out of the motel. She was powerless. She couldn't even get Fred to stop poking her with his elbow.

The day went slowly. The Revelation game started up again, and the four men played all day. People were still annoyed with Stephanie for finishing the puzzle. She was clearly a very nice person, and she wasn't used to people being angry with her. She kept offering to take the puzzle apart so everyone else could work on it again, but no one wanted that.

Caitlin was coming to an unhappy realization. She had indeed become the popular girl, the queen bee, Miss Congeniality. People—sane, adult, mature people—wanted to sit next to her, be doing what she was doing, have her approve of what they told her about themselves. When at lunch she had gone to an empty table, hoping to sit with Marcus and Seth as she had done at breakfast, April and Heather instantly moved from their table to sit with her, and Stephanie followed.

April was getting married in the fall, which meant that Heather had to talk about every wedding she had ever been to, heard about, or read about. Stephanie wanted to know if Caitlin had a boyfriend. Stephanie and Heather didn't either, but they wished that they did, and they wanted to talk about that...even though there was nothing to say.

\* \* \* \*

The deputies had brought pizza for lunch and promised tacos for dinner. Subway, McDonald's, Chinese, pizza, tacos, and the motel breakfasts, that's what they had had to eat so far. Caitlin asked if someone could go to the grocery store and buy some microwavable bags of fresh vegetables. There was a microwave in the breakfast room.

But the deputy said that the judge would have to authorize it.

Sally came by in the middle of the afternoon, looking even more exhausted than the day before. She did have good news. The first was that their families would be allowed to visit on Sunday. The jurors would be taken to a nearby park so that their location would not be disclosed.

"Like they can't all figure it out?" Keith said.

Sally ignored that. Family members had been told that they could bring more clothes for the jurors, and enough had wanted to bring food that it would probably be like a picnic.

"Do you know who is coming?" Yvette looked worried. Caitlin knew how unwelcome Yvette felt in her sister's mobile home.

Sally shook her head, but Delia and Joan both said that Yvette didn't need to worry. Their families would bring enough food to share.

When Andrea came on duty in the evening, Caitlin couldn't see how she could engineer a private conversation to ask the deputy about joining the morning run. But even if she could have, she didn't want to. She wanted Seth to ask. She wanted him to be thinking about her, trying to take care of her.

But he obviously did not. It was clear on Sunday morning that he had had another long, satisfying run, and no one else mentioned having gone.

Well, this was hardly the first time he had put himself first.

\* \* \* \*

Their first kiss had been the start of a magical time that third summer. The overgrown, chained property at the lake started to feel like theirs. They brought a bucket and a broom to scrub the pollen and moss off the dock. They tested the rocks along the shoreline to find an easy path into the water. They bought old lawn chairs at a yard sale and hid them back among the trees.

And it wasn't long at all before Caitlin was ready.

Her boss moved her to the day shift, and they had every evening together. Their families were used to the two of them being together as much as possible so there was only one question, and that was from MeeMaw.

"Do you love him?"

They had never talked about love, but Caitlin could answer instantly. "Yes."

"Have you told him?"

She shook her head.

"I suggest that you should tell him. You're too young to be making promises, but you should at least tell each other that."

So in his car outside the Dairy Queen the next afternoon, she said, "We weren't going to play games with each other, right? We were going to be straight."

"Yeah." He sounded puzzled, as she had already been straight about having sex.

"Then I want to say this. I love you, Seth."

"Oh." He was surprised. He hadn't thought about this. "Oh, *yes.* Yes, of course. That's what this is." He waved his hand between the two of them. "It's love, isn't it?"

Then two weeks later, it was over. He was gone.

He followed obsessively what was happening in the snowboarding world. He knew who was training where, who was practicing which trick, who was getting hurt. Most of the top US snowboarders were together in New Zealand while Seth was stuck in North Carolina.

A couple of the hopefuls apparently weren't making the progress the national coaches had expected. "See," he said to Caitlin, "they should have asked me."

"I thought that your parents didn't want you to train year-round."

"Some guys said that that was the only reason I wasn't asked. I know I am as good as three-quarters of those people."

Then suddenly his dad got a call. Nothing had really been said, but his dad had gotten a call. And he hadn't ruled it out.

"Why would your parents change their minds?" Caitlin asked. "What's different?"

"The company. The factory. It would be huge if I got on the Olympic team."

"But you're only sixteen. I thought you were aiming for four years from now."

"Well, sure, but..."

She knew Seth. And Seth really liked being on top, one of the best.

His mother took him all the way across the state to the Duke Medical Center so he could be tested and poked by sports-medicine doctors who concluded that her maternal instincts were far too cautious. There was no reason why Seth couldn't go back to training.

So the people who ran things in the snowboarding world were sending him a ticket to New Zealand.

Of course he was thrilled. "I wish you could go with me," he said to Caitlin. "That would make it perfect if you were there."

"Seriously? Like that would ever be possible?"

She must have sounded a little sharp because he drew back and after a moment said, "You know that I have to go, don't you? For the company and all."

"Don't bullshit me, Seth. Your parents talked to the doctors because of the company. You, you're going for yourself."

Caitlin knew that there was never any question of him staying in North Carolina for her. And really there was only a month left to the summer, actually only three and a half weeks. He would have been nuts to give up this opportunity for another twenty-five days with her.

Yet still...couldn't he have minded more?

"It's going to be different from now on," he said. "We aren't kids anymore, and we love each other. We're starting to have our own money. We can figure out how to see each other during the year. We won't have to wait until next summer. I promise."

But MeeMaw had been right. They were too young to make promises.

* * * *

A different bus was waiting to take them to the park to meet their families. Yvette was clinging to Caitlin; there was no way not to sit next to her.

"Do you think my sister will come?" Yvette asked.

"I don't know." Caitlin tried to sound cheerful. "But Delia and Joan said that their grandchildren are likely to be there. You can help with them."

"Oh, okay." That seemed to comfort Yvette.

The two of them were sitting near the back of the bus, and when they got to the park, the people in front of them were taking forever to get off. It turned out that the light outside was so bright that each person unthinkingly paused at the door, waiting for his or her eyes to adjust.

They had all turned into moles with no idea what to do in the sunlight.

Her parents and MeeMaw were waiting under a tree. They had brought lawn chairs, and there were four chairs. They had brought one for her.

Of course they had. It was common decency. But it seemed like so much more than that, someone trying to make something right for her, someone caring about her. By the time she reached them, she couldn't help herself. She was crying.

"Caitlin, sweetheart." Her mother pulled her close. "Baby, what's wrong? Is it that bad?"

"No, no, it isn't." Caitlin still clung to her. "It's just boring, and the water's so horrible." *And Seth, he's running with a deputy. I can't talk to him. I can't be alone with him.* MeeMaw handed her a tissue. "I don't know why I am crying. I just want to be home."

"Oh, honey, it's going to be a—" Her mother broke off and then forced her voice to get all bright and mom-like. "It's going to be fine."

But that wasn't she had started to say. She had started to say *it's going to be a while.*

Of course it was going to be a while. Caitlin knew that. They hadn't even had a full day of testimony, and the dick lawyers seemed determined to drag things out as long as possible.

"Here you go." Her dad handed her a bottle of water. "Tom Street brought a couple flats of water. He figured that you were at the Best Western and that their water might be bad."

Caitlin turned the bottle to look at the label. It had the Street Boards logo with its "& Snow" red graffiti. And the water was wonderful, coming from the pure underground streams of the Blue Ridge Mountains. Caitlin felt it flooding through her body, down her arms and legs, into her cells, cleansing, restoring.

There was an insane amount of food. Big aluminum pans of potato salad and macaroni and cheese, a platter of Dave's smoked meats and fish, two casseroles, brownies, and cookies, all of it homemade. Fortunately her parents had brought a big green salad.

Caitlin would have liked to sit in the sun, drink water, eat salad, and let her mom hold her hand and her dad put his arm around her. Jurors weren't supposed to touch each other. She wanted to be touched. She wanted to be a little kid, to be taken care of. But she had to sit at one of the picnic tables and go over business. Seth and his family were at another table; they had papers spread out in front of them too.

Trina had been working hard. She had forwarded to Caitlin's parents every email she had sent or received, and Caitlin's parents had printed them out. But much too much of the work had involved farming out ongoing projects to other designers.

"You're going to take a big financial hit, aren't you?" her dad asked.

She nodded.

"Do you know if you are allowed to sublet your apartment? Trina suggested if you could sublet it for a month—"

"A *month?*" Caitlin was horrified.

"I'm not saying that's how long the trial will last," her father said quickly. "You can always stay with us afterward or go visit your sister. Do you know if you are allowed?"

She nodded. She had started out subletting the place herself, but now she had a "master tenant" lease. Since her rent was by far her biggest expense, subletting the apartment would help a lot. So she suggested that her parents contact her friends Richard and Peter. Peter was a real estate agent.

It was hard to get all their business done, as the other jurors were interrupting, wanting to introduce their families. Some people knew MeeMaw was Dr. Thurmont's wife, and of course everyone commented on how Caitlin and her father had the same dark eyes.

Far too soon the bus pulled up, and reluctantly the jurors got back on. The shopping bags and suitcases that the families had brought went into the hold. Deputies would have to search them. People were allowed to take only the food that they could keep without refrigeration in their rooms. Apparently health department regulations wouldn't allow the leftovers to be stored or served in the motel's breakfast room.

On the bus she was sitting with Yvette, but Seth was across from her. He was wearing a watch again. His parents must have brought it for him. It looked new and very ordinary. The black strap was so shiny that it had to be vinyl. He shot her a quick glance and raised his eyebrows. It was a signal of some sort, but she didn't know what it meant.

In the parking lot back at the motel he knelt down to tie his shoe. He wanted to talk to her. So she told Yvette to go on ahead—fortunately Yvette didn't ask questions—and she reached Seth just as it would have looked strange for him to be fussing with his shoe any longer.

Had he seen her crying? Was he going to ask about that? Was he concerned about her? She would laugh it off. *Oh, my parents brought a fourth lawn chair so I cried.* But he would have noticed. That mattered.

"What do you think I should do about the water?" he asked.

Oh. He hadn't noticed. Well, water was the source of life and all that. "Do? What do you mean?"

"Only you, Marcus, and I really care. This is what Keith and Yvette drink all the time, and the others all seem delighted to have free soda."

"Some people do have to watch their pennies more carefully that you do." She knew that she was sounding a little schoolmarmish. "But you aren't suggesting that we hold the water for the three snobs, are you?"

"I was asking what you thought."

She was suddenly angry. "I'm thinking that you could start being more of a team player."

"Team player? What are you talking about?"

The other jurors had gone inside, but some of the deputies were unloading the bus and didn't seem to care that Seth and Caitlin were still outside.

"That stupid game you men have been playing all day. That's all the four of you have done, and you won't include anyone else. And your parents brought you a watch."

"So? What does that have to do with being a team player?"

"You could have asked them to bring one for Marcus. He doesn't have any family around."

"Oh...I guess I should have."

She had landed a body blow. So she hammered on. "And the running... Once again you didn't take anyone else out."

"I asked Andrea about that," he said. "But she said that she was only authorized to go out with one person."

"That's crap. The smokers go out with one deputy all the time."

"Oh." He paused. "That's right, isn't it?"

"Yes. She's being completely unprofessional. She's training for a marathon, and she knows that the rest of us will slow her down."

"She may have a bit of an agenda," he acknowledged, "and I'm sorry, I really am, but my not going with her probably won't change anything for everyone else. She'll just wait until she is off duty and go by herself."

"I suppose," Caitlin said grudgingly.

"And the game. Haven't you noticed that every time we stop, Fred tries to pick a fight with Teddy? At least the game is keeping that from happening."

What had he said at the end of the third summer? *I'm doing it for the company.*

"Don't bullshit me, Seth," she said, just as she had said back then. "You're having a grand time, and that's really what you care about."

\* \* \* \*

Okay, Caitlin thought as she freshened up after the picnic, to the list of godawful citizen, ungenerous sister, bitchy juror, and resentful puzzle owner, she could add—what?—stupid-ass, lovesick teen.

No, that wasn't right. She didn't love him. She wasn't wallowing in bitterness about what had happened years ago.

It was simply that she was disappointed in him. She had expected better of him.

In every crew a few rowers have longer arms than the others. They can stretch forward farther and pull back more, giving their oars a few more precious inches in the water. But they can't stroke to their maximum. All eight oars have to catch and release at exactly the same instant. Each rower must do exactly what the person in the stroke seat is doing. Few other sports require such precise teamwork.

But snowboarding? It was as individual as a sport could get.

# CHAPTER SIX

Where did Caitlin get off being so pissed off at him? Telling him that he wasn't a team player? Him, of all people?

He and his friends were dedicated to keeping snowboarding what it used to be. The medal podiums now were dominated by the people who practiced in secret, who lived to win, who had entourages instead of friends. He, Nate, and Ben, they weren't like that at all.

Okay, so maybe Caitlin had learned the names of everyone's kids and pets, and he hadn't. What was she doing, running for prom queen?

Wait, no. He didn't want to be angry with her. Of all the people here, she was the one he should be getting along with.

She was the one he had known forever. She was the one whose brain he could trust, whose heart he could trust. She was the one he had once loved.

He was determined not to make too much about that two-moments-at-once feeling he had had out at the lake. It had simply been a memory, he kept telling himself. That was all.

But what a powerful memory it had been. It did make him wonder if she was the new Colleen.

It was funny, their names being so similar, Caitlin and Colleen.

A couple of summers ago a woman named Colleen Ridge had come to the resort to translate for two Norwegian coaches. She and Ben had known each other a little bit as kids, not as boyfriend and girlfriend, nothing like he and Caitlin had had.

Everyone adored Colleen; she was lively and cheerful, but also smart and grounded. Knowing her from before, Ben had the inside track, and she was really good for him. He lightened up around her; he talked more, he stopped analyzing everything all the time.

But Ben was Irish American. He said that that made him a realist; the rest of them called him a pessimist. He didn't trust that anything good was going to last. So he had managed to push Colleen away even though she probably was the best thing that could ever happen to him.

*Is she the new Colleen?* That became the standard by which he, Nate, and some of the other guys assessed women. "She's no Colleen, but she's fine for right now." A Colleen was the real deal, the one you could see yourself sticking with, the one you would finally grow up for. He had never come close to finding a Colleen.

But what if Caitlin were it?

Talk about the wrong time, wrong place thing. It was like they were doomed. The boredom in the courtroom, the friction at the motel...they were bound to end up wanting to strangle each other.

He had no space in his brain for anything but trying to survive this mess.

He watched her cross the parking lot and then offered to help the deputies carry in all the stuff that people's families had brought to the picnic. His family had brought him books, DVDs, and high-resistance exercise tubing. Another woman had a big plastic tub of scrapbooking supplies. The two older ladies had yarn for whatever they were doing. Caitlin's family had probably brought her a water filtration plant. But no one was getting any of it.

"We're going to have to lock it all up until tomorrow," one of the deputies told him. "We have to search everything, and apparently they're trying to cut back on all our overtime."

"That's not going to sit very well with people," Seth said. Some of the jurors were having budget problems of their own.

Teddy was the biggest baby about not getting his stuff. He wanted to watch the Japanese animated feature film that his wife had brought for him. He was trying to cajole one of the deputies to give it to him. He had seen them load it into one of the storage closets. It was right on top.

"It's just one DVD," he kept saying. "What is there to search? It won't take you a minute."

Fred was, of course, the first person to attack him. "Why should they get your crap, and no one else's?"

"But it's for all of us," Teddy protested. "We can all watch it."

"You don't think the rest of us want to watch foreign shit, do you?"

Seth certainly didn't, but he wasn't going to take Fred's side on anything.

"She went to so much trouble," Teddy bleated, "and I—"

"What's that to anyone else? You're a pussy-whipped little pansy, you know that?"

"There is no call for that kind of language." Delia spoke in her extreme church-lady voice, a voice that had probably terrified three generations of little boys.

"What's it to you, Aunt Jemima?"

*Aunt Jemima?* Seth froze. He was never around racism this open. What were you supposed to do?

"I've had it with this bullshit." Fred pushed back from the table so sharply that his chair tilted back. He had to grab hold of the table to keep his balance. "I'm quitting. I'm going home."

"The judge will need to—"

"Screw that." Fred interrupted the deputy. "Here. See how the judge likes this." He pivoted and shoved Teddy's shoulder. "Or this." He hooked his foot around the leg of Teddy's chair and jerked it backward, then shoved Teddy again, sending him sprawling on the floor.

Seth shot out of his chair. This he understood.

"Don't touch him." The deputy's voice rang out with authority. "Don't any of you touch him."

People, tables, chairs were in Seth's way. He had to push the chairs aside, weave around the people and tables. This felt good, to be moving, to being physical.

"Step back, all of you." It was the deputy again.

"Seth." This time it was Caitlin speaking.

Her voice made him stop. He looked around. The other men had already stopped, putting their hands up, showing that they hadn't touched Fred. Keith and Dave were military veterans; they knew when to take orders. Maybe he should follow their lead. He stepped back, put his hands in the air too.

The deputies grabbed Fred's arms. Even with his arms trapped, Fred was able to shoot his foot forward. He kicked Teddy. Teddy shrieked.

"Stay in your seats. Stay in your seats," one deputy ordered.

The jurors all sat down in the closest chairs and watched the deputies march Fred out to the hall.

Teddy sat up, then, gripping the edge of a chair, struggled to stand. No one dared help him.

One deputy returned. He stood in the doorway, trying to keep his eye both on the jurors and on his partner and Fred out in the hall, while using his radio to call for help. He asked Norma to assess Teddy.

"I'll have to touch him," she said.

The deputy nodded. That was fine. Norma took his pulse, peered into his eyes, and asked him a few questions.

"I'm fine," Teddy protested. "Really."

"There doesn't appear to be anything immediately life threatening," she said, "but he should be checked out. He didn't just fall. He was kicked."

"No, no, I'm fine," Teddy repeated. "I don't need to see a doctor."

This was what the deputies wanted to hear. Seth figured that if Teddy said that he wasn't hurt, then he wasn't. He didn't seem to be the most stoic of fellows.

As soon as another deputy arrived, the jurors were told to put away their—that is, Caitlin's—things and go to their rooms. Only then did Seth realize that Andrea, his new running partner, hadn't reported for the evening shift on Sunday.

That was a surprise. She had talked as if she were going to be on duty all week. He hoped that nothing was wrong. But he didn't suppose there was any point in asking. No one would tell him anything.

\* \* \* \*

Monday was grim. Even though people had gotten their yarn, craft supplies, magazines, and movies, nothing could make up for the fact that they were spending the Fourth of July in a windowless hotel breakfast room.

April, the redhead with the shrieky laugh, was bummed over some wedding-planning details her family had told her about; apparently everything was more expensive than they had imagined. Heather, the one who talked so much, was yammering on about the *People* magazine pictures of celebrity weddings. Seth doubted that this was going to help April with her budget problems.

At lunch he sat with Marcus. "Hey, man, it was crappy of me not to ask my folks to get a watch for you. Shall I tell them to get one for you if we're still here next weekend?'

Marcus smiled, but shook his head. "Caitlin already offered."

Of course she did. "Do you need anything else?"

"Thanks, but Delia had her family brought me some contact lens solution yesterday."

Well, crap. How could you compete with women in the thoughtfulness game? A guy was always going to be outclassed in that race.

At least they didn't have to deal with Fred. Keith, his roommate, confirmed that a deputy had come to pick up Fred's stuff.

At dusk they were ushered onto a bigger bus to go down to the river to watch the fireworks, but they weren't allowed to get off. That's why, they were told, the court was paying for the bigger bus so that they could each have a window on the river side.

Whoop-dee-do.

*  *  *  *

The whole time they had been at the motel, no one had been tempted
to discuss the case; they weren't thinking about it. They could have been
marooned on a spaceship; they could have been trapped by a snowstorm or
quarantined for fear of a disease; they could have been political hostages.
Why they were stuck in the motel didn't matter.

But they were jurors, and Tuesday morning they were getting back on
the bus.

They arrived at the courthouse before eight and settled into their chairs in
the jury room. Sally was there with her clipboard. She did confirm that Fred
had been excused and that the judge needed to see Teddy in his chambers.

"Me?" Teddy looked surprised. "Why?"

Did he honestly think that she was going to answer that? And indeed,
she didn't.

Teddy was back in ten minutes. The judge had wanted to be sure that
he was okay, not too traumatized by Fred's attack to continue serving. "I
told him it was nothing."

Good for him. Maybe he wasn't as big a baby as Seth had been thinking.

Sally was addressing them again. "And now the judge would like to
see you, Seth."

"Me?" Seth drew back. "Why?"

Hadn't that been exactly what Teddy had said? But Seth was surprised.
Why would the judge want to talk to him? They had been told that they
could raise their concerns in individual notes to the judges. He knew that
Caitlin and Marcus had sent notes about healthier food. Dave had asked
if they could get the box scores from the Durham Bulls and the Atlanta
Braves. Others had been concerned about their prescriptions running out.
But Seth hadn't sent any notes about anything.

Under the cover of the table Caitlin nudged him. So he stood up and
followed Sally through the empty courtroom to the judge's chambers.

The room was paneled in dark oak although the wood in the courtroom
itself was birch. There was an Oriental carpet on the floor, and the furniture
was leather. Seth guessed that he was supposed to feel like he was in the
library of an English country house.

He didn't.

The judge did not look up when Seth had entered. He continued to read
something for another moment or two before acknowledging him. Then

he pushed away from his desk, tilted his heavily padded chair back, and linked his hands behind his head, keeping his elbows out, taking up as much space as possible.

"So, Mr. Street."

What an Oscar. Out on the slopes that's what they called people who were always strutting about, pretending that they were more than they were. They deserved an Oscar for acting.

There were two chairs facing the desk. The judge had not invited Seth to sit down. Seth did so anyway. He spread his legs and lifted one ankle to cross the other knee. The chair had arms, so he propped one elbow on one and hooked the other elbow over the chair back, making himself big too.

Two could play this game.

"This trial, Mr. Street, is not a promotion opportunity for your company."

Seth had no idea what he was talking about. "Sir?"

"It is my understanding that you have been distributing branded products among the other jurors."

"You don't mean the water?" Seth noticed that he was suddenly sitting like a normal person. Apparently the judge had won this round of the who-has-the-biggest-dick game. But, really, how could he be objecting to bottled water?

"Yes, the deputies will be telling your family that they can pick up the remaining bottles."

This was insane. If they were so worried about cost, then why not accept this donation? "What about if the labels were removed?"

The judge didn't answer that. He didn't have to. He wasn't an Oscar. He wasn't acting as if he had power and authority. He did have power and authority. "Now there is a second issue," he continued. "It has been reported that you left the hotel without approved supervision."

"No. No." Seth was going to defend himself. "I did go out running with a deputy, but I was with her at all times. We were off the main roads so there was no chance of seeing newspapers. No, sir. I was supervised at all times. Sir." He needed to be polite.

"But she was off duty at the time. Therefore you were not technically under court supervision."

"I had no idea that she was off duty. She never said anything about that."

"I believe that I cautioned you early on about not treating my courtroom as a singles bar."

Was he serious? A singles bar? This was even crazier than the water. "I know that, sir. I never approached her about anything. She came to me. It was her idea."

Was this ungallant of him, to blame her? But he was telling the truth. She had been the one exploiting her professional position. He was not going to have the face of Street Boards to be thrown off the jury for something plain old Seth hadn't done.

And there was no way the judge was dismissing him. Otherwise he would have done it at the start of the conversation.

Something had gone terribly wrong with this trial. Clearly this sequestration had not been planned—or budgeted for. They had had less than one day of testimony, and they were down to one alternate. Unless the judge wanted a mistrial, however much he hated Seth, he was stuck with him.

Suddenly Seth realized that he had some power too.

It wouldn't take much. Two people had to break, that's all, and there would be a mistrial. Seth himself couldn't be the one of those dismissed, but how hard would it be to get two others to crack?

Teddy was tougher than Seth realized, and Yvette was actually happy to be here. As godawful a place as the poultry plant was to work, she was actually getting her paycheck while on jury duty. But the jigsaw-puzzle person—Stephanie?—was still feeling absurdly guilty for having finished the puzzle. Keith was worried about his family and the farm chores. Dave had that payment coming up on his rig. Norma and Marcus seemed impervious, but sometimes those people who seemed so strong snapped because they couldn't bend. Delia and Joan, the two older women, were probably as resolute as Caitlin. Seth didn't know much about the other two young women, but he could find out.

He looked straight at the judge. *Okay, buster, sir, sir buster, you get this trial moving, or I torpedo it.*

"You may return to the jury room, Mr. Street."

But the judge had broken eye contact first.

"It was about the water," he told the others back in the jury room. "Apparently the court can't accept donations that appear to be promoting a commercial enterprise." He didn't know if that was the actual truth or if the judge was just being a jerk because the enterprise in question was Seth's.

"What if the labels were removed?" Marcus asked.

Seth shrugged.

The other jurors asked Sally about the notes they had sent to the judge. He had read them, she said, but had not had a chance to address them. That annoyed people.

"I'm not asking to see the newspaper," Dave protested, "or even read about the games. Can't one of you sit down at a computer and print up the box scores? What could be the harm in that?"

Sally too could only shrug.

\* \* \* \*

Once testimony got started again, the judge did seem to be trying, urging the lawyers to move along in their questioning, dealing with objections quickly, allowing fewer sidebars, but sometimes it seemed that there wasn't much he could do.

With Fred gone, Seth was sitting next to Caitlin now. He could tell that she was developing a glossary, keeping a list of the terms she didn't understand, then gradually filling in—or crossing out—definitions.

He needed to talk to her, but he had to be careful. Even during the sidebars, the jury was being watched, both by lawyers and by people whom he supposed were journalists. There wasn't any chance at lunch either. Everyone wanted to stand with her, sit with her, talk to her.

He figured his best chance was back at the hotel during the evening meal delivery...which sounded like prisoner-think, *when will the guards be the most distracted?* But prisoners were the best role model he had, so during the bustle of foil pans and serving utensils he asked Caitlin if she would recommend one of the books that her parents had sent.

Her boxes were in the corner. "What is it?" she said as soon as they had their backs to the room. She knew that his parents had sent him books, that he wouldn't need any of hers.

She really did have the most beautiful eyes. There was a little halo of green around the pupil, which shaded into the rich dark brown, which was flecked with bits of gold. And to be standing so close to her. Her hair smelled like grapefruit and lime.

He had to force himself to step away. *Wrong time, wrong place.* "You know we are down to one alternate. So it will only take two people and then this whole thing is over."

"Two...wait, you aren't suggesting that you and I—"

"No, no. I can't. But—"

She straightened. "I am certainly not doing anything dishonorable."

"Can you keep your voice down?"

"I will not discuss this." At least she was speaking more quietly, but from the way she was standing, you'd think that she had gone to the Naval Academy. "Not now. Not ever."

Well, crap. Now she was even madder at him. What had he expected? She might wear leather miniskirts and carry a hip messenger bag, but she was a military kid, the daughter of a judge; she was going to follow the law.

Why did he keep screwing this up? He wasn't trying to turn her into a Colleen. He simply wanted them to work together. He couldn't even manage that.

* * * *

Dinner was awful. It was supposed to be a well-balanced meal from a local family-dining restaurant, but the salad was soaked in a sweet dressing, and the chicken was swaddled in cheap tomato sauce and rubbery cheese. Then they all felt that they had to watch Teddy's Japanese animated movie with him. It was every bit as incomprehensible and tedious as the trial.

Wednesday morning it was clear that Teddy was in pain. He was moving carefully, taking shallow breaths. Seth guessed that he had a broken rib. Snowboarders broke ribs. Most were fractures that got better on their own, but they could hurt like hell while they were doing it.

Thursday morning he was coughing and running a fever, and Norma told the deputies that he had to go to the ER immediately. He probably had pneumonia.

The judge delayed testimony on Thursday, clearly hoping that Teddy would return, but after lunch the jurors filed into the courtroom, and another witness was called.

They were down to twelve.

The judge had to do something. The trial wasn't progressing any more quickly, and the jury wasn't doing well. People were growing stiff from the worn mattresses and the hours of sitting. Marcus and Caitlin were losing weight while others were gaining. No one seemed interested in watching movies or playing games. The women who had been trying to learn to knit or crochet stopped. April's laugh seemed louder. Seth couldn't tell if it actually was louder or if the rest of them had gotten more quiet.

Thursday afternoon they were told that they all had single rooms. But Seth was the only one who bothered to move. The rest were too weary to care. At dinner the deputies had printed up the box scores as well as newspaper articles about major national events, something that could have been done a week ago. A week ago people might have still cared, but now not even Dave cared about the scores.

It was too little, too late. Yes, the food was awful and the hotel dreary, but the problem was sitting in court, listening to repetitive, obscure testimony, watching the lawyers bicker. *Just declare a mistrial and send us all home.*

But the judge probably couldn't do that, not while there were still twelve jurors.

Thursday evening two of the women revealed something Teddy had told them. He had tried so hard to stay on the jury because his wife was going to write a book about her experiences during the trial. "She thought that that's what people would really be interested in."

"In *her?*" Seth couldn't help himself.

Apparently, yes. She had always thought that she deserved to be famous and this was her chance.

*The wrong place. Seriously wrong.*

\* \* \* \*

Friday morning Sally came to their 6:00 a.m. breakfast and told them that the court would, once again, not be holding a Friday session. "But"— she didn't give them time to protest—"you will be moving to a different facility today so you need—"

"Oh, no," Keith interrupted. "You aren't sending us to the Dixie Motor Court, are you? That place is trash."

"I heard it had bedbugs." Delia was horrified. "You can't do that. You *can't.*"

Bedbugs. It occurred to Seth that there might be some utility in bedbugs. If the jurors got infected, they would carry the little creatures into the courtroom—in fact, Seth would lovingly escort his—and then the courthouse would have to be closed and fumigated.

Of course his mom would shave his head and make him strip buck naked in the driveway before she let him into any house of hers. And maybe not just his head.

Sally was smiling. "I think you'll be very pleased. We have been working on this for several days. It is a bed-and-breakfast on the other side of town. You will be the only guests, so you will have more freedom. There will be an exercise facility, and you will be able to sit outdoors."

*Exercise...outdoors...*

"You don't mean the Wildflower Inn?" Joan asked. "I hear that's lovely."

"Isn't that closed for renovation?" Stephanie asked. "Our bakery used to sell to them, but not for a couple of months."

"I can't confirm where we are going," Sally said. "Indeed, there will be workmen there during the day while you are at court, but not in the evenings or weekends."

People were excited. No one had actually been to the inn—it was a high-end place—but several of them knew a lot about it. Each room was named for a Carolina wildflower, and each one had toiletries scented with the fragrance of that wildflower.

"Do you think that they will give us the products?" Heather asked. "I really hope so, but they probably won't because they are super expensive. A friend of mine won a raffle basket at the St. John's school fair. She didn't know anyone, she was only there because she had gotten a ticket from this person—"

Seth stopped listening. He got up to get more coffee, and on his way asked Keith about the inn.

"It's been open about three years and hasn't been doing great. It's got new owners, and they're adding on a ballroom, trying to get into the wedding business. So they probably gave the court a really good deal since they're closed."

"Are there going to be holes in the roof and no hot water?"

"Anything's better than the Dixie Motor Court."

Seth traveled enough that he could pack quickly. As soon as he was finished, he went back to the breakfast room to help Caitlin organize her boxes. Stephanie was already working on it.

"Do you believe," she asked, "when the deputies packed up Teddy's things they took the Revelation game? Apparently he told them to be sure and get it because it was his."

"Oh, I do believe it." But he didn't mind. He never wanted to see that game again.

From the front seat of the van—they no longer needed a bus—Sally explained the new room assignments. There were eleven rooms and no elevator so Joan and Delia would share the ADA-compliant room on the first floor. Three of the rooms were on the third floor, and Sally had decided that Caitlin, Marcus, and Seth were the most suited to those rooms because the last flight of stairs was difficult.

"I made these decisions," Sally said. "I am taking full responsibility. But I'm open to discussion."

Someone accepting responsibility? Someone thinking the jurors were capable of having a thought?

But the plan was a good one. After Delia assured Joan that the only thing that could wake her was a child who needed her, those two ladies confirmed that they would rather share a room than subject their knees to stairs. Marcus, Caitlin, and Seth didn't mind the stairs.

The trip seemed to be taking a while, and soon the jurors who knew the area said that they couldn't be going to the Wildflower. It turned out that the van driver was lost, so Keith had to move to the front to tell him where to go.

Maybe the whole trial would be going better if the jury could be in charge.

\* \* \* \*

The Wildflower Inn was in a small village nestled in the mountains. The inn itself was an old white-shuttered stone building that sat close to the narrow Main Street. The front porch was marked off with caution tape, and the back parking lot was full of construction vehicles and a dumpster.

They came in through the back door, but the rear entry was luxurious and welcoming, a freshly painted square room with a high ceiling and stone floor. In the center was a round hall table that held a flower arrangement, brochures for local activities, and a dish of foil-wrapped chocolates. Two armchairs, comfortably padded in a flowery fabric, sat on either side of the double doors. Along one wall was a coffee station, and in the far corner was a freestanding water dispenser with a five-gallon jug of springwater inverted on top of the cooler.

Fresh water... Marcus was already at the dispenser filling a glass—a glass made of actual glass. The motel had only had disposable glasses.

The air was full of the light floral scent of the flower arrangement and the warm sweetness of something baking. The motel had smelled of burnt toast, pancake syrup, and lemon-scented disinfectant.

He had stayed in plenty of places as nice as this, but clearly most of the others hadn't. Keith and Dave, farmer and trucker, stood together, looking as if they were expecting someone to come tell them that they didn't belong here. Yvette looked frightened, but everyone else seemed to relax. Tensed shoulders went down, breathing deepened.

A middle-aged innkeeper invited them into the breakfast room.

How different it was from their last breakfast room. Tall windows on one side filled the room with light while the front wall had French doors leading out to the porch. Fresh cranberry scones sat on a platter next to a silver coffee service.

The scones probably had as much fat and sugar as fast food, but Seth didn't care. They were worth the calories.

The innkeeper told them there was an exercise studio across the parking lot, but they needed to be careful of construction traffic. Unfortunately, the front porch was not stable, but there was a patio in the back, and most of the rooms had balconies. There were sitting rooms on both the first and second floors, but they were adjacent to the construction work. They were not to talk to the construction workers, and the construction workers had been warned not to talk to them. He then apologized for having to remove the televisions from the rooms. The inn would provide breakfast, but they didn't have the staff for the other meals.

"Can we use your kitchen?" Marcus asked. "If we clean up afterward?"

The innkeeper shrugged. "I don't see why not."

Sally then spoke. Because the jurors would be staying on three separate floors with several places to spend their free time, they could not be as closely supervised as before. But she had assured the judge that no one had shown any inclination to discuss the case. One of his concerns was that they not splinter themselves into factions, so she hoped that they would be mindful of that. Again they were not to enter each other's rooms.

"But aren't all the rooms different?" one of the younger women asked. "I want to see them."

Everyone seemed to agree, and Sally promised that she would arrange a time for that.

Clearly she had stopped feeling that she needed the judge's approval for everything.

Marcus had already disappeared into the kitchen, so Seth and Caitlin followed Sally up to the third floor without him. The staircase between the second and third floor was stacked against an exposed brick wall. The treads were unfinished, a few of the risers were missing, and the railings were raw two-by-fours. Sally assured them that it was safe.

At the top of the stairs she stopped. Through the mass of the brick wall Seth could hear the faint grind of a power saw.

"Listen, you two," Sally said, "I don't have the manpower to put a deputy up here all the time. The obvious thing would have been to put three men up here or three women, but every time I tried to do that, I ran into problems. Either the stairs would be too much or I was going to be setting up factions. And I am aware that some of you are more resilient emotionally than others. So this is the arrangement I could live with, but it involves trusting you."

"You can," Caitlin said instantly.

*Yeah, she hates me way too much.*

Yesterday in line outside the courtroom he had asked her if she was still mad at him.

"No, I'm not mad," she had said. "I am disappointed."

That had stung. Sure, he disappointed himself like when he suddenly stopped being able to land a trick he had been doing for months and months, but other people? When had other people been disappointed in Seth Street?

Except Caitlin when she had been in high school and he had stopped returning her calls. She would have been disappointed then.

"You're both young," Sally was saying, "you're attractive, and you're bored. It wouldn't be surprising, but I have to ask you to think of this as part of your juror's oath and also as something personal from me. I trust you. Please don't let me down."

Seth wasn't sure that the juror's oath meant a thing to him anymore, but an individual pledge to Sally...oh, yeah, that counted.

He put out his hand. "We know that this is a bitch for you too."

She blinked in surprise...and then blinked again as if she was trying to fight off some tears. She shook his hand with a nice firm grip, then moved on, probably uncomfortable with the emotion of the moment. "There's one room in the front and two in the back. The front one is much bigger so you might as well take that, Caitlin."

Caitlin was shaking her head. "Part of your calculus had to be Marcus needing to escape from the crowd. Give him the bigger room, especially if he is going to cook sometimes."

Sally nodded. She didn't care. So Seth was in the Mountain Laurel room, while Caitlin was across the hall in the Iris.

Seth's dad had once shown him how straight grained the wood from a mountain laurel bush was, but the bushes never grew large enough to be of much commercial use. The blossoms were pink and white, so Seth assumed that his room would be overpoweringly girly, but it was done in soothing neutrals and sage greens with only a few touches of pink and maroon. The bathroom was awesome with a heated floor, a glass-walled shower with multiple heads, a whirlpool tub, and a toilet that raised its lid as you came near.

This would make a difference. But would it be enough? Perfumed bath salts weren't going to make it much easier to sit through the lawyers' little reindeer games. There were times during court when he wanted to stand up and break his chair over someone's head.

He had seen pictures of beautiful mountains destroyed by logging or mining. He knew of places where the discharge from chemical plants had polluted the water. The courtroom, someplace that was supposed to be noble, was like that, full of corrupt politicians, greedy financiers, and asshole lawyers.

Did it have to be this way? Didn't the country stand for more than this? He had worn the American flag on his sleeve at the Olympics.

If you got a silver or bronze medal in an international competition, you had to be a complete shit not to want the gold to go to your teammate. That way during the medal ceremony, you heard your own national anthem. What a moment that had been, seeing all three Stars and Stripes being raised. Halfway through "The Star-Spangled Banner," the guy on top had pulled the other two of them up with him, and the three of them had put their arms around each other's shoulders and listened to the rest of the anthem.

So maybe he was a player, careless and irresponsible. Not in the sexual sense, like Caitlin probably thought, but in the whole citizenship department. He didn't have a clue what was in the tax return that he signed every year, and when he had registered for the draft at eighteen, he had done so without a moment's worry. He wouldn't be called up. The country had an all-volunteer military. Other people could put themselves in harm's way on his behalf. National security was their problem, not his.

But justice...maybe this was where he had to step up, where he had to take some responsibility.

# CHAPTER SEVEN

One of the many random things that Caitlin knew was that wild irises were called dwarf irises because they only grew six inches tall, but she supposed that "dwarf" wasn't a word that evoked much elegance, and the Iris room was elegant indeed. The heavy drapes, the bedcover, and the chair had a purple-blue Regency strip on a cream background. Cream-painted wainscoting circled the room, topped by a iris-colored chair rail; the crown molding was also painted iris; the carpeting and other accents were moss green.

The decor was too traditional for Caitlin's taste, and her romantic alter ego Aurora probably would have liked to add a gauzy canopy over the bed and some pretty ribbons, but it was a wonderful improvement on the blandness of the Best Western.

The bedroom was king sized with a light layer of memory foam supported by a firm mattress. The bathroom was bigger than her kitchen in San Francisco, much bigger. The toilet had a motion-activated lid and a bidet feature controlled by a panel on the wall. The towels were on a heated rack, and behind the door hung two thick white bathrobes embroidered with the inn's logo. The claw-foot tub was so deep that there was a little stool to help you get in, and the glass-walled showers had six different heads, all with adjustable spray patterns.

This was a room for romantic-weekend sex, for anniversary sex, for first-time-away-together sex.

What had Sally been thinking, putting her up here with Seth?

*I need to know that I can trust you,* Sally had said.

Surely there had to have been another arrangement. If you started with Marcus being up here because he needed more alone time than anyone else, then why not put Norma up here with Caitlin? Norma could do the stairs...but maybe Sally wanted Norma to keep her eye on Yvette, and you wouldn't want to isolate Yvette up here. What about some pairing of April, Heather, and Stephanie? No, separating two of them would lead to a faction. What about...

Every combination Caitlin could think of had problems.

So this was it. Only two doors and a narrow, unguarded hall lay between her king-sized bed and Seth. And the fact that Sally trusted them.

Caitlin looked around the room again. The Queen Anne furniture was starting to grow on her. And to be here by herself. No one would want to talk at her, no one would say, "Oh, are you warm?" when she had taken her sweater off or ask her if she had gotten cold when she went to put it back on. Best of all, she could actually make a few of her own decisions. She could sit in the first-floor lounge or the second-floor library. She could even open the door and go out to the patio or gym without violating a court order.

She changed into her exercise clothes and went out into the hall. No deputy watched her close the door. She started down the makeshift stairs. No other juror asked her where she was going. It was so delicious that she wanted to go back to her room and lather, rinse, and repeat.

Only when she had gone through the second-floor hallway and reached the front steps did she see anyone.

"Isn't this place amazing?" Heather enthused. "Have you looked around yet? It's like being in a movie. The chairs in the sitting room—that's what they call the one on the first floor, the sitting room, and the library is up here. Or is it like being in a game of Clue? They are building a ballroom, you know. Are you going over to the exercise place? Have you seen the schedule? Sometimes we can be on the first floor with the machines because they're giving classes in the yoga studio. Then sometimes we need to be in the yoga studio because they have members who use the machines. I've never done yoga. Have you? Do you think you could teach the rest of us? My sister said that yoga would help us sit in the courtroom all day."

Caitlin was shaking her head. She knew a few poses, but had never had much formal instruction.

The fitness center wasn't large. There was one weight stack in the center of the room. Seth was using it. He was facing its tower, extending his arms, then pulling a bar down to his shoulders. He didn't notice her coming in. The other machines were placed to face the windows: two stationary bikes, a treadmill, a Pilates reformer, and a rowing machine. Caitlin was curious about the reformer, but she had no idea how to use it. The rowing machine was similar to the ergometers the crew team had used in college. She would use that.

It took her a long time to warm up, but eventually the endorphins kicked in, flooding her with a sense of well-being, making her feel focused and alive. She could do this forever. She was going to do this forever. Her form was good; she had her core engaged, her shoulders—

"Ah, Caitlin?"

She glanced over her shoulder. It was Yvette.

"I've never been in a place like this," Yvette said timidly. "Where should I start?"

Caitlin stopped at the top of the drive, keeping her legs straight, her arms holding the tension. She looked around the room. Norma was on the treadmill. April and Heather were side by side on the two stationary bikes, but Heather was talking, not pedaling.

"Heather looks like she is done. Go ask her to get you started."

Yvette looked uncertain.

"No, it's fine. She's just sitting there."

Caitlin started to row again, but she watched as Yvette approached Heather. Heather clearly had been so busy talking that she hadn't noticed that she had stopped exercising, which of course made April laugh her hacking laugh. Heather started pedaling furiously again. A minute later Yvette left the studio.

Caitlin couldn't recapture the glow. She tried for another ten minutes and then gave up. Seth was still using the weight machines, and once again Heather had stopped pedaling.

She wiped down the machine. Norma asked her if she would like to use the treadmill. Caitlin shook her head. April pointed to the reformer and asked Caitlin if she knew what it was. Caitlin told her, but said that she didn't know how to use it.

"Do you think Seth does?" April asked.

They all looked at him. He was doing legwork. His T-shirt and gym shorts were gray, both sporting the Street Boards logo. The shirt was marked with sweat, and the ends of his hair around his neck were dark and damp. He was absorbed in the exercise, exhaling regularly with each exertion, putting in extra effort at the end of each rep to keep the weight stack from crashing down.

"He's more likely to be able to figure it out than the rest of us," Caitlin answered. "Why don't you ask him?"

"Oh...would you ask him for us?"

"You can ask him yourselves." After living with him for a week, were they still thinking of him as a star? "He won't bite."

Back in her room Caitlin took a bath. The tub was so deep that the water came up to her shoulders. The Iris products had a sweet, creamy scent. She swaddled herself in the robe and sat down in the armchair to read. She liked reading in a comfortable chair, and the chairs at the Best Western had been designed to use at tables.

She must have fallen asleep because she suddenly jerked awake. There was a steady tapping on the wall behind her shoulder. Was it construction noise?

No, the construction was on the other side of Seth's room and the stairs. This must be Seth.

She should ignore it. That was the smart thing to do. And the honorable decision. Sending messages through the wall didn't seem like a great start on living up to their pledge to Sally.

The tapping continued.

She tapped back.

The return tapping started moving, tracing a line toward the back on the hotel. Oh, the balcony. He wanted her to go out on the balcony.

The door was so heavily curtained with the purple-and-cream drapes that she hadn't thought to check it out before. She lifted aside the fabric and opened the door. The balcony was small, cut off on one side by the wall of her bathroom. A chest-high fence-type railing protected the front, and a four-foot brick wall divided her balcony from the one belonging to the room next door.

Seth was standing on his side of the wall. His hands were linked, and his forearms were resting on the balcony's front railing—since what was chest high on her was a lot lower on him. His hair was rumpled as if he had dried it with a towel, but not combed it, and he was wearing khakis and a Street Boards rugby shirt.

Well, crap. Crap, crap, *crap*.

Sequestered-jury sex, Mars-expedition sex, even the friends with benefits idea...thinking like that suggested that sex was sort of a joke, something that you could control, something that had no power. But it wasn't. Not at all.

Seth's shirt fell loosely from his shoulders. If he tucked it in, she would see his lean torso and the finely shaped muscles at the back of his khakis.

Her room with its dense, soft sheets and sweet, earthy fragrances was about magic and heightened moments. It was about mystery and intimacy, about reaching and yearning, imagining and longing.

"I hope you weren't tapping Morse code," she said lightly. She needed to keep things that way. "I don't know it."

"You think I do?" He looked at her, a quick grin flashing across his face, and she had to force herself to breathe.

Then he turned back to look at the parking lot; his voice changed, becoming low and serious. "This is the only balcony on this side of the inn. There's nothing odd about us chatting out here."

"No." What was he getting at? "Although I probably should have gotten dressed first."

Why had she said that? *Look at me; I don't have any clothes on.*

He glanced at her again, but the big white robe covered her more than any of her clothes. "Yes, but it would be weird if you went in and came back out. I don't know if anyone can hear us, but they can see us."

Down in the parking lot, the construction workers were getting into their vans. If any of them looked up, they would certainly see the balconies, and the plate glass windows of the fitness center's second-floor yoga studio gave an even better view.

"Look over there"—he pointed to the west—"so it looks like we are talking about the mountains."

"Okay." Over the roof of the fitness center she could see the western mountains. On the lower slopes the trees were shaded from a light yellow spring green to a green that was rich and dark. In the distance the higher peaks were smoky blue against the clouds.

But he wasn't out here to discuss the view. "Obviously they brought us to this place because there aren't any more alternates. But I don't think that this pampering is going to be enough."

The beauty of the hills and trees was dissolved, swamped by the sounds of construction vans' doors slamming shut and their engines grinding. "Seth, I told you I was not going to have any kind of conversation like this."

"No. No. Please. Hear me out. This is a million times better than the Best Western, but I am not sure that it is enough. I still think if there is going to be a mistrial it is better to have it sooner rather than later."

She pulled her sash tighter. "You have made that very clear."

Why did he have to be like this? Why couldn't he be perfect? She wanted him to be perfect.

No, no. She didn't want him to be perfect. It was safer to be mad at him.

"I do know when to cut my losses. Maybe this doesn't have to be a loss. But the only way I can see to all twelve of us making it to deliberations—"

"Make it to deliberations? I thought that was the exact opposite of what you wanted."

"We're another week into it now, and maybe this is throwing good money after bad, but if we are going to hang in there, we need to work together."

"Work together? *You* are saying that?" This felt good, being mad at him. "Didn't you spend the entire afternoon monopolizing one machine?"

He drew back. "I would have gotten off if anyone had asked."

"And who is going to tell Mr. Professional Athlete to get off so that they can do a three-pound bicep curl?"

"Now, wait." He was sounding pissed off too. "I have never played that card."

"You don't have to. Everyone knows who you are."

He took a breath. "This is my point. If you and I are at each other's throats already, then something's going to blow up unless all twelve of us decide to pull together."

Caitlin jerked at the sash of her robe. She was not at his throat; she was nowhere near his throat. "What in the name of everything holy do you think I have been doing for the last week except to try to keep everyone happy?"

"Right, but it's just been you trying to keep everyone happy, people wanting to sit next to you, talk to you, take their troubles to you. Everything runs through you, and you're exhausted."

That was true. She was tired, tired of playing the games she didn't want to play, tired of feeling guilty that she hadn't helped Yvette on the machines, tired of not being touched, tired of never being alone, but always feeling alone.

*If I'd wanted to be a navy wife, I would have dated sailors.*

"What are you suggesting?" she asked. This was hard for her, having a conversation without looking at him. She was so visual. She didn't only listen to people's words, but watched their faces, the play of their lips, the rise and fall of their eyebrows.

"That all twelve of us sit down and figure this out together," Seth said, "what we need to do to make it. We won't talk about the case, we will do it in front of the deputies, but all twelve of us will do it together."

"I hope you aren't expecting me to lead this meeting?"

"No, of course not. I'll do it."

But he had paused, leaving her wondering if that had been part of his original plan.

"Then I think," she said, "it's important that you just be speaking for yourself, not for the two of us. If this is 'our' plan, people aren't going to feel like equal partners. This conversation has to have never happened. As long as it doesn't seem like we're working together, I will have your back."

\* \* \* \*

The inn stocked only breakfast items for the guests, but the innkeeper and his wife did have a store of groceries for their own use. They told Marcus that he could use their personal supplies for this first night, but their financial arrangement with the court only covered breakfast.

Dinner began with a cold carrot soup, spicy with ginger. Marcus apologized for the ginger being powdered, but no one cared. He served a roasted vegetable medley, apologizing the portions were small. The entrée was chicken in Thai peanut sauce. He apologized that the chicken had been frozen in a bag and he had had to start with processed peanut butter. No one cared. People were thrilled with the food, with the rooms, the fitness studio, the library, the bath products, the chocolates on the table, the filtered water, the fancy toilets, the wonderful mattresses, the showers, the whirlpool tubs.

For dessert Marcus had melted some of the candies from the front hall and dipped orange slices in the chocolate. He apologized that the chocolate didn't have a glossy finish. No one cared.

Seth hadn't said much. So apparently this open, problem-solving, rally-around-the-flag discussion wasn't going to happen. That was good. How much easier it would be for her to go on being disappointed in him. They could be cordial through the rest of the trial, then go their separate ways. She would be the one who wanted things to end; she would be the one in charge, the one with power.

*You disappointed me. I don't want you.* That was power.

People started talking about evening plans. The inn had movies they hadn't seen, books they hadn't read, games they hadn't played.

"Count me out." Dave pushed back from the table. "I'm going up to my room. That chair is the first comfortable place I've sat since this whole thing started."

Others were scooping up their silverware, getting ready to help clear the table. Caitlin did not look at Seth. *This is on you. I'm not going to push.*

"Could you all please wait a bit?"

It was Seth. So he was going to come through.

"There's something I would like us all to talk about."

Ryan, the deputy who had been sitting in the corner of the dining room, stood up.

Seth spoke to him. "I am not going to talk about the case. Trust me. I'm not. In fact, if Sally is still around, ask her to come in. We want witnesses to the fact that we aren't talking about the case."

Ryan said something into the radio clipped to his shoulder, and an instant later Sally and another deputy rushed in, alert, worried, expecting a problem. Ryan shook his head. "They're going to have some kind of meeting and want us to listen."

"Are you sure that's wise?" Sally asked, looking at Seth.

How did she know that he was the one behind this? Because he was the only one who'd had his face on a magazine cover?

No. Sally was observant; she was smart. She would know that an Olympic medal didn't mean a person had leadership skills. She must be seeing something in Seth that Caitlin wasn't. And Sally wouldn't have forgotten that he was a Street of Street Boards, the town's biggest employer. No one would think it odd if a Street took charge.

"I think I know where the lines are," Seth was saying to Sally. "But stop us if we get close."

She nodded and went to stand against the wall. She'd had a long day; her hair was flat, her shirt was coming untucked, and her pants had big wrinkles at the top of her legs.

Seth looked around the table, then started. "It's clear that we have no more alternates, and the court is worried. The question for us is how committed are we to making it to deliberations. Do we have that as a common goal? If we don't agree on that, we should just tell the court that it's hopeless. Don't spend any more money on us; start over with another jury."

"You mean we would leave here?" Yvette sounded frantic. "No. *No.* I've never been anywhere like this before. I don't want to go home."

All the others were taking his question seriously and nodding their agreement.

Caitlin watched each one of them, trying to judge their commitment. They were all on board. As different as they were, there was one thing that the twelve of them had in common—they were the sort of people who showed up. They didn't oversleep and get to work late. They didn't say that they'd pick you up at the airport and then forget. They didn't promise to bring cookies and then instead turn up with ice cream that needed bowls and spoons. They did what they said they were going to do. All of them.

Video games were full of heroes. But wasn't this the first part of any kind of heroism? Showing up? Before storming Omaha Beach, before ripping your petticoat to make tourniquets for wounded soldiers, before drawing your gun on a gravity-heavy planet, you had to show up. And the twelve of them showed up.

"It's not enough to agree on the goal," Seth continued. "What do we need to do to make it happen? What's our biggest concern? What do we need to have happen?"

The food. Everyone agreed on that. After Marcus's dinner this evening no one wanted to go back to fast food.

Marcus had thought about this. If the deputies were willing to go to the grocery store instead of restaurants, he believed he could provide far better meals for less money. Stephanie said that she would help with the prep or cleaning up. "Because of what I do at the bakery, I have had the Food Handler's training if anyone is worried about that."

No one was. Sally said that she would need to talk to the judge, but if it didn't change the budget, she couldn't see why he would refuse. Ryan pointed out that grocery shopping once every few days would save a lot of man-hours over having to pick up fast food twice a day. "The judge is really going to like that."

"We have to stay healthy," Norma said. "Watch the basics. Wash your hands a lot. And I mean it. Sing 'Happy Birthday' twice while you are doing it."

*Happy birthday to you, happy birthday to you...*Caitlin started to run the song through her heard. "Twice? That's a lot."

"Well, do it. And tell me if you think you're getting a cold, a prickly throat, anything. Don't suffer in silence. I'm sure that there will be some way to get you on an antibiotic fast if that's what you need. And everyone needs to get more exercise, even if it is just walking around the courtyard."

Boredom and passivity was another issue. Dave asked Caitlin if she could resume art lessons. Keith wondered if there were any projects around the inn that they could help with; he was tired of not being productive. April said if people asked their families to bring in photos, she would help them make scrapbook pages. Gradually they developed a schedule of activities.

"And we have to stick to it. We can't let ourselves mope around like we did this week," Joan said. "But there's something else. Our interpersonal dynamics, how we get along. We have to see if we can fix that."

No one said anything.

"People are getting on each other's nerves," she prompted. "We need to have it out in the open."

She was right. Of course she was. She had spent years watching third graders on the playground. But was Caitlin really supposed to tell April that she hated her laugh, that she wanted Heather to shut up for five minutes, and that would everyone please, please stop looking at her like she had all the answers?

More silence. No one wanted to go first.

Okay, she had told Seth that she would have his back. She needed to say something. Not the truth, of course, but something. "Seth, I would have liked to have gotten your help on the exercise equipment."

"I'm happy to do that," he said. "We can add that to the schedule. And we need to stretch at lunch, do some yoga or something, so we can sit the rest of the afternoon. I will lead that; it's no problem. But I'm not sure that that is addressing Joan's issue."

Actually it did. *People find you unapproachable. You're a celebrity, an Olympian, a Street of Street Boards.*

But she hadn't said that, had she?

More silence.

Finally April spoke. "I don't know, I mean, maybe I'm overreacting, but Caitlin—"

Caitlin sat up.

"—I feel like you don't like me."

Oh, no. No, no, no. Everyone was looking at her. What was she supposed to say?

"I feel like you're always trying to avoid me," April said. "You won't sit near me. That makes me feel horrible."

Caitlin wanted to lie. She so wanted to lie. But Joan was a teacher, and even when Caitlin had been pretending to be a depressed art student, she had done what teachers told her. "I don't dislike you, and I know that I am not getting to know you, but your laugh does grate on me. It's loud, especially during the movies. It's not anything else about you; it's just the sound. I'm so sorry. I really am."

"And," Keith added, "you're smiling all the time."

"What's wrong with that?" April asked.

"It just doesn't seem sincere."

"As long as we are doing this," Heather said. She had become April's friend. If April had been attacked, Heather was going to attack someone else. "Seth, I hate the way that you sit. You hook your arm across the back of your chair, and your foot sprawls out. Sometimes you even put your foot on the rung of someone else's chair."

"It is the man-sprawl thing," Marcus said in his quiet way. "You do seem to feel entitled to take up a lot of space in the world."

*He wasn't as bad as Fred.* But Caitlin was going to let Seth defend himself.

He didn't. "Ah...I usually run with a pretty competitive group of guys. And I don't want to sound full of myself here, but when you want media attention, that's what you want to do, be big. It becomes automatic. But I can try."

"I've always wanted to ask you what it was like to be famous," Stephanie said. "I can't imagine it."

"Then ask. You can ask me anything. If I've come across as something other than one of the twelve trying to get through this, I'm sorry. I'm just a regular guy."

"No, you aren't." Keith shook his head. "I wasn't going to say anything about this, but you went out running with that deputy girl. We were roommates. I woke up one morning, and you were gone. I looked out the window, and the two of you were off. "

Now everyone was looking at Seth, heads cocked, eyebrows drawn close together. No one liked the sound of that. Seth tried to explain, that Andrea had told him she could only go with one person, that he hadn't known she was off duty, that the judge had called him on the carpet about it. "I did ask her if other people could go. Really I did."

"Is that why she stopped being assigned to us?" someone asked.

Seth nodded.

"She must have been disappointed by that," Delia said.

"But when you came back from your meeting with the judge," Keith said, "you only told us about the bottled water."

Seth grimaced. "Honestly, I was ashamed. I got a special privilege that no one else did, and that wasn't right."

"I think the lesson is that we shouldn't keep secrets from each other," Joan said. "Let's stop sending individual notes to the judge. Let's act as a unit."

Everyone seemed to agree with that.

"Can I explain?" April suddenly said. "About why I am laughing so much? I'm doing it on purpose. We all seem so dreary. I know that some people say I don't have a nice laugh, but I was trying to make it seem like we were having fun. There's nothing wrong with that, is there?"

"We aren't having fun," Joan said gently. "So there's no reason to make it appear like we are. It doesn't help."

"It did occur to me," Delia said, "that if you breathed differently and took some singing lessons, your laughter could be...ah"—Delia was obviously struggling for a polite term—"more melodious."

"Really? You can change your laugh?"

Delia nodded, and singing lessons were added to the schedule.

Then Keith said that he was uncomfortable with the way Delia had kept correcting Teddy on his manners. "It didn't seem like your place."

Delia admitted that Teddy had pushed her buttons. It wouldn't be hard to be more respectful of everyone else.

"So is that it?" Joan said.

No, it wasn't, and everyone knew that it wasn't.

"I know I was wrong to finish the jigsaw puzzle," Stephanie said, "and I am really, really sorry about that."

That was not the issue.

Finally Norma had the nerve at least to get close. "I don't watch many of the movies, but when I do, I don't want there to be a lot of conversation."

"Sometimes it would be nice to have some quiet," Seth agreed.

"I suppose you are talking about me," Heather said. "Everyone says I talk a lot."

She was looking around, waiting to be told, that no, it wasn't a problem, that everyone liked hearing from her.

No one said anything.

"We know you have a heart of gold," Delia said, "but it's too much. It is."

Heather looked mortified.

"And we know that's your coping mechanism," Joan said. "You can't take a vow of silence and expect to survive this. But if you could keep from telling so many stories about your friends and your sister's friends, that would help."

"Do I do that?"

"Oh, yes."

"We know you like people," Caitlin said. "You want to engage. So maybe you could occasionally ask people questions about themselves."

This was, she thought, a nobly self-defeating thing for her to say as she was thoroughly sick of having to explain what she was doing every time she stood up to get a glass of water.

"Heather's not the only one at fault there." Dave spoke for the first time. "It seems like all you young people have written Keith and me off as old farts not worth knowing. Caitlin's been nice about the art business, but she's the only one."

That was true. Everyone knew it. There was nothing for anyone to say except to promise to do better.

Joan volunteered to draft the note to the judge, and everyone else descended on Dave, trying to appear interested in him, but he escaped with Keith to talk to the innkeeper about the construction project.

The "one for all and all for one" spirit kept Caitlin downstairs for longer than she would have liked, but eventually she felt able to excuse herself. She knew that Seth had seen her leave, so she went straight out to her balcony.

The sun had already set. The mountains were shadowy masses, and the streetlamps were on. The gym's local members were leaving the fitness center, calling good night to each other.

A few minutes later she heard Seth's door open.

"We missed the sunset," she said.

"But it sounds like we're going to have plenty of other chances. My sense is that everyone is on board. Joan was really solid, wasn't she?"

"Yes, and you did a really good job, Seth. I was impressed."

"You were?" He seemed pleased.

"Do you think that you'll run Street Boards someday?"

"Me?" He sounded surprised. "Why are you asking that? Mom and Dad are doing such a great job."

"But not forever. Do your sisters or their husbands want to take over?"

He had to think for a minute. "They're good at what they do. Really good, but they're implementing Dad's ideas."

"My dad is really enjoying retirement, and he didn't think that he would."

Seth was shaking his head. "I can't imagine my dad retired. He's been working since he was fourteen. Look, I know in some tiny rational part of my brain that there will come a day when no one wants me to hobble onto a snowboard, but just because my name is Street doesn't mean I can run anything."

# CHAPTER EIGHT

The families were scheduled to visit Sunday afternoon. The need to conceal the jurors' location had eased—apparently no Mafia hit men were after them—and the families were allowed to come to the inn. All the jurors made their beds and left their doors open so that the families could see all the different rooms.

Caitlin's parents brought her papers to sign. Her friend Peter had found someone who was thrilled to find a short-term furnished rental in San Francisco. By law she could only charge the rent that she was paying, but Peter had tacked on a separate fee for the rental of her furnishings. The fee seemed absurdly high, but it would take care of her August health insurance and her cell phone bill. What a relief that was.

"I'm not criticizing you," her mother said, "but I couldn't believe how much you were paying for such a small place."

"It does make me wonder why I live there," Caitlin admitted.

Then Monday came, and the testimony was as tedious as ever, the lawyers as infuriating as ever. Caitlin continued to work on her glossary. In the middle of the afternoon she realized that the prosecutors were calling something an agreement while one defense lawyer was calling the same thing a document and the other one was calling it a letter. Three hours of testimony now made more sense. She would have liked to have shared her finding with the others, but of course she couldn't.

During the sidebars and other breaks, she started to design a new font—not that the world needed another typeface, and if it did, there were computer programs that took much of the tedium out of the work. But there was something satisfying about doing it by hand, although it would have been nice to have a ruler.

In the evenings at the inn the jurors stuck to their new schedule. Seth led fitness classes, Caitlin taught art lessons, Delia had them all singing scales. The construction foreman left them projects, sanding trim or taping drywall. Stephanie appointed herself in charge of cleaning the public rooms so that the innkeeper didn't have to hire extra staff.

People were also careful about where they sat. Instead of Joan looking to sit next to Delia, and Heather next to April, they systematically filled the seats on the van and the places about the tables, not making any effort to sit with someone particular.

Each day Caitlin and Seth found a few minutes to be out on their balconies. They never talked about the case or anything that happened in the courtroom. Instead they kept tabs on the other jurors. Should one of them say something to Marcus about a few people finding his food too spicy? No, Marcus would notice what was left on the plates. What about trying to get people to include Yvette more? Yes. Was Joan getting a cold? Yes, but she had already talked to Norma. And Heather? Seth thought she had seemed out of sorts today, and she was usually so sunny. Caitlin said that Heather had mentioned that PMS hit her hard once for a day or so each month; she'd probably be starting her period tomorrow. Seth said that he didn't want to know that.

"Too bad," Caitlin said.

These conversations weren't what Team Jury was supposed to be about. People weren't to have secrets; everything was to be done by consensus. But teams needed leaders. So they each stood at the railing of their own balcony, looking out at the mountains, always waving to anyone on the patio, talking in low voices. Working with Seth like this felt great. He might be short of perfect, but he was trying. People he would have never paid any attention to before, people who would have been invisible to him, he was treating with respect and consideration.

They talked about other things as well: indie music, graphic novels, their lives in Oregon and San Francisco, where Seth had traveled, where Caitlin would like to travel. She talked about her work; he told her about the two guys he lived with. They talked about their families, and she made him laugh when she told him how uncomfortable it had been to hear her grandmother talk about her grandfather's physique.

"I guess we were lucky," he said. "Grandpa only talked about the first time Granny let him hold her hand. He never forgot it. He said it seemed like the softest thing he had ever felt."

Caitlin looked at her hands. They were resting on the handrail. There was still enough light that she could see the ink stain on her right index finger. She had been helping April and the others letter their scrapbook pages.

Seth's hands were also on the handrail.

The railing ran continuously from her half of the balcony to his; the wall stopped just short of it. If she slid her hand along toward his side, would he move his hand to meet hers?

*We've had sex. Why am I thinking about letting him hold my hand?*

The sun was setting behind the green-topped mountains. The blazing ball of saffron was melting into a swirl first of corals and pinks. It would soon fade into lavenders and grays. The sunset in San Francisco was a thin band of fiery yellow slashing across the ocean horizon.

"Do you ever think," he asked quietly, "if we—our generation—have screwed things up for ourselves by making sex so easy?"

"That it doesn't mean enough?" She had to look at him. She couldn't talk about this looking at the mountains.

"Something like that, yeah."

Was he regretting that time at the lake? At least he had tried to make it meaningful. He had tried to connect it to what they had shared in the past.

"I did that the night we were together, tried to turn it into a nothing hookup."

"Oh." He took a step back and clasped his hands behind his neck. "I'm sorry you feel that way."

Was he hurt? His hands weren't on the railing anymore. "No, you don't understand. It was special to see you, and I didn't want it to be. I wanted to show you—myself—that I was in control, that I was this cool chick you couldn't hurt."

"You didn't trust me." His voice was flat.

"That wasn't fair," she said urgently. Why was all this coming out now, just when she was starting to respect him so much? "I didn't know you, not as you are now."

He dropped his hands. When he looked at her, his grin was mischievous. "Can I point out that having sex with me is kind of an odd way to keep me at arm's length?"

"I never said that it worked."

* * * *

Among the requests that the jury had submitted to the judge on Monday had been to be allowed to drink alcohol on Friday and Saturday evenings.

The innkeeper had offered to purchase wine. Because the jurors were helping with the housekeeping and some of the construction, he was saving money on staff.

None of them had felt very strongly about needing alcohol. They had included the request because they assumed that the judge would need to refuse at least one thing to show that he was in charge. So they were surprised that during the return van ride on Friday, Sally told them the inn would be hosting a happy hour. There were rules, of course. Jurors could not drink in their rooms, and they were restricted to the wine that the inn provided.

"Is there a two-drink maximum?" Seth asked.

Sally looked at her clipboard. "No, there's nothing about that."

"What was that about a two-drink maximum?" Caitlin asked him as they were crossing the parking lot.

"I don't think that this is such a good idea," he answered. "Is drinking going to bring out the best in us?"

"Maybe not, but honestly I don't care."

"Then prepared to be annoyed."

He had a point. April was trying to breathe while she laughed, and someone had given Heather a rubber band to wear around her wrist. Every time she started to speak, she snapped the rubber band to remind her not to tell stories about friends of friends, but to ask others about themselves. It was helping a lot, but after a glass of two or wine, everyone would almost certainly revert to usual habits. She imagined that by the end of the night Seth himself would be man-sprawling all over God's green earth.

The innkeeper had laid out a spread of cheese and smoked sausage, along with apples, grapes, and crackers. Everyone told Marcus that he wouldn't need to cook.

There was a red wine and a white wine. Caitlin chose the red. It didn't have any of the complexity of what she drank with her friends in San Francisco, but at least it was more fruity than sweet. She stayed on her feet, drifting in and out of conversations. Stephanie was carrying around both kinds of wine, topping off people's glasses. Caitlin would have found it hard to keep track of how much she was drinking if she was trying to keep track, but she wasn't. She felt lovely and relaxed.

She drifted over to the table where some of the other women were looking at April's bridal magazines. It was amazing how people who didn't even have a boyfriend already knew what they wanted in their weddings.

"What about you, Caitlin?" Heather asked even without snapping her rubber band. "What kind of flowers do you want?"

"I have no idea." She had never given it a minute's thought. Honestly, she couldn't imagine herself having a wedding.

Stephanie came over to refill the glasses. Caitlin sat down and joined the conversation about wedding cakes because Stephanie had promised that her boss at the bakery would give April a deal on her cake.

"Decorate it with fresh flowers," Caitlin suggested. "It's cheaper."

Her sister had had fresh flowers on her cake. It had been pretty. In fact, Caitlin had liked everything about her sister's wedding. There had been twenty people in MeeMaw's backyard. Trina had worn a shell-pink tea-length gauzy dress, and since there weren't any attendants, Caitlin had been able to wear her most amazing thrift store find, a boldly geometric Emilio Pucci silk minidress from the sixties.

It suddenly occurred to Caitlin, if she liked everything about her sister's wedding, her sister probably hadn't. Trina was a personalized-cocktail-napkins-in-the-wedding-colors kind of girl. Caitlin felt bad for her. Why shouldn't she have had a fluffy white dress if that's what she had wanted? What bride was a virgin anymore?

Caitlin suddenly decided that it would be nice to be in her room. She could lie on her bed and let the world float around her. Her bed would feel like a magic carpet, tilting in the wind. She stood up.

"Do you need some help?" Keith asked.

"No, no, no, no." Caitlin liked the sound of the *o*'s, how you could draw them out. "Noooo, nope." "Nope" was fun too; the *p* popped, exploding her mouth open. She said "nope" again, noticing how her head jerked back a bit. That was interesting. She should try it again. "Nope. Nope." She put her hand on her neck. Cords tightened and lengthened with the *p*. This was really interesting.

A warm hand closed on her arm. "Let's go, girl."

It was Seth.

His hand felt nice, warm and strong. She missed having people touch her. She missed him touching her. She let him guide her to the stairs.

Halfway up the first flight she stopped. "Have you ever said 'nope'? I mean, really said it like those mindfulness Buddhists want you to do, really felt it?"

"I don't think that the Buddhists are big on 'nope.'"

At the rough stairs up to the third floor Seth gestured for her to go first.

"I thought a gentleman always went upstairs first so that you wouldn't seem to be looking at a lady's but-tocks." She drew out the last word, putting the accent on the second syllable.

"That probably assumes that the lady in question isn't drunk and likely to fall down the stairs."

"I'm not drunk."

"Yes, you are," he said.

"Then I will go first, but only because an hour a day on the rowing machine is giving me my San Francisco fanny back."

"I noticed," he said.

San Francisco fanny. That was cute. Frisco Fanny. That's what she would call herself if she ever became a Wild West bandit.

Halfway up the stairs she stopped and looked back at Seth. "Did your sisters have personalized cocktail napkins at their weddings?"

"Personalized what?" He shook his head. "I have absolutely no idea. Keep walking."

She made it up the rest of the stairs successfully, although it took a surprising amount of concentration. But as they were walking down the hall she did stumble.

Seth grabbed her arm, and she felt his other arm circling around her to steady her waist. She leaned against him. He was warm. That was nice. More than nice. She turned and let herself go limp. He had to hold her more firmly.

Wasn't this what these beautiful bedrooms were designed for? The tub was big enough for two, and the bed...oh, the bed with its four pillows, high-thread-count sheets, and soft blankets. Who cared about meaning? Weren't high-thread-count sheets meaning enough?

She was facing him now, lifting her arms, resting her hands on his shoulders.

His hands closed around her forearms, not pushing her away, but not letting her move closer.

"You know, we've never been in a bed together," she said. She was flirting, teasing, trying to move her body closer to his.

"I am well aware of that."

"Or seen each other completely naked."

"We aren't doing this, Caitlin."

"Why not? Who will know? They never come up here anymore. They never knock on doors."

"We promised Sally."

*Sally.*

Caitlin hated the judge, she hated the lawyers, and right now she didn't care about her juror's oath, but Sally? Sally, frumpy, dumpy, dear, dear Sally, was stuck between the judge and the jurors; she was trying so hard. She was probably risking her job with some of the freedom she was giving them.

Caitlin stepped away. "Then it is good night."

"Yes."

* * * *

She woke at 2:00 a.m., which always happened to her when she drank. She forced down several glasses of water, hoping to flush out her system, but then she had to get up at four to pee. The motion-activated toilet lid, rising to meet to her, seemed like some female-eating porcelain creature in a bad horror movie. Poor Frisco Fanny. What a way to go.

When she woke up again at eight, she tapped on the wall, but there was no answering tap. She went out to the balcony to see if Seth was already there. He wasn't. In the courtyard she could see the fitness center's local members entering the lower level to use the machines. At this hour the jurors needed to use the second-floor yoga studio. Caitlin leaned forward to look through its big windows. Seth was there, lying on his back on one of the big balls, doing big sweeping leg circles.

How on earth was he staying on the ball? She would have rolled off the minute she had her legs in the air.

He was probably alone. This would be a chance to talk to him. She went downstairs in her workout clothes, waved to the people in the breakfast room, and crossed the parking lot. She went up the stairs to the yoga studio. The studio was washed with the morning light. Neatly rolled yoga mats, stacks of step platforms, and bins of leg weights were stored against the walls. Seth was doing side crunches on the ball, his body perfectly parallel to the floor.

What an amazing body he had. She didn't know the names of every last muscle, but she could draw them and she knew how they moved under the skin, contracting and lengthening. But she knew it all from pictures, diagrams, and videos. It was different to be watching. And to be watching him. Seth.

He saw her. He swiveled on the ball and started to stand up.

"Don't get up." She rolled one of the balls over and sat down across from him. His ball was red. She had a green one. "I put you in a horrible position last night, and I am sorry."

"It's okay. I quit after one glass so I could still think straight. And we would have been found out. I met Marcus on the stairs. He had realized that if someone was going to escort a beautiful young woman to her bed, it ought to be him."

"What would he have done if we were already in the room?"

"Probably been disappointed. He did look relieved when he saw me coming back down."

"It would have made a joke of Team Jury, wouldn't it?"

He nodded. "We have to behave ourselves until the trial is over."

"And what then?"

She shouldn't have said that. They weren't ready for this conversation.

"I wish I could answer that," he said. "You deserve an answer, but—"

"No, no." She was mortified. "I shouldn't have asked."

"Please hear me out." He was leaning toward her. His eyes, usually a light green, looked dark and more blue. "I've done hard stuff before, but nothing like this. It's all new to me, and sometimes all I want is to go back and be myself, a guy who lived in the moment all the time."

"You have had to be that way." She knew that when he was out riding, the slightest loss of focus could actually get him killed.

"Trying to understand what the witnesses are saying and keeping track of ten people—and I said ten, not eleven. I'm not even counting you as one of the things I have to worry about."

"I hope not," she murmured.

"Your saying that us having sex at the lake meant nothing to—"

"No, no. I didn't say 'nothing.' I didn't say that at all."

"Then that's my point. I don't know what you said. I would have to think about it, try to understand it, and I can't. I know that that isn't what you want to hear, but it's all I have."

What did she want to hear? She didn't know. All those years ago, MeeMaw had said that they were too young to make a promise. Were they still?

He waited for her to speak. She didn't. She had nothing to say. *Stop worrying about the trial and all these people. Think about me.*

Except if he did that, she wouldn't respect him. What a mess. If he did stop and think about her, she wouldn't want him anymore. She started to stand up. The big green ball rolled behind her. She lurched forward. Seth reached out to steady her just as she was sitting back down.

His hand landed on her thigh.

The palm of his hand was broad against her narrow leg. She could feel its weight.

When he lifted weights, he wore open-backed gloves. Today his hands were bare; he wasn't even wearing the vinyl-strapped watch. The heel of his palm was just above the hem of her bicycle shorts. An inch lower and his skin would be touching hers, his flesh pressing against hers. How that would feel.

She hadn't appreciated it out at the lake, the wonder and warmth of a man's hand. Of his hand. That's what mattered, it being his.

"I'm not supposed to be doing this," he said.

"No."

They were both looking down. His fingers were slightly arched; she could feel the pad of each fingertip. Gradually he spread his fingers, flattening them so that there was more contact, more touch.

*Forbidden.* That wasn't a word she used much. Things were illegal, wrong, stupid, mean, harmful, even dangerous, but what was forbidden? This. His hand on her leg.

She could have stood up; he would have let his hand fall away. Or she could have moved his hand herself; he wouldn't have fought it. But she couldn't. She needed him to lift it himself.

* * * *

She had loved him once, and she had been shattered by it.

After Seth left for New Zealand during that third summer, Caitlin set about earning as much money as she could. She worked double shifts at the Dairy Queen, and she babysat. She was a responsible fifteen-year-old, very experienced with babies and toddlers. She made a lot of money babysitting. She liked that. Money was going to let her see Seth.

She got to San Diego two weeks before school was to start. The skate park near her family's new house was awesome, with ramps and bowls, stair sets, even a half-pipe, things Caitlin had seen in magazines, but had never tried. As soon as she had unpacked, she went over with one of the new boards Seth's father had given her. As she signed in, the attendant said, "We do have girls' time, you know."

Caitlin looked through the fence; there were a lot of guys, all skating aggressively, goading and taunting each other. "Is this a men-only time?"

"Oh, no, but you'd probably be more comfortable coming then. I can refund your money."

"I'll be fine."

As she walked in, many of the skaters stopped and stared at her. As much as she wanted to try the half-pipe, she headed toward a more familiar ramp. The guys who had been waiting in a rough line drew together in a knot, so there was no telling where the line was, where she should wait. She kept walking back to what had to be the beginners' area.

"Keep on walking, that's right," she heard someone call.

"Ramp tramp."

Caitlin flipped her board around. *This is a Street Board, assholes.*

"Yeah, anyone can buy an expensive board," someone jeered.

*I didn't have to buy it.* She pushed off and did as much as she could in the beginners' area. They would have to see that she had solid skills and eye-catching style. Of course, she knew that there was no chance they would suddenly forgive her for being female just because she was good. She stayed for an hour, long enough to show them and herself that she wasn't going to be scared off.

She called Seth. He had gotten back from New Zealand and was spending a few days in North Carolina before heading up to Oregon.

"Amateurs can be jerks," he said. "You didn't let it get to you, did you? You have to be as good as half of them."

"How did you feel when you were the only little kid in the room?"

"I wanted to be like them."

"Well, I don't want to be like those guys, believe me, I don't."

"And I don't want you to."

It turned out that the girls' sessions were for the under-twelve crowd. She found out where the professional women practiced, but those parks were too far away. She also discovered that she couldn't skateboard on the sidewalks with the freedom that she had in Virginia. There were so many skateboarders in California that their activities had to be regulated, and those regulations were enforced.

Her sister was going to enroll at a community college. Trina hated the thought. Trevor, Dylan's father, was back in Virginia attending a big state school, going to football games, and pledging a fraternity. Because of how expensive houses in California were, this was one of the smallest places the family had ever lived, and they all felt squeezed.

So Caitlin wasn't feeling great about the world when school started.

Military kids are supposed to be good at starting new schools, but because her dad had spent six years at the last place, she had gotten out of practice. She couldn't figure out how to fit in here. The art classes were full of kids who were high all the time, and the computer lab was full of guys who were terrified to talk to a girl.

She ached for Seth. She couldn't seem to take a deep breath; the air stopped just below her collarbone. It was as if her heart wouldn't let it pass.

She kept thinking she saw him in the halls. A flash of a broad shoulder, the turn of a slender torso...but it was always one of the surfers, shaggy haired, but not Seth, so not Seth.

She needed something more than her schoolwork. She knew that. But she wasn't going to start doing drugs just to get friends. Her mother kept suggesting that she join clubs. But what clubs? Chess? Cheerleading? Young Life?

Two weeks into school her gym teacher asked her to go meet with the crew coach.

"Me?" Caitlin didn't think any of her own teachers even knew her name. "Why?"

"She's an English teacher. She's in room 426."

With nothing else to do, Caitlin went to room 426. There were a number of girls lounging around the room. They were all big, tall with broad shoulders and long arms. Caitlin wondered if she was supposed to be their lunch. She started to turn around and leave, but one of the girls noticed her.

"Oh, Coach, here's that cox you were looking for."

Cocks? Caitlin knew that she wasn't the most feminine person on the planet, but most people generally figured out that her anatomy was not that of a male, much less two males.

"Yes, yes." The coach stood up from her desk. She was every bit as small as Caitlin. She told the other girls to clear the room, and then she said to Caitlin, "I hear that you are a skateboarder."

Oh. Caitlin must have made more of an impression than she had thought. "Do you have a skateboard team?"

"No, I'm sorry. I wanted to talk to you about trying out for crew."

She explained what a coxswain did, steering the boat, implementing the race strategy, motivating the rowers. In terms of powering the boats, the coxswains added nothing, so they were usually small and light.

The coxswain for the senior boat had quit, so one of the coxes from the junior varsity boat would move up, but that would leave the JV boat short. Rather than throw a freshman in there, the coach was hoping to start with someone a little more mature. "And you must have a good spatial sense if you can skateboard the way people say you can."

"I don't know about that, but I'll try anything."

It turned out that she liked being out on the water, feeling the sunshine and the wind, gliding along with the current and then rowing back against it. Of course she had a lot to learn, but learning new things was one thing Caitlin was always good at, and fortunately the actual racing season wasn't until spring.

"So being skinny and sitting on your butt," Seth asked, "that's a sport?"

They hadn't yet made any plans to visit each other even though she had enough money. He was too busy. They weren't even talking that much. Seth couldn't think about anything besides the Olympic trials. The two top US snowboarders were the best in the world–they just were–and so the competition was for the third spot. Four guys had a shot at it, and Caitlin knew that Seth must have been disappointed when he was named as the team alternate for the half-pipe.

"You're only seventeen," she said when he finally called her back.

"That's what everyone says, but the doctors say I'm still growing. All my uncles on my mom's side are over six three. Snowboarders aren't tall."

But within a week the third guy on the team ripped up the ligaments in his shoulder, and Seth was officially on the US Olympic team.

He wasn't expected to medal. The top two Americans had a lock on gold and silver. Sweden, Norway, and France were battling for bronze. Seth was, however, getting lots of media attention. The two top men were not handsome, and Seth was photogenic. He was a good interview, cheerful, funny, endlessly willing to make fun of himself. He also had a crowd-pleasing all-American story—his blue-collar, factory-employee dad making his boards in the garage.

And then the amazing thing happened. The weather had turned warmer than the top competitors were used to, and the Europeans floundered. Seth, who had first learned on even warmer slopes, put together the runs of his life. He squeaked into bronze. Thanks to him, the USA had swept the event. Three American flags flew during the medal ceremony. "SETH SWEEP" was the caption on the front of the weekly magazines, showing him pumping his fist, laughing joyfully in front of the flags.

Caitlin called him, and the voice mailbox on his phone was full. But she was sure he would call her back when he got back to the States. He didn't.

She sent him an email, and three days later got a form reply. "Hi, Friends! Weren't the Olympic Games great for the whole USA team? We..." She tried again a couple of weeks later, and he still didn't answer.

And after a while she used the money that she had saved to buy herself her own computer.

It was a difficult spring for her. The girls in the JV boat resented that they had to give their coxswain, who was one of their friends, to the senior boat. As hard as Caitlin had studied the sport over the winter, she made a tactical error in one of the first races of the season, and they wouldn't let her forget it. She longed to talk to Seth about it, to tell him how isolated she felt, to see if he had any advice. How could she motivate these rowers who hated her? But Seth had abandoned her.

She had to figure it out on her own. And she did.

* * * *

No one on the jury or any of their immediate families worked at Street Boards, but many of them had friends and neighbors who did. It made Seth realize how important his family's company was to the town. Street Boards had saved the town when the furniture factory had closed. No wonder his father had made such a big deal about keeping jobs in North Carolina, not opening a factory in China or contracting with an outside manufacturer to produce boards to Street Boards specs.

What would happen in the future? His sister Abby and her husband ran the factory; Becca and her husband managed sales and distribution. His parents developed the new products, supervised the marketing campaigns, made the strategic decisions, all that. Didn't they ever worry about what would happen when they retired?

No, he suddenly realized, they didn't...because his parents, especially his dad, were taking it for granted that Seth would take over.

That was nuts. Surely you'd have to be a big-picture thinker to run a company, planning years ahead. That wasn't him.

Except what about the parts, the videos? Didn't he always start with something big, a feeling he wanted to create, a vision, even geometry? But there were actual pictures. He could think big for them.

Maybe he could do strategic planning or whatever it was called—he was certainly surprising himself during the trial—but maybe he would run the place into the ground. He had visited Nate's hometown once. It was in the coal-mining region of West Virginia, but the mines were closed. Half the storefronts on Main Street were vacant, and the used-car lots were full of cars people couldn't afford to keep.

He did not want to be the guy who made that happen here.

His parents had always emailed him the company's monthly numbers. He never even opened the files. Last week they had brought him hard copies. At least he hadn't thrown them away. That was something.

The spreadsheets were easier to understand than he would have thought. The company did well at the middle and lower ends of the market. His parents respected those customers; they had never forgotten having to save up for Seth's first board. But the professional line didn't come close to breaking even. Seth supposed that his dad would say that they needed the high-end boards to promote the other products, but was that really true?

The boards that Seth himself used were as good as anything out there, but for how long? The big companies were investing so much in research and testing. Did Street Boards have the resources to keep up with them? Probably not.

When his parents arrived for the Sunday visit, he tried to talk to them about the long-term viability of the high-end market. Yes, he had actually used those words, "long-term viability."

The conversation was awkward. He thought that his mom was getting it, but his dad wasn't. Toward the end of the visit when his dad was chatting with Caitlin's dad, his mother spoke to him softly. "Don't forget, Seth, that for Dad the heart of all this is you. He has made boards for every level of your career. He has always lived vicariously through you."

*What?* Seth stared at his mother. Dad? Living vicariously?

"It took a lot of talking to convince him that you needed to get out of competition."

This was not cool. His dad didn't need to live vicariously through anyone. Look at what he had achieved, going from being a high school graduate building boards in his garage to being the president and CEO of Street Boards. And he was nothing like some of those parents who were ultra stage moms, sucking up to the big-time coaches.

But, on the other hand, wouldn't his mother know?

His getting that bronze medal had taken three other guys, guys who were better than him, underperforming. You couldn't count on that in sports, not ever. But Seth had been seventeen, and seventeen-year-olds were cocky. If luck broke your way once, why wouldn't it always? And pretty soon you stopped thinking about luck at all. Surely it was all you; surely you deserved all the credit.

So he had come back from the Olympics, believing himself the crown prince, the heir apparent of American snowboarding. That's what the mainstream media kept saying. He was Seth Sweep.

But inside the snowboarding world he had a hard landing. "It was great what you did for the sport," people told him. "Grab your endorsement deals while you can."

His coach eventually told him the hard truth. There were kids, thirteen and fourteen, who were already almost as good as Seth, and they didn't have uncles who were six foot three. Seth's big swooping moves were going to be a joy to watch, but in terms of speed, height, and the tight twisting flips that won the Olympics, he had probably peaked. He still had a bright future in the Big Air competitions, but not the more traditional ones.

"I don't care what anyone says," Seth answered. "I'll show them."

But the next time he went home, his parents, for the first time ever, didn't seem to be on his side. It was his mother who talked to him. Of course they would support him in whatever choice he made, but if he was going to pursue the Olympics again, Street Boards would have to diversify their marketing and promotion. Everything couldn't be about Seth.

"So you want me to stop at bronze?"

"You know you'll do well at Big Air, and the videos you make...people love them."

It took Seth another six months to see that his parents were right. Nate with his explosive power and Ben with his precise technique were starting to score better than he was. He also knew that the sport was changing. The extra little quarter twist that made a trick immeasurably more difficult meant everything to the judges and nothing to the general public. The future was in five- or ten-minute videos that people could watch on their home computers.

Seth now knew that he was one of the best in the world at what he did, seeing the possibilities in the beautiful backcountry settings, planning runs that harmonized with the landscape, finding exactly the right music. But for almost a year, filming the parts had felt like failure.

That's why he had let things fall apart with Caitlin. He had been too miserable, too confused, to talk to her.

Right now, watching her saying goodbye to her parents, he had to think that that had been a pretty high price.

Maybe that was the real point of Ben and Colleen. A Colleen was the perfect woman for you and the one you had let get away.

He caught Caitlin's eye and jerked his head toward their balcony. She nodded.

It usually took her a long time to get upstairs because so many people wanted to talk to her, but this time he had only been out on his side of the balcony for a minute or two when he heard her door open.

"What's up?" she asked. Her voice was soft. She had sensed that something was wrong.

"Do you think my dad lives vicariously through me?"

"Your dad?" She stopped and thought. "I don't know, but would it be so surprising? Wasn't he working at the furniture factory even before he had graduated from high school?"

"I guess. He didn't have many choices."

"Do you feel guilty about that?"

"A little," Seth admitted.

"I get that, but what can you do? The kids who should feel guilty are the ones who've screwed up, who threw away everything that their parents had done for them. You didn't do that."

"But what if all this vicarious shit is leading him to making bad decisions now?"

"That would be a problem," she acknowledged. "What's going on?"

He told her how the company might need to rebrand itself, focusing on the Walmart customers, getting them to spend a few dollars more for a board that was twice as good as what else was there. "But I don't know. My dad doesn't want to talk about it. It's kind of ironic. My parents have this vision that I will swoop in and do a great job of preserving the family legacy, but the first time I ask a question, it's too threatening."

"Do you want me to do the usual women-are-from-Venus thing and listen sympathetically, or shall I pretend I'm from Mars and offer a suggestion?"

"Suggest away." At least as long as she held on to being from Venus too. There were aspects of that he liked a lot.

"You jumped in there with something pretty global. That would make anyone uncomfortable, but they'd probably love it if you came up with a smaller, more concrete idea."

"If I had one of those I'd suggest it, but I don't."

"Well, I do. This is the one thing I know about. Did you sign away any rights with that old video game?"

"I should know that," he admitted.

"Yes, you should. If you do a video game for kids, little kids, and sell it cheaply or even distribute it for free, you'll get some good data from the downloads. Does it tank completely? Is there initial velocity, then build? Does it do better in one part of the country than another? It will give you information. Every company needs information."

"But Street Boards...we're trying to get kids outdoors, we want them to be more active, not spend more time staring at a screen."

"Then make it educational. Have the kids think strategically, see patterns, work systematically, process information, all that."

It did sound like a good idea. "I don't know much about this."

"I know plenty," she said confidently.

\* \* \* \*

Sunday evenings were always a little dreary. The jurors found it hard to say goodbye to their families, and none of them were looking forward to another week in the courtroom. April was particularly unhappy. Her parents and sisters had told her that she was going to have to make a difficult decision. Either she postponed her wedding or she let them start making some decisions for her.

"My sister and I are the same size," she was saying when Caitlin had come into the library. "Do I let her go try on wedding dresses for me?"

"Does she have your coloring?" Caitlin asked.

"No, not at all. So if the color looks good on her, it will look terrible on me."

"This just isn't right," Delia said. "Did the judge have any idea what he was asking us to give up?"

No one had an answer to that.

Out on the balcony Seth asked Caitlin if this wedding-dress shopping was a big deal.

"It is to April, but I don't know that there is anything we can do about it."

"Maybe there is. Before she had to start traveling with me, my mother did the alterations for that wedding shop near the VFW hall. She is still chummy with the owner. I bet if Mom asked, Mrs. Kressley would open up late sometime and let April come in by herself."

"Oh my God, Seth. That's a great idea. It really is."

"I'm glad you think so. Who knows if the judge will approve it, but I will suggest it to Sally."

* * * *

Another week passed. They had been at this for a full month.

One morning they were gathering in the back lobby, waiting for the van. Caitlin was listening to Marcus asking Joan and Delia about their grits recipes. April suddenly burst in, shrieking Seth's name. In violation of a great many rules, she threw herself on him, hugging him, thanking him rapturously.

His hands closed around either side of her waist. April's shirt was densely patterned with tight clusters of red and violet flowers. Seth's sun-warmed hands looked strong and masculine against the riotous print.

This was what he had done to help Caitlin get down from the tree; he had put his hands on her waist. Would that ever happen again?

Now he was smiling down at April, not with his naughty little boy grin, but with a sincere happy adult smile.

*That should be me. He should be holding me that way, smiling at me that way.*

April had already broken away from him to tell the others. Seth's mother had set up a private session at the bridal salon on Sunday morning for April, her mother, and her sister. By promising to stay with them the whole time, Sally had gotten the judge to approve.

"It's hard to believe," Delia said, "but that judge must have a heart."

"Or a daughter," Keith added. "A girl and her wedding...You say, 'Yes, dear' and keep out of the way."

April was back by noon on Sunday. She'd had a glorious time. Seth's mother had brought champagne and mini-muffins, and Mrs. Kressley was giving her a huge discount because she felt so bad about April's jury duty taking so long. April was able to look at dresses that would have been way out of her price range otherwise.

Sally had taken pictures of April in all the different dresses and had then stopped on the way back to the inn to get the pictures printed. All the jurors—at least all the female ones—spent the hours before the family visits, looking at them, giving April their opinions. Even though Caitlin wouldn't have been caught dead in any of the dresses, she had a good time looking at them. Heather was steadily popping the rubber band, her cue not to tell stories about friends of friends of friends, and maybe it was the music lessons or maybe it was that April was feeling genuinely happy and secure, but her laugh seemed less forced and annoying.

"I hope the court is paying Sally for printing the pictures," Joan said. "It can be pricey."

"Honestly," April leaned forward and whispered, "I'm not sure that she's even putting in for her hours. She's just a really nice person."

\* \* \* \*

Each day there were fewer observers in the courtroom. The public was apparently losing interest in the case. Caitlin couldn't blame them. The prosecution was building up to its big finish with an array of witnesses sneaking in comments about the defendants' characters and lifestyles when the testimony was nominally about something else. At the start of the trial Caitlin might have enjoyed the juicy gossip. Now she knew that it was irrelevant and yet another waste of time. At the start of the week in August the prosecution rested, doing so shortly after an afternoon break. That was a crappy trick. The defense teams wouldn't want to begin their cases at 3:15 p.m. But the judge wanted to keep things moving.

One of the defense lawyers had made his opening statement at the beginning of the trial. Now the other one had a turn. His gist was that this was a political witch hunt.

*Well, duh, we figured that out a long time ago. But that doesn't mean they are innocent. Or that they are guilty. We are still obliged to listen to the evidence.*

The first witness was called. It was clear that several lines of questioning had been ruled out. The defense lawyer would start to ask a question, and an instant later someone from the prosecution team would be on his feet objecting. The judge would rule in favor of the prosecution, and the defense lawyer would look shocked, which he couldn't possibly be. Caitlin was surprised at how uncurious she was at the excluded information. *Please, please, please just give me what I need, and let's get done.*

Finally the judge called the lawyers to the bench. Caitlin stared blankly at them. One of the prosecutors still had a little stain on the lapel of his suit jacket. He had gotten it at lunch last Tuesday. He had worn the suit again on Thursday and now on Monday.

*We are bored enough that we notice your dry cleaning.*

The one female defense lawyer was wearing a different suit. It looked new. Caitlin supposed that she had gone shopping over the weekend. Why hadn't she bought new earrings too? She wore the same ones day after day. She was saying that the prosecutors didn't need—

*Wait.* Caitlin's heart stopped. Why did she know what the lawyers were saying? The judge had turned off his microphone and flipped the switch that sent white noise through the courtroom speakers.

She looked at him. He was speaking to the prosecution team so his face was turned toward her.

"Yes, I am awash fat..."

Awash fat? No, it must be "aware that."

*Oh my God, I am lip-reading.*

It made sense. Much of her work involved observing how people moved, including their facial muscles. During the trial when she listened to the witnesses, she watched their mouths. Unconsciously she had been putting it together.

She glanced at the observers. Most of them had turned to their neighbors to chat. She couldn't tell anything from a profile view, but those who were directly facing her, yes, she was making out a word here, a phrase there, nothing very coherent, but with time...

What should she do?

# CHAPTER NINE

Seth heard Caitlin gasp.

"Are you okay?" he whispered.

She nodded, but something was definitely wrong. She was staring intently down at her lap, her hair falling over her face. When the testimony started again, he nudged her foot. She flinched and then looked up, but she wasn't okay.

What could be wrong with her? He had no idea. But if he watched her, if he tried to figure it out, the lawyers or the reporters would notice.

The best thing he could do for her was to ignore her. What kind of gallantry was that?

When they got back to the inn, instead of helping the construction workers tidy up their tools and sweep as he and some of the others usually did, he went up to his room and out to the balcony without tapping. Caitlin would come out.

A minute later she did. She was clearly worried. Her features seemed narrow instead of delicate, and her dark eyes were pulling the life out of the rest of her face.

He gestured over the railing, reminding her that there were people in the courtyard and the parking lot. "What's up?" he asked softly, careful not to look at her.

"I can lip-read. At least a little."

"What do you mean?" His eyes jerked toward her, and he had to force himself to look away. "No, I know what you mean. But did you just figure this out? I don't get it."

She explained how she had been learning unconsciously. "I don't know what to do. I don't want to tell the judge. What if he thinks he has to declare a mistrial? I don't want all this falling apart because of me when I haven't heard anything. And I will make sure that I don't."

"But what if it comes out afterward?" he asked. "Couldn't that be grounds for an appeal?"

"Why would it have to come out? I wouldn't tell anyone."

*You told me.* "What if one day you reply to something that you couldn't have heard? And you know how carefully they are watching us. Somebody is going to notice how you never look up during sidebars. They'll wonder why."

"So what should I do?"

He wasn't sure. Secrets sucked. The top riders in snowboarding practiced in secret now, not wanting others to know what they were working on. Seth hated that. It seemed against everything that sports was about.

That argued for telling the judge. You'd think he would declare "no harm, no foul," but maybe he was the one person in the state of North Carolina who didn't follow basketball. Wouldn't it be a bitch if he took it in his head to declare a mistrial when they had all been trying so hard to keep that from happening?

"Maybe this should be a group decision," he suggested. "We agreed to discuss everything as a team." The deputies were leaving them alone a lot.

"Then we will have twelve people knowing. How can twelve people keep a secret? It would definitely come out then."

She didn't say much at dinner, and later that evening she tapped on the wall. He went outside. "I gave Sally a note for the judge."

"So you made up your mind?"

"It was awkward because Sally knows that we decided not to send individual notes to the judge. I could tell that she didn't want to take it, but of course she had to. I felt bad about putting her in that position."

Sally was hardly the issue. "Why did you decide to tell the judge?"

Caitlin shrugged. "I thought about my dad. He was a judge. He would say that you don't keep stuff from the judge. You have to trust the judge."

"What if the judge is a jackass?"

"That's what appeals are for."

* * * *

As soon as they got to the jury room the next morning, Caitlin was called back to the judge's chambers.

People were surprised. Seth had been called back about the bottled water, and Teddy had been asked if he could continue after Fred had kicked him, but since then the judge hadn't spoken to any of them individually.

What was going to happen? Seth supposed if the judge were going to declare a mistrial, the remaining eleven jurors would be led back into the courtroom. Ten minutes went by, then twenty.

"What could be taking so long?" people were asking. "What do you think they are talking about?"

Finally the door opened, and it was Caitlin. She met his eyes for a brief instant, then looked down. It took him a moment to understand. She was fiddling with her necklace, but her thumb and forefinger were forming an open circle. She was signaling that everything was okay.

"He wanted to ask me about our morale," she said. "I told him that we were trying really hard, but that we were sacrificing a lot."

"Why did that take half an hour?" someone asked.

"Because doesn't every five-minute conversation around here take at least thirty?"

People laughed, but then someone else asked, "Why did the judge call you?"

She shrugged. "I don't know. Maybe it had to do with my mom sending me all those boxes at first."

"We do rely on you too much," Norma admitted. "Maybe that's something we need to work on."

During the rest of the day it was clear to Seth that the judge had discussed Caitlin's lip-reading with the lawyers. During sidebars they all kept their backs to the jury, and when they were whispering among themselves at their tables, they lifted a piece of paper or a file folder to cover their mouths. Caitlin also did her part. Unless a witness was actually testifying, she kept herself busy with her notebook.

So it had been no harm, no foul.

Wrong. There was plenty of harm.

The question came from Joan, experienced observer, wrangler of eight-year-olds. When Stephanie jumped up after dinner to start cleaning the table, Joan asked her to stay for a moment.

"Caitlin." Joan's voice was gentle, even sad. "Are you keeping a secret from the rest of us?"

He wanted to answer for her. He had practice at these impossible questions. *Seth, Seth, why aren't you... Olympics... Seth, Seth, how do you feel when other guys...* Caitlin didn't. She bit her lip and bent her head.

Then she sat up and pushed her hair back. "Yes, I am." She was looking around the table. "But the judge asked me not to say anything to anyone else. That's why the meeting took so long. I kept telling him that he was putting me in a nightmare situation."

"Can you tell us anything?" someone asked.

"No. He was really clear."

No one liked this.

"I can't imagine what it would be," Heather said. "Was it about the drinking the first night? I know I had too much."

"I don't feel I can even say what it wasn't about. "

"Did you go and say something about the rest of us?" Keith asked.

The room was quiet. No one liked that idea.

"I would answer that if I could," she said.

People were still quiet. Then April looked at Heather, Keith at Dave, Joan at Delia. Seth knew what they were asking. *Can we trust her?*

"Wait a second," he said. "Stop and think. We know Caitlin. Don't you trust her, of all people, not to be some kind of traitor?"

"No, not Caitlin," Yvette cried out. "Never. She would never do anything wrong."

But the more alert people were drawing back, now wondering how well they really did know each other.

"Seth." This was from Norma. "Do you know?"

"No." Caitlin spoke instantly, before Seth had a chance to react. "No, he doesn't. Why would he?"

Norma shrugged.

It was a toxic question. It put a thought in people's minds. *Caitlin and Seth, Seth and Caitlin...of course...young and single...the two out-of-towners...the two who play in a bigger ballpark than the rest of us...*

Over the next few days it was clear that things had changed. People were less comfortable with Caitlin. What if she were an informer, a tattletale? They were cordial; that was part of being on Team Jury, but, except for faithful Yvette, they didn't seek her out, they didn't chat with her. No one decided to go to the gym because she was going. People asked her if she wanted to join in a game, but they were being polite. No one hopped up to rearrange chairs when she came in the room. When the construction foreman left jobs for the jurors, Caitlin was always working by herself.

It was so wildly, so desperately unfair. She had done so much to keep them all happy in the early days. Seth wanted to defend her, protect her. But that would increase the suspicion that the two of them had a private bond...which, of course, they did.

He had no idea what to do. That was the trouble with being educated in the bro-school of gallantry. You didn't learn squat.

"This is really hard on you, isn't it?" he said out on the balcony.

She shrugged. "I've been an outsider before. In fact, I've *always* been an outsider: the kid with the pregnant sister, the only girl in the skateboard park, the one person in the boat who doesn't row, the only straight person. This was the first time I've been the popular girl. But people don't trust me anymore. That's what really bothers me. I haven't had that since my first season as a coxswain."

That would have been in high school after her family had moved to San Diego. "Why didn't they trust you? I thought you were really good."

"I had to learn, and the rowers didn't know that I don't make the same mistake twice."

"Crew races in the spring, doesn't it? So that would have been right after the Olympics. When I stopped calling."

"It doesn't matter now, Seth."

\* \* \* \*

He had been trying to write it off as a strong memory, that strange episode out at the lake when he had felt both like himself now and like a fumbling, enraptured kid. The power of memory. Period. That was it. Nothing more.

But sometimes when he was out on the balcony in the early morning, watching the shadows slide off the mountains and the mist dissolve into the air, he would think that it had to be more. It was as if the love he had felt for her back then had tunneled its way into the present, making the two moments actually happening at once.

But he felt empty inside; he was a kid staring up an empty blue sky, knowing that it wouldn't snow today.

This trial, this goddamn trial. They didn't have a chance.

\* \* \* \*

Managing Team Jury was now pretty much all on him. His mom should be proud. All those lectures about not being so full of himself... well, look at him now. Out on the slopes he and his crew would have had contemptuous labels for the different jurors—bowling pins, gnats, herbs, spores, chumples—but here he had to be respectful and engaged. April's fiancé was rebuilding a car; Seth looked at the scrapbook pages she was making about that. He talked about smoking and grilling meats with Dave, soil fertilization with Keith. He played Scrabble even though he was bad at it, really, really bad. He used his own workout time to lure Joan and Delia into the gym. He put them on a regimen of insanely mild strengthening and flexibility exercises in hopes that their knees would feel a little bit better.

He needed to get them to start trusting Caitlin again. She would be essential to the deliberations about guilt or innocence. His parents were in favor of trying another video game, and so he rolled out the idea with—he thought—greater marketing sophistication than they had had for the actual launch of the old one.

He waited until Caitlin was not around. Joan, Yvette, and some of the other women were sitting on the patio. He pulled up a chair. He shared the concept of the game, presenting it as entirely his own idea, and asked Joan, the retired teacher, about making it educational. When she asked him to explain, he started drawing stick figures, deliberately making them even more awful than his limited artistic gifts would have normally produced.

"I would think"—Joan couldn't help herself—"that a person with such a large head and short legs would have trouble walking, much less snowboarding."

"Let's get Caitlin." Yvette jumped up just as Seth knew that she would. "She can draw it for you."

Caitlin was chill, acting as if this were the first time she had ever heard about a Street Boards video game. That job in Silicon Valley must have prepared her for other people taking credit for her ideas. She knew that any indication that she and Seth had talked about this beforehand would increase suspicions that the two of them were having private conversations.

Which, of course, they were.

But people were happy to have something new to think about. Over the next few days, all of them were busy working with Caitlin to imagine a game in which a young user could arrange a course that would cause a pixilated Seth either to land a triple cork or to eat snow, boomph, asspass, buff, bonk, and generally have a Leonard kind of day.

\* \* \* \*

The trial slogged along. The lawyers had sunk into a morass of petty bickering. The judge was trying to move things along, but the lawyers would always find another way to slow it all down. But to give the lawyers credit, they were trapped. If one side tried to be reasonable, the other side would go for the three-point shot.

On Sunday evening, Caitlin reported that the guy renting her apartment wanted to keep it for another two months.

"Two months?" Seth didn't like the sound of that. "Do your folks think that the trial will last that long?"

"They don't let on. They pitched it in terms of knowing what my rent is and said that I could stay with them or go visit Trina until I got my apartment back."

There was something in her voice. "You do want it back, don't you?"

"I don't know. But this does give me another two months without having to worry about my monthly bills."

Monthly bills...was that what it would be like for his family if Street Boards went under? Going back to having to worry at the end of each month?

* * * *

Monday, Tuesday, Wednesday...more tedious testimony, more late starts, more angry sidebars.

Thursday started like any other. They got to the courthouse and sat in the jury room. Then sat some more. And some more. Lunch was brought in.

At last they were escorted into the courtroom.

Something was different, very different. There were fewer lawyers at the tables, and none of them had any papers out. No one had given the jurors their notebooks.

"Ladies and gentlemen," the judge said, facing the jury as he spoke. "I apologize that we have kept you waiting yet again."

He didn't usually apologize for that. "The attorneys involved have informed me"—he was no longer looking at them—"that the case has been settled. So you are excused with the thanks of the state of North Carolina."

*Settled?*

Seth felt himself jerk in his chair. Caitlin had her hand over her mouth. Other jurors had their hands in the air. *Settled?*

"You may be contacted by members of the media and perhaps by the lawyers—"

It was over? Just like that? What the fuck?

"—and you retain your First Amendment rights. You may speak to anyone about anything, but you also don't need to. Of course, you may want to return to your homes—"

Go home? How could this be happening?

"—but we have arranged for you to have another night in your accommodations, and the deputies will ensure that you will not be harassed.

I strongly advise that you take this time to organize your thoughts. So now you are indeed excused for the final time."

"No." Delia had stood up. "Why were we sequestered?"

But the judge was already leaving; the high padded back of his chair swiveled toward them, the back of his black robe a blank slab as it disappeared from the courtroom.

Sally gestured for them all to return to the jury room.

Everyone was frozen. Was this a joke?

"Please," Sally said. "Please come."

Obediently they stood. This was insane.

The front row always went first. Those of them in the second row waited.

"What does it mean?" Yvette was asking Caitlin. "That they settled?"

"Probably that they pleaded guilty to some of the charges and got less of a sentence than if we had found them guilty of everything."

"I guess I had heard of that," Yvette said, "but doesn't that usually happen before the trial?"

"That would have been nice," Caitlin answered.

Seth agreed with her. It sure as hell would have been nice.

He had had to give up that New Zealand shot, and it was possible that it would never again make sense for Street Boards to finance such a big-deal part. And people like Caitlin and Dave not being able to earn? And April? She had had exactly one morning of fun in planning her wedding. Back in June Seth would have thought that that was nothing. Now he knew what a big deal it was, that some brides and their moms enjoyed the planning as much as the wedding itself.

In the jury room, Sally said that of course that any of them could walk out immediately, but the sidewalks were clogged with reporters, and they would have to return to the inn eventually to pick up their belongings. She advised them to go back in the court's van. It would be here soon. Then she handed Marcus the sealed bag with his computer, phone, and watch. Everyone else had had family to pick up their things.

"Can you go online?" someone asked Marcus. "And find out what's going on?"

He nodded and switched on his computer. "It will take a while to boot up."

"What about our notebooks?" Caitlin asked Sally. "Can we get those back?"

Sally shook her head. "They are being shredded right now."

"Shredded?" Caitlin sounded a little sick.

No wonder. Her notebook had been her companion throughout all this. She had developed that glossary that might have gotten them through deliberations; she had been designing a font, and once she had realized that she could lip-read, she had kept her eyes down during all the sidebars, drawing these super-elaborate designs. Of course she would want that back.

But why should anything good come out of this mess? He was beyond disgusted. Why had he even tried? They should have let everything fall apart at first. It would have saved weeks.

Marcus apologized. His computer was updating itself; it would be another few minutes.

"I'm ready to go," Keith announced and pushed his chair back from the table. "I'm not afraid of some reporters."

"Me either," Dave agreed.

"You should be," Seth said bluntly. They didn't know what it was going to be like out there. He did. "The judge is right. We don't know anything. It's going to be a piece of cake for someone to make us sound like idiots, and there will be people who want to make us sound like idiots."

"Why would they want to do that?" someone asked.

"Because it will sell papers."

"I can't believe that this is over," April said...and she didn't laugh.

"Why don't we all go back to the inn and have dinner together?" Joan suggested. "We've stuck together this long. Let's figure out our next move together."

Marcus's computer was finally on. "Does anyone remember what date we were sequestered? It may be easiest to start there."

During their last day of "freedom," the judge had learned that the big newspaper in Charlotte was about to publish a story based on the supposedly secret details of pretrial plea negotiations. Both defendants had been willing to plead guilty to some of the charges; they had even been willing to do some jail time rather than go to trial, but the prosecution had been inflexible. The district attorney had wanted to go to trial. This was an election year.

"Wait a second," Dave said. "Are you saying that we ended up exactly where they could have started?"

"It looks like it," Marcus said mildly.

This was beyond wack. What a waste.

The judge had been heavily criticized from the beginning, Marcus continued. Some commentators thought that he should have made the lawyers agree to a deal.

"Are they kidding?" Keith said. "How could he have done that? He couldn't get them to shut up."

When the van came, Marcus switched to reading on his phone, following the case in the local newspaper. After taxpayers started to realize how much sequestration was costing, the judge was criticized for that as well. The jurors weren't supposed to be reading about the trial, so how would they have found out about the plea negotiations? And if they did, couldn't the judge instruct them to ignore it?

That seemed impossibly naïve.

"What about the lawyers?" Caitlin asked. "Aren't people criticizing them?"

"Yes. Apparently...hmm, this is taking me a minute...oh, okay, North Carolina has some statewide prosecutors who specialize in financial crimes. But the district attorney was trying to make the case that out here in the western part of the state we can handle our own stuff."

He certainly hadn't made such a great case for that, now had he?

There were people with notebooks and cameras outside the entrance to the parking lot. Deputies were keeping them off the inn property.

"How would you... Did you... Tell us..." Questions were being shouted from the sidewalk.

The innkeeper was waiting inside with a tray of champagne flutes.

What on earth were they supposed to be celebrating?

# CHAPTER TEN

There was a glass of champagne in her hand. Caitlin didn't remember taking it.

The innkeeper was saying that he had put the phones back in the rooms. If people wanted to talk to their families in actual privacy, they could go call.

"Can we take the champagne with us?" someone asked.

"Of course," he answered. Apparently they were normal people again, able to make phone calls and drink unsupervised.

Caitlin's glass was almost empty. She didn't remember drinking any. She held out the glass for a refill.

Up in her room, she called her parents. They had heard the news. "So do you want us to come get you?"

"I don't know...I suppose not. I think we are all trying to get some kind of closure."

"It's important to say goodbye," her mother said. "You learn that in the military."

Caitlin felt confused. She didn't want to go on being sequestered. Of course not. But what was she going to do next? Her apartment in San Francisco was sublet for the next two months. She could probably stay with friends if she were desperate to go back, but she wasn't sure she wanted to go back at all.

Her parents were still talking. The whole trial was being viewed as an election-year stunt, and the lawyers on both sides were being blamed for time-wasting courtroom antics. After a while she stopped them. "You know, I don't really care."

"We've saved all the articles for you. You can read them when you get home."

Caitlin couldn't think of anything she would want to do less.

She tapped on the wall. There was no answer from Seth. Maybe he was already on the balcony. She opened the door and peered out. No, he wasn't there. Maybe he had been in the bathroom. It was going to be hard to break that singing "Happy Birthday" twice habit. She went back in to tap again.

And then remembered that she didn't have to tap. She could knock on his door, go into his room.

She crossed the hall and knocked. It felt very strange. How could something that had been completely forbidden just this morning be okay now?

He opened the door. Over his shoulder she could see that his suitcase was almost completely packed.

His expression was tight and hard. She had never seen him look like this. All the puckish openness to new adventures, the friendliness, the easy play of facial muscles, had contracted into something fierce.

"Can I come in?"

"Oh, right. We are independent adults again." He sounded bitter, but he stepped back so she could come in. "This was some kind of big joke, wasn't it?"

"It does seem that it was a waste."

He drew back. "Aren't you angry?"

"No." *It seems like you are angry enough for both of us.* "It happened. It's over. I'm going to look for the good."

"The good? What good has come out of such a mess? Do you believe it? The whole trial, everything could have been avoided if the DA hadn't been such a dick."

"His political career is probably over."

"Who the hell cares about that?"

"Seth, why are you so angry?" It made her uneasy. "This isn't like you. I thought the code on the slopes was not to look back, not to waste time in regret."

"That's for snowboarders. Tell me what I have done that has anything to do with shredding? Do boarders need to know how installers are assigned at Sears or what it takes to become an assistant manager at the Nine West store at the outlet mall?"

Those were April's and Heather's jobs.

One thing about being a military kid was that your parents didn't protect you from failure. They taught you how to deal with it. Make a mistake that cost your boat a race, and you knew what to do next.

Seth's parents, by getting him out of the very technical competitions, had kept him from failing. It had been the right decision for his career and for their company, but it had left him here, at twenty-five, not even understanding what failure was.

"Seth, you didn't fail."

"I set a goal, to get all twelve of us to deliberations, and that didn't happen. Are you going to try to spin that as success?"

"Well, no," she admitted. "But it wasn't your fault. It wasn't in your control."

"What difference does that make? Technically it wasn't my 'fault' that I medaled in the Olympics. Other people messed up. So why do I get to claim that as a big personal success and not get pissed off about this?"

Caitlin had no idea. She couldn't follow his logic. There probably wasn't any.

There was no point in talking. He wasn't thinking clearly. She took his hand and started leading him toward the reading chair. "You can't like feeling this way."

"No."

Words weren't going to help. She pushed him back into the chair, circled behind him, and put her thumbs on the back of his neck and threaded her fingers through his thick hair. She had no training as a masseuse, but she knew the human body. At first she used her fingertips, feeling his scalp shift over the bone of his skull. Then, with firmer pressure, her thumb followed the muscles along his neck, muscles that connected his head to his shoulders.

Even those muscles were strong. Snowboarders turned their heads constantly while wearing a helmet. Along the rest of his upper back each muscle group was cleanly defined, and his core, his glutes, his hamstrings, all those must be even finer, more perfectly developed.

She leaned forward and unbuttoned the top button of his shirt so she could slip her hand down the front of his torso, following the contours of those muscles. She leaned forward and kissed his neck, letting her iris-scented hair brush against his face. Immediately his hand came up to touch the side of her face, hold it, cradle it. Her body grew soft and heavy with longing.

Then suddenly he jerked away, almost lurching out of his chair. The buckle of his cheap watch caught her hair, and she winced.

What was going on? Why had he stopped? Didn't he want this as much as she did? Hadn't he lain in his luxurious bed night after night and thought of her?

After the Olympics, back when he wasn't returning her messages, had she given up too easily? She had wondered that several times after college. Should she have tried harder to understand why he wasn't calling? Maybe she would have found out that it had nothing to do with her. But she had been a kid herself; of course she had been wounded by his rejection.

But she wasn't a kid any more. She was a grown woman who cared deeply about a man who was struggling, feeling defeated. That was the richness, the meaning, the magic, that she hadn't felt in June.

His back was toward the bed, so she touched his chest, letting her fingertips rest on the warmth beneath his open collar. She pushed gently, easing him back until he was sitting on the bed.

"Caitlin." His voice was thick. "No. It wouldn't be—"

Be what? Fair? She knew he was feeling weary, wrung out. She didn't care about herself. She pressed her fingers to his lips. "No, let me." She dropped her hands to his shoulders, pushing him back. Now he was lying across the bed, his arms stretched across the sage-green coverlet, the buttons of his shirt straining. His eyes were half-closed, and a pulse throbbed in his neck.

She slipped out of her panties and shimmied her skirt up over her thighs. She straddled him, and as she leaned forward to kiss him, his response was immediate.

By the time she had his belt buckle undone, he was so aroused that she wasn't sure she could free him from his clothes, but he lifted his hips, and in a moment his erection was pushing against her leg, moving, searching. She shifted, trying to lower herself onto him. She gasped at first, but all she had to do was look at his face, his much loved face, with his eyes now fully shut, and her body softened.

She began to move. His arms curved upward, and he gripped her hips, moving her to his rhythm.

How strong he was. He wasn't hurting her, but he had taken control. For a moment she wasn't sure that she felt human. Was she just something that he was moving up and down on his penis? A second later he thrust deep into her, shuddered, and climaxed

His arms fell back to the bed, and she began to lift herself off him. "No, wait." His voice was still thick. "Give me a minute."

She didn't want a minute. She didn't want her "turn." That hadn't been what this was about. Not for her. She murmured a few words and then moved herself back to stand up. Her skirt was twisted about her belly. She tugged it back in place and left, at the last minute remembering to pick up her panties.

She set the six jets in her glass-walled shower to a gentle rain and let the water flow caressingly down her body. As she had done the first afternoon at the inn, she wrapped herself in the big white robe, then looked around the room. How much stuff she had accumulated—the crocheted pot holders Delia had taught her to make; the one scarf she had knit. She had done it in a garter stitch, row after row of knitting. She had wanted to do the stockinette stitch, a row of knitting, then a row of purling, but Joan had said that beginners should not be too ambitious. Normally Caitlin would have resisted that—*I can learn anything*—but part of Team Jury was going along, not arguing about every little thing, so Caitlin had obediently knit the whole thing.

All the games and videos her parents had brought were in the library. She supposed that she should pack them up. Maybe the innkeeper would let her leave them for future guests. She didn't want to see them again.

And her clothes. She never wanted to wear any of them again. They felt like a prison uniform.

* * * *

The innkeeper had prepared dinner for them, grilling steaks he had been given by a caterer up in Boone, who was eager to have some of the future wedding business. He also announced that he was hiring a new assistant manager and head of housekeeping—Stephanie.

Stephanie was flushed and happy. She had liked working in the bakery, but she was going to have so much more responsibility. One night a week she would be at the inn by herself, completely in charge. Her new boss had already given her a notebook to read, and she was going to take a CPR course. Signing up for that had been her own idea.

Despite this good news, the jurors were picking at the food, cutting their steaks slowly, leaving their baked potatoes wrapped in the aluminum foil.

Seth had come downstairs just as they were taking their places at the table. His hair was damp, and he was wearing his narrow, square-rimmed glasses. He apologized for being late. He had fallen asleep.

A couple of people said that they were surprised at how tired they also felt. Then someone brought up the trial, and everyone acknowledged that they had no idea how they would have voted. They would have had to listen to the rest of the defense, then go through the charges one by one and for each of the defendants. It would have taken a long time, but they all would have rather done that than to be like this, sitting here in front of steak and a baked potato, feeling like it had all been a waste of time.

"Okay, Seth," Keith said, "you're the most experienced at talking to reporters and such. So tell us what we should do."

Caitlin wondered how Seth would answer. He was weary. He felt like a failure. He didn't want to be the leader anymore.

He took off his glasses and rubbed his eyes, but then he came through. "Decide what your purpose is, why you are talking to them. I know that right now my purpose would be to punish everyone involved. I want to criticize the judge and all the lawyers. But that's not going to achieve anything, and that's not the kind of person I am. So I am going to keep my mouth shut."

"I would like people to know how great Sally has been," April said. "Taking me dress shopping and all."

"Yes, but we don't know what the office politics are. Public recognition could get her in hot water. You should touch base with her first."

They talked about it for a long time. Some people thought that they should all agree to talk to no one. Others didn't like that idea. Still others weren't sure. It wasn't a rancorous discussion, and eventually everyone agreed that they should talk about it again at breakfast the next morning.

"One more thing," Norma said. "Caitlin, can you lip-read?"

Caitlin stared at her. "How did you know?"

"After you met with the judge, all the lawyers kept their mouths covered. It was the only explanation, especially since you know as much about the movement of facial muscles as some plastic surgeons. But why didn't you tell them from the beginning?"

"Because I couldn't when I started." Caitlin explained what had happened and how she had anguished about whether or not to tell the judge.

"I thought that this was the sort of thing that we were all supposed to talk about together," someone said.

"The thing is, if I decided not to tell the judge and then it came out later, that could be grounds for dismissing the verdict. And asking twelve people to keep a secret forever—"

"You could have asked these twelve," Delia said. "We could have done it."

Caitlin wasn't sure what to say. She hadn't trusted them. There was no getting around that.

"I asked this before," Norma said, "and Caitlin answered, but now you answer, Seth. Did Caitlin talk to you about this?"

He sighed and ran a hand through his hair. "Yes."

"I was the one who lied about that," Caitlin said quickly. "Not him. I didn't want people to think that we were working behind the scenes."

"But you were," Joan said flatly.

"So those times when we would see the two of you, up on your balcony," Stephanie asked, "were you talking about the rest of us?"

No one liked the sound of that.

"I started it," Seth said, "and it was always in the context of making sure that everyone was okay."

"But weren't we supposed to do that as a team?" Stephanie answered.

There was no answer to that.

"I don't know," Heather said. "This makes me feel creepy. Like all this Team Jury stuff was a fraud."

"I thought that tonight was going to be a happy time," Yvette said.

"We'll try again in the morning," Delia promised her. "We will all be here for breakfast."

That seemed like a good choice, for everyone to go upstairs and pack tonight. Then the celebration, the closure, the whatever, could be in the morning.

\* \* \* \*

Caitlin had finished packing everything that she wouldn't need in the morning when she heard the familiar tap on the wall. Curious, she went out to the balcony.

"You could have come to the door."

"I know...but listen, I have called my parents. I'm cutting out tonight. Do you want to come?"

"Aren't you going to say goodbye to people? It's what they are expecting."

"There's no way we are going to have a happy little party and pledge to be BFFs forever. We got together to do a job. We did our part. And that's the end of things. Except for you, I'll probably never see any of them again. So do you want to leave tonight?"

Leave tonight? Of course she wanted to go with him. But what would it be like for the other ten if she and Seth weren't there in the morning? It would be strange enough to have him disappear, but at least she could try to explain. She could make up something about him needing to go to New Zealand.

She shook her head. "No, I'll wait with the others."

"Then I'll be seeing you tomorrow night. I think our mothers are organizing something."

She nodded. Her mother had already told her.

"And about last night—"

It had actually been this afternoon.

"—I saw that some of your hair was caught in my watch."

What did that have to do with anything? "It didn't hurt."

"Looking at it made me feel bad, like I'd used you."

"You didn't."

He waited for her to say more. She didn't. "Okay, then, I will see you tomorrow night."

"Of course."

\* \* \* \*

She could have gone out to the balcony and watched his parents drive up. His mom would have hugged him while his dad started to load the car. But she didn't. She stayed in her room and thought about him turning his wrist to unbuckle his watch and seeing her hair caught in the buckle.

Hadn't he noticed that she was using her own shampoo again? That she had switched back as soon as he said that was the one he liked?

# CHAPTER ELEVEN

People were going to ask why Seth had left. They would expect her to know...and of course she did. But what could she say? Others had also been eager to get home, but they were staying, knowing that it was important to the group.

*Well, yeah, he put himself first. What could you expect from a snowboarder? He's way too cool for the likes of you.*

They—she—might have expected that he had changed.

Ultimately she didn't have to explain anything. As she came down from the third floor in the morning, she saw a cluster of people gathered around one of the second-floor rooms, looking worried.

It was the Goldenrod room, Yvette's room. Apparently she had sat up all night, nearly catatonic. She hadn't packed, showered, slept, anything. She couldn't stand the thought of leaving her spacious room with its sunny walls, heated towels, claw-foot tub, and glass-walled shower. She couldn't bear to leave the charming breakfasts and interesting dinners, the quiet evenings in the library, and, above all, the attention, the kindness, the concern.

Even Seth, she had told Stephanie earlier in the evening, *Seth Street*, had spoken to her every day, every single day.

Since then she had said almost nothing.

Caitlin knew that Yvette lived in her sister's mobile home. She used to have a bedroom of her own while her sister's two kids shared the other room with their mom. Then the sister's boyfriend had moved in; the kids took over the second bedroom, and Yvette was on the sofa...even though Yvette paid half the rent and half the groceries, and the boyfriend paid nothing.

How could Caitlin complain about her apartment being so small?

"Have we called—" Caitlin broke off. They weren't Sally's problem anymore.

"911?" Norma finished for her. "It isn't medical. And really there's nothing we can do. She just doesn't want to go home."

"I can't blame her there," Caitlin acknowledged. "Her sister's probably gotten used to not having someone sleep on the sofa."

"Stephanie went in with some water, trying to get her to drink something," Norma said. "That might help." She gestured for the rest of them to go downstairs.

The four older people were in the breakfast room. They looked up eagerly when Caitlin came in, but she shook her head. No news.

"I was wondering," Keith said, "if one of us should take her in—we've all got extra rooms with the kids being grown—but Joan says that that just delays the inevitable."

"The rest of us have done something with our time here," Joan explained. "Stephanie's found a new job, and Dave is really enjoying his art. That rubber band is working for Heather. She's not talking so much, and April is trying to breathe while she laughs. I learned how I miss teaching. Delia and I are thinking about linking up with the mothers who are homeschooling. She could do music, and I can work with the struggling readers. But Yvette put her head in the sand. She hates her life. She wouldn't think about how to fix it. And we can't do it for her."

No. Caitlin hadn't been able to make her sister happy...her sister had had to do that herself.

But that hadn't kept Caitlin from wanting to. "I'd be willing to ask Seth's dad if he could find her a job at the Street Boards factory." For all her passivity, Yvette was a diligent worker. "It doesn't solve her living situation, but at least working conditions are better."

"That's good of you," Joan said, "but she still has to decide if she has any boundaries with her sister."

* * * *

Caitlin expected that her parents would arrive early, and they did. Her father went up to get her luggage. She took her box of art supplies into the breakfast room, wanting to give them to Dave. But no one was there. So she wrote his name on the box and went out to the car with her parents. That was it. It was over.

In the car, her parents were eager to talk about the trial. They kept asking her if she had any questions. Her father reminded her that she could say whatever she wanted now.

"I just don't care. I really don't."

"It was badly handled," he said. "But the district attorney is facing a strong challenger in the election this fall. It's time to clean house."

Caitlin agreed.

"It's a woman who's running. We've contributed to her campaign, but she needs to reach out to the young people, you millennial types. Since you're going to—"

Caitlin wasn't listening. She wanted to see Seth. That was the only thing she could think about.

Now her mother was talking. "I got you a hair appointment. But you don't have to go. We can cancel. Elena will understand."

Hair? In San Francisco she left hers long and went to a beauty school twice a year to have the students trim it. Did she want to go sit in a salon today? She didn't know. Apparently former prisoners had trouble learning how to make their own decisions again once they were released.

So she let her mother decide.

Elena, her mother's stylist, suggested that she cut Caitlin's hair to emphasize her eyes. Caitlin said that that sounded fine. The stylist knew that Caitlin had been on the jury, and she was dying to talk about it. Caitlin had to explain how weary she was of it all. She should have brought headphones so she could listen to music on her phone, but she had forgotten that she was now allowed to do that.

She watched as Elena cut and cut and then cut some more. Surely she was cutting too much. Was she punishing Caitlin for not wanting to talk about the trial? Caitlin knew that she should try to stop her, but apparently she had also forgotten how to speak.

Her hair ended shorter than it had been since elementary school. It was layered and fringed; she looked nothing like herself.

"Oh, honey, you look so pretty," her mom exclaimed when she got home. "The way those side layers call attention to your eyes...do you like it?"

Caitlin shrugged. She had no idea if she liked it or not. She put on an apron to help her mother with the beet and orange salad they were taking out to the lake house.

She thought about calling Seth. Find out how he was doing, see if being home was making him feel any better.

No, she could wait. It would be better to see him in person. On the phone he would say that he was fine.

She decided to call her sister instead.

There were hundreds of texts and messages queued up on her phone. She ignored them.

"Can you talk?" she asked as soon as her sister answered. Trina worked at a lighting-design firm and was in the middle of a huge contract.

"Actually, yes. Our computers are down. How are you? I'm dying to come see you. I wanted to throw myself in the car the minute I heard, but school's already started, and you know Dylan. He's in a million sports. We will be there Labor Day."

"You won't recognize me. Mom's hairdresser cut my hair."

"That took some courage. Send me a picture."

Obediently Caitlin turned her phone around, took a selfie, and sent it to her sister. How strange to be able to communicate like it was the twenty-first century.

"Oh my God," Trina gushed a minute later. "I love it. That's so cute. It's totally you."

"Totally me?" Caitlin turned the phone again to look at the picture. "It's a 1970s shag."

"I know. It's retro, it's hip."

Caitlin turned to look at herself in the mirror. On the streets in San Francisco, would she stop that girl and ask where she had gotten her hair done?

Fat chance.

Trina squealed that her computer had come back on. She had to hang up. Caitlin went to her room to get ready for the picnic. She hadn't even opened her suitcase. She was sick of everything in there. She went down the hall and leaned over the banister. "Mom, does Trina keep any clothes here?"

Her mother came out from the kitchen, drying her hands on her apron. "Only pajamas and workout clothes. Otherwise she borrows from me. Do you need something? I have a Lilly that I stopped wearing because I think it is too short for someone my age."

Ten minutes later Caitlin was in an aqua-and-taupe print Lilly Pulitzer sleeveless sheath dress. Her mother was two inches taller than Caitlin, so what had been too short on her was a ladylike knee length on Caitlin. Then her mother had handed her some thin gold bangles and a pair of strappy pink flat sandals.

Caitlin looked at herself in the mirror on the back of her parents' closet door. She didn't look hip, she didn't look retro; she looked like she was going to a luncheon for the Palm Beach Hospital Auxiliary's gala planning committee.

* * * *

Seth's family was waiting on the terrace that spanned the roadside of the lake house. Through the backseat window of her father's car she could see Seth standing by the railing. He was in loose khaki shorts, something he had never worn at the inn, and a blue button-up chambray shirt. He was wearing Sperrys without socks. The shirt was untucked, the sleeves were rolled up, and he had his own sleek watch back on.

He looked like a magazine ad...which was no surprise because this was straight out of a magazine ad. She had seen one of Seth and his two friends horsing around on a beach, all of them in Street Boards gear. Seth's shirt would have a small Street Boards logo above the pocket. Except for the fact that he had been barefoot in the ad, this had been exactly what he had been wearing.

It made him seem unreal, like someone she didn't know.

Mr. Street—Caitlin was having trouble calling him Tom—had come around the car to open the door for MeeMaw. He noticed that Caitlin was trapped under a big, foil-covered pottery bowl. He signaled to someone to come open her door.

Becca, Seth's sister, got there first. She reached in the car to get the bowl.

"Well, look at you!" she exclaimed. "Your hair. You look so pretty. What a difference."

Caitlin thanked her as she slid out of the car. She tried to take the bowl back.

"No. No. Seth, come take this. Watch out. It's heavy. Did you see Caitlin's hair? Doesn't she look great?"

Seth stepped forward to take the bowl. "Did you get my text?" he asked Caitlin softly.

She shook her head. "I turned my phone on, but there were a million messages. I couldn't face them."

Before he could say more, her mother cautioned him not to tilt the bowl. "It's got beets. They'll stain."

Then his mom asked her mom how she kept her hands from turning red when cutting beets. "Latex gloves," her mom answered, and they talked about beet juice as they went into the house.

How right this felt, their two families at a picnic together. She suddenly wished that Trina were here along with Trevor and Dylan. Dylan would call her "Aunt Caitlin." The little Street kids would call him "Uncle Seth."

This was the reason not to go back to San Francisco, not because her apartment was small or because the city was expensive, but this...family.

"So are you glad to be home?" Seth's sister Becca asked her when they were in the kitchen together. "Seth seems to be numb."

"Me too."

"I'm worried about him. I wish he weren't leaving so quickly. It's like he's running away."

Caitlin froze. Seth was leaving? "I beg your pardon?"

"Didn't he tell you? He's going back to Oregon tomorrow morning."

*What?* The shock was like an electric current, sizzling through her, jolting her awake. Seth was leaving? He couldn't. He simply couldn't.

She went looking for him. He was on the lakeside deck where his father was lighting the grill. There were enough people out there that no one seemed to notice when she signaled him to come over to the steps.

"What the fuck, Seth?" So what if she were wearing a ladylike Lilly Pulitzer? "What the fuck?"

"I tried to tell you."

He needed to go back to Oregon. His parents had kept some bad news from him. Nate had injured himself again, and Ben had had some kind of major public flameout, criticizing the entire snowboarding establishment.

So? Wasn't Nate always injuring himself? He had told her enough about his friends for her to know that. And if Ben had a PR problem, what was Seth going to do about it? She couldn't see that that was any reason for him to leave.

What had she expected? Just yesterday he had left the inn early, not caring what she or the others thought.

"You know," she said when his explanation trailed off, "we've had this conversation before, back when we were kids. You were saying how you had to go to New Zealand for the good of the company when you wanted to go for yourself." At least that time he had had a better excuse; that program had put him on the ladder to the Olympics. "Your sister is right. You're running away."

"What are you talking about? I'm not running from anything. Nate's family needs pro riders out on the slopes. The guests expect it."

And there was absolutely no other professional who would be willing to come to the one place in the United States that had snow year-round? "They can't need you as much as your own family does. What about the rebranding? And the game? You know that once we talk to someone who knows children's games, we will have to start over."

"That's just it. We don't know enough to design a game ourselves."

That annoyed Caitlin. "Once an educator gets me on the right track, I know plenty."

"Okay, so you do. But I don't. All that stuff I was talking about rebranding and our reverse inventory logistics, what do I know about any of that?"

Enough to know that his parents needed help.

Speaking of branding...why was Street Boards making chambray shirts? All the other guys in the ad had looked like snowboarders, wearing grungy hoodies and insane neon colors. But a chambray shirt? Seth didn't look like a snowboarder. He looked like a North Carolina preppy, a lazy-ass, smug, entitled, North Carolina preppy.

"You could learn," she said.

"You don't have any reason to think that."

They were fighting, and it felt good. Fighting was better than talking about oranges and beets or not talking at all. But she wasn't going to do it in front of their families. She walked away.

The rest of the evening was difficult. Once the children were settled, the other adults wanted to talk about the trial. The consensus among trial observers was that while the defendants were apparently guilty of some charges, they were innocent of others.

"It seems impossible that you could have sorted it out in the jury room," Becca's husband said.

"We would have done our best." Caitlin felt obliged to defend her fellow jurors.

"I heard that most of you hadn't finished college."

"Well, that would include Seth, wouldn't it?' she said sweetly.

At the end of the evening she found herself standing on the front terrace with him, waiting for MeeMaw to finish the interminable round of Southern thank-yous and goodbyes. The porch light was on, but the summer evening was still light enough that the lamp wasn't drawing too many bugs.

"Your hair, that dress, you look so different," he said. "It's like talking to a stranger."

She shrugged. She didn't have anything to say to him. He was abandoning her. Again.

"I think we were set up to fail. The jury, I mean. I think about the original sixteen. There was no way we could have come to a verdict. Someone must have been okay with that."

"I figured that out before we'd heard any testimony."

"You did? How?"

She had paid attention, that's how. She hadn't sat there all wrapped up in herself.

That wasn't fair. It might have taken him forever to learn April's name, but then he had found a way for her to try on her own wedding dress. "It doesn't matter now, Seth."

"You could come to Oregon with me, you know."

*What?* Did she hear him right? Did he ask her to come to Oregon with him?

She couldn't breathe. Wasn't this what she wanted? For him to ask her to come with him?

No. She wanted him to say that she mattered, that he wasn't running away, that he had to go to Oregon to think and he couldn't do that without her.

Instead he had said it as if it had just occurred to him, as if he were thinking about whether or not to have a second cup of coffee.

*I need to be more than that.*

\* \* \* \*

"We didn't want to start an argument with the Streets' son-in-law," her mother said in the car on their way home.

"Argument?" What was she talking about? "Oh, about the jurors being clueless? Well, we were."

"Some of the columnists were saying that the lawyers were making it more confusing than it needed to be, but your dad kept saying that you would find a way."

"That's nice of you," Caitlin murmured.

"I meant it," her dad said. "Look at you, constantly figuring things out for yourself, getting your way paid to Stanford, supporting yourself on your own. I knew that you would find a way to come to a decent verdict."

Caitlin had to blink. That was nice to hear. At least her parents thought she was worth something. "I was trying." She explained about her glossary. "And I could tell a lot from the witnesses' body language, which ones were being straight with us, which ones were trying to shape their story, which ones were ashamed to be there."

"That's my girl," her dad said.

\* \* \* \*

Her mother knocked on her door as she was getting ready for bed.

"Your dad doesn't like to talk about this, about how little money we had for your education. The night you signed with Stanford, he felt so guilty.

So we decided then that we would make sure that you could have any kind of wedding that you wanted."

"Wedding?" Caitlin stared at her. "Wedding?"

"You do know what a wedding is."

"Yes, but—"

"I know Trina's was very quiet. At first she wanted something bigger, more traditional, but even she came to understand. When it came to a big wedding, it would be your turn."

This was insane. Why was Mom talking about a wedding? Caitlin wasn't getting married. April was getting married. April was marrying that nice apprentice electrician she had met working in the installation office at Sears. Caitlin didn't know any nice electricians. She only knew a snowboarder, and he had just abandoned her. She had been seduced and abandoned...although technically she had done the seducing, but not the abandoning, *so* not the abandoning.

"Mom. You are way ahead of yourself." *Just like with the birth control pills.*

Caitlin looked at her watch as the door closed behind her mother. Her sister would still be awake.

"Did the computers get fixed?" she asked when Trina answered.

"Yes, then no, then yes again. I'm still at the office."

"Is there anything I can do to help? I could come down."

"That's so sweet of you." Her sister sounded surprised. "But no...this is the biggest assignment I've ever had, and I want to show my boss—and myself—that I can handle it. But do you need to come here? Are Mom and Dad driving you nuts?"

"Not Dad. But Mom has started talking about my wedding."

"And that surprises you? Don't forget that she grew up in North Carolina."

"What does that have to do with anything?"

"Oh, honey chile." Trina faked a Southern drawl. "The navy might have taken the girl out of the South, but ain't no one can take the South out of the girl. " Then she returned to her normal voice. "You're going to get a big-ass Southern wedding with ten bridesmaids and a cake the size of Tennessee."

"That's nuts. Why would I want that? Even if I had someone, which I don't."

"What about you and Seth?"

"No. Absolutely not. I don't know where you got that idea."

"From Mom. Where else?"

Sweet Jesus. Her mother was thinking she would marry Seth? Well, soon enough Mom, Trina, and Southern girls everywhere would know the truth. Seth was going back to Oregon.

\* \* \* \*

Caitlin couldn't sleep that night. A big-ass Southern wedding? She didn't want that. She would settle for a guy who hadn't run off, looking for snow at the height of the summer.

When she came downstairs in the morning, her parents were at the breakfast table, their heads bent close together over the newspaper. When she saw Caitlin, her mother grabbed the paper, scrambling to fold it up.

Her dad stopped her. "She's going to see it, Sharon. You can't protect her."

"What is it?" Caitlin held out her hand for the paper. She didn't need to be protected.

Through the weeks of the trial the local paper had criticized the judge, the lawyers, the defendants, the DA. The jury had always been off limits.

Not anymore. The paper hadn't quite called the jurors bone dumb, but it did question whether they had the intelligence and education to be the vehicles for justice in such a complex case.

*The lawyers chose us. Blame them.*

Only four of the jurors had undergraduate degrees, the paper had learned, and five had never attended college at all. Courtroom observers reported that that some had difficulty staying awake while others seemed to be daydreaming and one was doodling in the court-supplied notebook.

Caitlin folded the paper and handed it back to her mother. "I was the doodler, but only during the sidebars."

"Don't you want to say that, then? Don't you want to answer them?" her mother asked. "Should she do something, Pete?"

Apparently Caitlin's father's opinion about what Caitlin should do mattered as much as Caitlin's own.

"No," he said. "It will blow over. Answering will keep the story alive."

\* \* \* \*

Seth's sister sent him a text with a link to their hometown newspaper. He was stuck on the runway at the Portland airport waiting for a gate to open up, and so he clicked on the link. At any other time he might have ignored it.

It was an article about the jury. He scanned it. Well, yeah, the jurors hadn't been qualified to render judgment on the issues...because no one had tried to get them to understand. The trial had been a complete-ass waste of time, insulting and—

No, he wasn't going to get angry again. He was done with that.

Ben was waiting for him when he got through security. His thick auburn hair was cut shorter than Seth had ever seen it, but his expression was alert as always.

"Hey, man." Seth punched him on the arm. "What kind of pickle did you get yourself into?" Ben's scorched-earth criticism had been about the pressure being put on the young kids and their parents. Snowboarding was becoming like gymnastics and figure skating where the coaches needed massive numbers of parents writing checks, unknowingly sacrificing their kids for the sake of the few who would succeed.

"You know I've thought all that for a long time," Ben answered. "This time I said it. But, listen, Nate's out in the van. This latest injury is a game changer for him. He barely escaped some serious spine damage. Another fall like that, and he's paralyzed."

"Oh, man...that's just...I don't even know what to say. It sucks so bad."

"Yes, but a part of him has got to be a little relieved."

"Relieved?" That was nuts. "What are you talking about?"

"He's not all creative like you or super technical like me. All he can do is go higher and bigger, and he's sick at the thought of pushing that envelope again and again. He's ready to be done with the insane stuff."

Seth winced. He didn't like hearing that.

Even with only the van's overhead light switching on, Seth could see that Nate was wearing some kind of body brace under his coat. The leg seam of his jeans had been ripped open because he had a hard plaster cast from his foot up beyond his knee. A pair of crutches was thrust over the console between the two front seats.

It took about an hour to get from Portland to Mt. Hood. Seth assumed that he would be glad to be home, but he was immediately bugged by the casual mess in the chalet he shared with these two guys. Everyone on the jury had been so considerate at the inn, never leaving empty coffee cups or Coke cans lying around, always putting their games and DVDs away.

The video queued up on the TV was about soccer. That was strange. "Are we trying a new sport?" he asked.

"It's a video about coaching girls," Nate said. "My mother and sister are trying to get us to do more for them."

"I'm game," Seth said, but as he was speaking, Ben left the room. He looked at Nate questioningly.

"Yeah." Nate picked up the remote. "None of the big training programs want anything to do with him right now."

That was a shame. Ben would have made a great coach. He could see so much and explain it all so well. They'd all assumed that he would eventually end up doing it full-time someday. He might have just screwed that up for himself.

It was like with Colleen. Whenever Ben got close to something good, he pulled out the grenades.

Seth settled down with Nate to watch the video. It focused on how critical young girls were of themselves. He thought about teaching Caitlin to skateboard. She had been supercritical of herself, but she had never doubted herself as these girls did. She had never given up.

Why hadn't she come to Oregon with him?

*Because maybe, you asshole, for the first time in her life, she's quitting on something. You.*

"What do you do when you mess up with a girl?" he suddenly asked Nate.

"Me? I run. I hide."

"I've done that. I'm doing it right now. What else?"

"Beats me. Send flowers. Women are supposed to like flowers."

"She'd take that as a kiss-off."

Nate pushed the Pause button on the remote. "I take it we are talking about someone specific. Is she the new Colleen?"

"I don't know...but I certainly messed things up as badly as Ben."

\* \* \* \*

Caitlin's parents didn't try to hide the Sunday paper from her. After labeling the jurors stupid on Saturday, the Sunday paper declared that they were self-indulgent crybabies.

They hadn't been willing to share rooms at the Best Western. They had demanded exercise facilities, more entertainment, and better food to the extent that the good, hardworking taxpayers of North Carolina had to pay to have them moved to a place of sybaritic elegance.

Accompanying the article were color photographs of the Wildflower Inn, showing the beautiful bedrooms, the luxurious bathrooms, and the comfortable common spaces. This was what the long-suffering taxpayers of North Carolina had coughed up their pennies for in hopes of keeping these twelve spoiled brats doing their civic duty.

There was nothing about the steeply discounted rate offered because the inn would have been vacant otherwise, nothing about how the jurors had done most of the housekeeping and had spent their weekends painting and sanding.

Reading this was painful. Caitlin wanted to call the newspaper and protest, saying that everything was slanted. But what good would that do? Whatever she said would get twisted.

She needed to talk to someone who would understand. Stephanie had gathered all the jurors' contact information. There had been copies next to the coffee that last morning. Had Caitlin picked up a copy? She couldn't remember. She checked the side pocket of her suitcase. Yes, she had.

Joan was an early riser, but wouldn't have left for church yet. Caitlin would call her.

"Bless your heart, honey lamb," Joan exclaimed. "Isn't it awful what they are saying about us?"

It was good to commiserate and find out what people were up to. Apparently Delia was having trouble getting back into the routine of fixing three meals a day. "Her family can't believe it, but she is telling them that they can sue her."

"That's a jury I'd be happy to be on. What about Yvette?"

Yvette had ended up spending Friday night in the hospital. "Say what you want about that chicken place, but they do have decent health insurance."

Then on Saturday morning Joan, Keith, and Keith's wife had sat down with Yvette's sister for a "come to Jesus" talk. If Yvette couldn't get her bedroom back, she would be moving in with Keith or Joan and would have to pay rent to them, not to the sister. "We wouldn't have actually charged her anything, but we wouldn't have let her pay her sister."

Yvette's sister had thrown out her deadbeat boyfriend and had given Yvette her old room. Yvette still felt that she had to pay half the rent and half the groceries even though the grocery bill included the little kids' diapers, which were apparently a bigger expense than Caitlin had realized.

* * * *

Monday's article was about the food, how the jurors' meals had been prepared by a private chef. The fact that this chef had also been one of the jurors was buried in the middle of the article.

Many of their meals had been vegetarian, but whenever Marcus had extra in his budget, he had prepared shrimp or good cuts of beef. Of course the paper made it sound as if that had been their nightly fare without ever noting that Marcus's cooking had actually saved the good, clean-living, overburdened taxpayers of North Carolina some money.

Caitlin was disgusted. What was wrong with this town? This was supposed to be the beautiful, wild High County. But the court system was about politics, not justice, and the newspaper was going to slant every fact to make people look bad. How could she consider living here?

Because maybe she could help fix it. There wasn't much she could do about San Francisco, how expensive it was, what a nightmare traffic and parking were. But here she could work to make sure that a trial like theirs never happened again.

That afternoon she borrowed her mother's car and drove to the law office of Deborah Cornerstone, the woman running for district attorney. The meager campaign staff was thrilled to have a young volunteer, someone who understood social media platforms and could design graphics. And then when they found out that she had been a juror—

"Is there any chance you could get Deborah an endorsement from Seth Street?"

# CHAPTER TWELVE

"I thought you said those notebooks had been destroyed."

It was Tuesday morning, and Caitlin's parents had gotten to the newspaper first.

"That's what we were told. What is it this time?"

The paper had printed facsimiles of pages from two of the supposedly shredded notebooks. No names were mentioned, but Caitlin could tell that one was Yvette's and the other one hers. Because of where they sat in the jury box, their notebooks would have been at the bottom of the stack.

Each day Yvette would carefully write down the date and then nothing else. The next day she would do the same thing. Each notebook page was line after line of dates. Caitlin had seen the notebook during court, and that's what was reproduced now.

*Don't criticize her.* Caitlin felt defensive. *She is a sweet, hardworking, ill-educated, spineless girl who wasn't up to this. Criticize the people who seated her.*

Caitlin's notebook could have been interesting to courtroom observers. The glossary with all its deletions and insertions would have shown how hard she was trying to understand the financial terminology. Her daily notes included her impressions of the witnesses, noting what their body language was revealing about their testimony.

But those weren't the pages the newspaper bothered with. Instead, it printed pages of the elaborate doodles she had done during sidebars once she had discovered that she could lip-read. The pages made it look as if she never paid attention, as if she sat in court all day drawing pictures.

Not at all. This was what she had done to keep the trial going. *I cared more about that than any of you.*

* * * *

His sister continued to send Seth the links to articles about the jury. He opened them, but then would have to stop reading. Getting his form back was enough of a challenge that he couldn't let himself be distracted.

Tuesday he decided he wouldn't open the links at all. Then in the middle of the afternoon the coaches out on the slopes told him that he had to quit for the day. He was getting tired.

How frustrating was that? He knew that he had started practicing again only a few days ago, but still...

He went to the resort's main lodge to find someone to complain to. Nate's sister listened to him for about five minutes, but then excused herself. He couldn't blame her.

He pulled out his phone. After glancing at the new messages, he clicked on the link in his sister's.

Whoa, Nellie. These images were from the notebooks. One page had to be from Yvette's notebook, and the others were from Caitlin's, not her glossary or her daily notes, but two of her flowing full-page doodles.

He enlarged one image on his phone, but it was still too small. Back in the offices was some good equipment that he used sometimes for editing video.

On that screen the resolution was surprisingly good. The first doodle had started with a little amoeba shape in the center and then had grown outward, the shape repeating, twisting, mirroring. Some of them were inside others, growing larger and larger like a set of Russian dolls. Others spun away from the doll set. Inside each little amoeba she had put three dots near the concave curve.

She had missed a few spots. She hadn't been doing this on the computer with a single command that would have put dots in every amoeba. She had taken her pen, lifted it, and tapped it down to make each one of those dots. He had seen her do it. She had held the notebook with her left hand, her big watch turned toward the floor, and her right hand had held the pen.

The next image was a mass of flowers, leaves, and vines. He touched the computer screen. The screen was cool. That seemed surprising. The drawing had so much vibrancy and life, even in cheap blue ink, that it seemed as if its warmth would have to come through.

He started to trace a line with his finger. It didn't start and stop, but curved and flowed, moving all over the page, this single uninterrupted line forming a blossom here, a vine over there.

He felt his body stir.

Oh, for God's sake. Was he lusting after a drawing?

No, it was her. Caitlin. Caitlin of the summers. He wanted her.

\* \* \* \*

MeeMaw said that she and her friends thought that Caitlin's doodles were pretty. "I know that you never liked the word 'pretty' when you were younger, but we can't help it. We're Southern. We like pretty."

Growing up, Caitlin had felt that she could never be as pretty as her big sister. Then when Trina got pregnant, Caitlin hadn't wanted to be anything like her. So for a long time she had dressed like a tomboy, and when she outgrew that, she had chosen the hip and edgy. She had always associated prettiness with Trina.

But now when she thought about it, of course she liked pretty. Softness, curving lines, watercolor hues, everything that had made the Iris room at the inn a soothing retreat. Why not celebrate all that?

She was suddenly repelled by the violence and aggression of the games she worked on. Could she support herself on the romance-novel covers? No, that wouldn't be enough. But what had her dad said about her? That she figured things out for herself. She could figure this one out too.

She sat down at her computer and signed into the account of Tlin, her game-designer, androgynous alter ego. She wrote a message to those clients. She would finish any ongoing projects, but would not be accepting more work of this nature. She signed off with her own name. Let them know that they had been working with a girl.

Then she called the Streets and set up an appointment to discuss an educational video game. This would be the first time she had ever worked on a game from start to finish. She began drawing up a budget for the outside help that she would need.

\* \* \* \*

Nate had an appointment with an orthopedist in Portland. Seth offered to drive him. The appointment didn't take long, but Nate didn't want to go back to the resort. He was getting restless. That was not good. Even at the best of times, Nate's impulsivity made him dangerous. But a bored, restless Nate?

Oregon was a beautiful, environmentally conscious state. Seth had been paying to North Carolina the taxes he owed to Oregon. The least he could do was protect the habitat from Nate.

"Let's be adults," he suggested, "and go visit the retailers."

He pulled up a list of the shops that carried Street Boards. Although Nate and his crutches were hardly a great advertisement for active sports, the store owners and managers were happy to see Seth.

"Am I crazy," he asked Nate after the first two visits, "or were they all more interested in the skateboards?"

"It's summer. That's what they are selling now."

Yes, but... "Skateboarding's on the short list to be an Olympic sport, isn't it?"

Nate nodded. "But it isn't likely. A lot of the best people don't want it. They're afraid that it will make them lose their authenticity, their street style...basically that they would turn into us."

Were skateboards the future of Street Boards? The low end of the market was strong, doing well in places where the snow sports weren't sustainable. The high-end market was certainly less mature than in snowboarding. God knows those pros were even hungrier for sponsors than the snowboarders were.

*But Seth*—he could hear his father's voice—*you are a snowboarder.*

*Yes, and I won't give up the sport, but it can't be about me, Dad,* he answered. *It can't be just about me. We, the family, we need to be a team.*

And he would show Caitlin that he could be a team player.

\* \* \* \*

Caitlin was busy. Seth's parents had agreed to the video more quickly than they should have. If they weren't interested in rebranding the company, there wasn't much point in doing this. They should have taken some time, thought about it more. But they were so pleased to have Seth interested in something besides filming his parts that they would have agreed to any of his ideas. They were eager to sign her contract.

She told her romance-writer clients her real name and started having phone conversations with them. She also became the volunteer director of volunteers for Deborah Cornerstone's campaign. The other volunteers were an oddly assorted group—college students home for the summer, stay-at-home moms, and older widows—but Caitlin scrambled them into some reasonable order. It felt good to think that if women like Deb assumed public office, the courtrooms would no longer be places for testosterone-fueled pissing matches.

This wasn't the life Caitlin wanted, borrowing her mother's car and telling MeeMaw that, yes, it would be nice if Caitlin knew how to play bridge, but she wasn't going to learn. However, she felt like she was headed in the right direction.

Caitlin had called April, offering to address her wedding invitations. "I know you were planning on using labels, but calligraphy looks so much nicer."

There was some usual Southern back-and-forth—*you're so sweet to offer...can't let you*—but Caitlin won.

Caitlin went over to April's mother's house to pick up the envelopes. April's invitations had a clean, contemporary look, and Caitlin gave her several fonts to choose from. As she was trying to make up her mind, Caitlin scanned the guest list. And saw her own name and Joan's and Delia's...and Seth's.

"You've invited the whole jury!"

"Yes, of course. We're friends, aren't we? I only have Seth's parents' address, but he's out in Washington State, isn't he? Do you know that address?"

"Actually it's Oregon, and I don't know the address. I suppose I could get it from his mother."

"Oh, no. I hate to bother you, and I don't imagine that he will come."

"Probably not." What had he said? *We got together to do a job. We did our part. And that's the end of things. Except for you, I'll probably never see any of them again.* So much for the "except for you." He didn't seem to be planning on seeing her again either.

"I was hoping," April sighed. "He was so great about my dress."

"For my part, I hope Sally comes." Caitlin had seen the deputy's name on the list. "I would love to see her again."

* * * *

Working on the Street Boards game was challenging, not creatively or technically, but personally. It was too much about Seth. It was important to Mr. Street that the character really seem to be Seth. So Caitlin was looking at hours and hours of video, trying to turn Seth into shapes. She drew lines across his shoulders, she followed the forward twisting of his hips, she tracked each shift of his head, ankles, knees, glutes. She tried to think of him as pixels. It didn't work. He was still Seth.

Then, surprisingly, she got a text from him. *Could you call me? Need to talk about the game.*

Okay, that was plenty clear. This was a business call.

Indeed, they exchanged no pleasantries. He got straight to the point. "How hard would it be to convert the work you've done on the game into skateboarding?"

His voice was so familiar. She remembered having to take the family phone into the hall closet to talk to him in private. "The math will all be different because of the speed, but the concept and the visuals...wait, why are you talking about skateboarding?"

He told her. His notion of the Street Boards rebranding was even more extensive than before. If there was going to be any focus on the elite athletes, it would be the skateboarders.

"Have you discussed this with your parents?"

"Not yet. I'm getting my ducks lined up. But they like you so much that I can see them saying that we had to go on with the video simply because you've been working on it."

Caitlin was charging an hourly rate. She would not lose if the project were canceled. "That's no way to run a business."

"It's worked for them, but they've been lucky."

* * * *

Trina and her family arrived Friday evening of Labor Day week. She hugged Caitlin, apologizing for not coming sooner.

"You've said that a million times. But what have you done with Dylan? Who is that monster truck you brought with you?" Caitlin hadn't seen her nephew since Christmas. He had grown into a mini linebacker since then.

"It seems like he needs a new pair of jeans every week." Trina shook her head.

"Did you ever think about having more kids?" Caitlin asked Trina once Dylan was out of earshot.

"Sometimes. We are fifteen, in some cases twenty years younger than his friends' parents, and the other moms always think that I am the au pair. But whenever there are any kind of parent-child athletic competitions," she went on, "Trevor and I are the most popular family ever. We can run up and down a soccer field without having heart attacks. But I want to talk about you. Are you really staying in town?"

"I do know that I am not going back to San Francisco."

"What about Seth?"

"What about him? He has nothing to do with this. He's back in Oregon."

"And is that okay with you?"

"I don't have a say in it."

"Well, why not?" Trina spoke urgently. "Listen, Caitlin, I never gave up on Trevor, not even when he was so hopeless those first few years. He was relieved when we moved to San Diego. Relieved. Can you imagine how that felt? He was terrified of the responsibility. But I loved him, and I never gave up on him even though everyone else thought he was a dirtbag."

She had a point. It was unfair that Trevor had been allowed to mature in a more normal way than Trina, attending college and all, but he had matured. Midway through college he woke up and realized what fatherhood meant.

"So why are you giving up on Seth?" Trina asked.

"I don't know what you are talking about." Caitlin felt herself go stiff.

"Are you in love with him?"

"Why on earth are you asking that?"

"Because I'm your big sister."

Caitlin suddenly flashed back to the halls of one of their elementary schools; it was the one with the wall of glass brick. She was in first grade, and she couldn't find her lunch money. She had been waiting in the lunch line, feeling frantic. What would she do when she got up to the front of the line? She didn't care about the food. Her stomach was churning too much to eat.

Suddenly Trina was there. She had been sitting at a table with third-grade girls and had noticed that her little sister was upset. She had come over and handled it. Caitlin was not the first and only child to have ever lost her money. The lunch lady wrote a little note and put it in the cash drawer. Instead of going outside after lunch, Trina came with Caitlin to her classroom, found the money in Caitlin's desk, and went back to the lunchroom with her. None of the teachers questioned the two of them walking through the halls together. They trusted Trina.

That's what a big sister does for you. When she is eight, she finds your lunch money for you. When she is fourteen, she lends you her clothes. When she is twenty-six, she asks you if you love him.

*I missed this. I missed this.*

"So?" Trina prompted.

The first time she had been in love with Seth, her grandmother had had to ask her. This time it was her sister. But she was as sure now as she had been then. "Yes, I do. I do love him."

"Then seriously, are you just going to wait until he has to come home? Caitlin, you have more initiative than anyone on the planet. Why are you sitting around?"

"What am I supposed to do? Go out there and beg him to love me? I am not going to do that."

"If begging were going to work, then you should do it, but it wouldn't. Go and figure out why he is there, if he really has been able to get his old life back. If you show up and he won't make eye contact, then you can turn around because you'll know."

"But the place is hard to get to, you have to fly—"

"Caitlin. Caitlin. Caitlin." Trina pulled out her phone. "We'll drop you in Charlotte on Monday. We're leaving early."

Caitlin refused to let Trina use her mileage points to pay for the flight. If she was going to go beg some guy to love her, the least she could do was pay for the flight herself.

She told both her parents and the Streets that she was going to Oregon to talk to Seth about the game. Surprisingly, none of them asked any questions, not even the Streets, who had a legitimate interest in the issue.

"I don't get it," she said to Trina on the way to Charlotte. The two sisters were in the backseat while Trevor and Dylan were in the front, talking energetically about the Braves' pitching rotation. "Why wouldn't the Streets at least ask me what I need to talk to him about, see if they could answer my questions? And Mom and Dad didn't ask any questions, and since when does Mom not ask questions?"

"Oh, Caitlin," Trina sighed. "Don't you think that they know perfectly well why you're going...or at least hope that they know? Mom says that the Streets want the two of you to get together as much as she and Dad do."

"Excuse me? They actually talk to each other about it?"

"Well, the moms do. Maybe not the dads, but Mr. Street is crazy about you, and Dad likes Seth a lot. And don't forget about the big-ass Southern wedding."

"That's what I'm supposed to tell Seth? That my mother wants to plan a big-ass Southern wedding?"

"Well, no," Trina admitted. "I wouldn't suggest that you start there. At least not right off."

\* \* \* \*

Okay, she wasn't going to beg him to love her, and she couldn't tell him about the big-ass Southern wedding with a cake the size of Tennessee and ten bridesmaids who hopefully wouldn't have big asses, but Caitlin wouldn't discriminate against them if they did. So what was she going to say?

She had no idea.

His mom had texted her while she was waiting in Charlotte to say that Seth would pick her up at the airport. Indeed, he was there, just beyond security, leaning against a pillar, his arms crossed, wearing a Street Boards hoodie over a loose flannel shirt. He hadn't shaved in a couple of days so his face was scruffy, more like the Seth of the pictures.

He straightened and stepped forward when he saw her...and then he looked nothing like his pictures. He was tired, his lips were narrow, his shoulders were hunched up.

*I don't want you to be unhappy,* she wanted to say...but she had a feeling her sister would tell her, *hell, yes, you want him to be unhappy. You want him to be fucking miserable when you aren't around.*

Would her sister ever say "fuck"? Not in front of her ten-year-old.

He reached for her...no, not for *her*, for her suitcase. She handed it to him. "Hello, Seth."

"It was good of you to come. I know that you didn't want to, that my dad was insisting."

"I beg your pardon?"

"My mom told me that my dad is concerned that you've never actually seen me ride in person, and that you said that since the game was on-screen, watching the videos was more important." He was talking too fast. "But I know how my dad can be."

Well. This was interesting. Caitlin had only told the Streets that she needed to talk to him about the game. She had given them no more detail because she had had no more detail to give. She wasn't a good liar. Mama Street apparently was.

"Now that you mention it," she said mildly, "seeing you in action live might be a good idea."

"What do you mean, now that *I* mention it?" He put her suitcase down. "That's what my mom said. Isn't that why you're here?"

"I guess it could be."

"And it wasn't? Then why are you here?" Now he was looking at her. His eyes seemed lighter than normal, almost a sea green.

*If you show up and he won't make eye contact, then you can turn around because you'll know.* But how could she have ever turned away from him?

He was still talking. "It's killing me that you didn't want to come. I get it. I do. It's Colleen all over again."

"Colleen?" This suddenly wasn't going so well. "You do know my name is Caitlin, don't you?"

"Of course I know your name. Don't be stupid. Colleen was Ben's ex-girlfriend. She was really great, and he pushed her away just like I've done with you. At least he told Colleen that he loved her. That's more than I've done. But for what it's worth, I love you, Caitlin. I'm sorry. I told myself I shouldn't say anything, not after I've been such a tool. I guess this will make things super awkward now."

"No. No, it won't." She couldn't think. Seth loved her. He loved her. He had started off by saying she was stupid, but he had ended up saying that he loved her. "Not awkward at all."

"Then we're cool." His voice was stiff, as if he didn't think for one minute that they were cool about anything.

She suddenly remembered that she still had April's wedding invitation. She had forgotten to get his address. She dug it out of her purse and stuck it out at him. "Here. I came to bring you this. That's why I came."

He looked confused, but took the invitation. "What is this? 'Mr. and Mrs. George Hibbert.'" He read the return address. "Who are they? I don't know them, do I? And why did you bring it? It already has a stamp on it. You could have mailed it."

"It's an invitation to April's wedding, and I brought it because I was afraid that you might not come."

"She invited me to her wedding?" He looked surprised. "Why would she do that?"

"She invited all of us. She thinks of us as her friends. You should go."

"Why? I really hope she has a great wedding, and I will send a gift if she's got one of those registry things. I'll even take care of it myself. But why do you think I should go?"

"Because you helped her get her dress, and I am going to be there, and weddings are so much more fun when you have a date."

"So you want me to fly all the way across the country to be your wedding date?"

"Pretty much," she said, and she was smiling. How could she not be smiling? They were in love.

He saw her smile, and the familiar warmth came back to his eyes; his shoulders relaxed. "I guess I can do that. Is there an RSVP card in this thing?"

"Those were too expensive. You need to email."

"That's easier than finding a mailbox. But are you—"

A voice shouted out, interrupting him. "There they are, there they are."

Caitlin turned. Two guys were coming toward them. One was on crutches, and the other was astonishingly handsome.They were both shaggy haired and dressed like Seth in careless layers. Caitlin knew who they were.

"What the hell are you doing here?" Seth demanded.

"I brought her a coat." Ben, the handsome one, unfurled a school-bus-yellow parka. "Newcomers always forget to bring coats."

Caitlin certainly had. Ben started to introduce himself, but she stopped him. "I know who you are."

"Do you speak Norwegian?" Nate asked.

"Ah...no." What an odd question. "Is that a problem?"

"No, not really. It's just that Colleen could."

"I actually know who she is, too."

Ben groaned. "Why does everyone—"

"Oh, shut up," Seth ordered. "Seriously, what are you two doing here?"

"You've been acting like there was no hope so when we heard that she was comin' round the mountain, we had to come out and meet her like the song says to do."

"And bring her a coat," Ben added.

"I don't suppose it occurred to you," Seth said, "that if there was any hope, you two clowns showing up wasn't going to help."

"So does he have any hope?" Nate asked her. "Are you the new Colleen?"

"I thought Colleen was history," Caitlin said. "I'm trying not to be history. Why do you think I'm here?"

"Then we've done our job," Nate said proudly. "Let's run along, Ben."

Ben hugged her—which Seth had not done—and Nate tapped her hip affectionately with his crutch. Then, by reaching far forward with his crutches, he was able to swing off in a stride so big that Ben was going to have to hustle to keep up.

"The coat," Caitlin called after them. "You can leave the coat." She had never needed a coat when she and Seth had been together before. It had always been summer.

Without turning around, Ben held the coat by the sleeve, swung it around his head like a lasso a couple of times, and flung it backward. It landed on a line of chairs about ten feet away from them.

"I don't know why he thinks he can throw." Seth shook his head as he went to get the coat. "None of us can."

Caitlin watched as he scooped up the coat, moving as easily, gracefully, effortlessly as ever.

Airport sex. She had never thought about airport sex before. It might not be as bad an idea as it sounded.

"I liked your friends," she said.

"I don't really care what you thought of them. What do you think of me? I'm getting a mixed message here."

"I don't know why you think it is mixed. I wanted to come here and beg you to love me, but my sister said that that wouldn't do any good."

He stared at her. "Was that what you wanted to do?" He shook his head. "So why did my mother say you didn't want to come? What did she know?"

"She didn't *know* anything, but according to my sister, this is what both our mothers were hoping for. She probably made up that story so you wouldn't show up at the airport all cocky."

"Fat chance of that. I thought you hated me." He started to drape the coat between the handles of her suitcase so that he could carry both and still have one hand free.

Caitlin noticed something slipping out of one of the coat pockets. She rescued it. It was an Endless Snow Resort envelope with his name on it. "Oh, look, you have more mail."

"This is weird," he said. "This is Nate's mother's handwriting. Those idiots forgot to give it to me." He ripped it open and took out a key card with a Post-It note attached. Caitlin looked over his arm to read the note.

*K3,* it read.

"Isn't that the mountain almost as high as Everest? Don't get your hopes up, Seth. I'm not taking that 'climb every mountain' thing literally."

"You're thinking of K2. No, this is the honeymoon chalet at the resort."

Oh. So her mom and his mom had an ally out here.

And honeymoon-chalet sex? There shouldn't be any such thing. Honeymoon chalets were for making love.

Out in the parking lot he opened the car door for her as he had done that night in the Dairy Queen parking lot so long ago. He put her suitcase in the trunk and then came around to the driver's side.

He put his seat belt on, then turned to her without starting the car. "Do you remember that night back when we were kids and we went to the park after you had to pretend that I was your boyfriend?"

"Of course I do. You opened the car door for me then, too."

"I guess I have the same question that I had that night—how far do we want to take this?"

"Pretty far, I should think."

"All the way to a ring and one of those fluffy white dresses?"

Caitlin blinked. "Seth...are you proposing?"

"Well, crap, it does sound like it, doesn't it? I guess that's something else I need to work on. Do you want to table it and let me try again? I can probably do better with a little prep."

"You can't be serious. People like us...do we get married?"

"Because we're too cool to make a promise?" He grinned at her. "No, we're way ahead of the curve here. The newest, hippest thing to do is get people to throw rice at you."

"You don't throw rice anymore. People used to think that it was bad for the birds. The rice swelled up in their stomachs, and the birds exploded. But it's an urban myth."

"Exploding bird guts? Caitlin, I may be bad at proposing, but you're worse at answering."

He had a point there. "Shouldn't we just live together for a while? That's what people do, isn't it?"

"Sure...when we are out here. No problem. But I'm going to need to be back home more, and isn't your mother going to bug you endlessly about a wedding if we get a place together there?"

"So you know about the big-ass Southern wedding?"

"I know about Southern mothers." He started the car, and then he looked at her again with that mischievous grin she had seen so little of during the trial. "So if we settle at home and have kids, you know what that will make you, don't you?"

\* \* \* \*

The first part of the drive to Mt. Hood took them through the eastern outskirts of Portland. It was still warm enough that big groups of families and friends were celebrating Labor Day with the last picnic of the summer, the last day at the pool, the last softball game. Summer was over for most of Americans.

It was never really summer on top of Mt. Hood. But that didn't matter to Caitlin and Seth. They could finally stop counting their summers.

# About the Author

**Kathleen Gilles Seidel** is a bestselling author of contemporary romances, two of which have won RITAs from the Romance Writers of America. She has a Ph.D. in English literature from Johns Hopkins. She grew up in Kansas and lives in Virginia. She and her late husband have two adult daughters.

Printed in the United States
by Baker & Taylor Publisher Services